Her Turn

Her Turn

Katherine Ashenburg

ALFRED A. KNOPF CANADA

Excerpts from *The Odyssey* by Homer, translated by Emily Wilson. Copyright 2018 by Emily Wilson. Used by permission of W. W. Norton & Co., Inc.

Library and Archives Canada Cataloguing in Publication

Title: Her turn / Katherine Ashenburg.
Names: Ashenburg, Katherine, author.
Identifiers: Canadiana (print) 20200334778 | Canadiana (ebook) 20200334794 |
ISBN 9780735280762 (softcover) | ISBN 9780735280779 (EPUB)
Classification: LCC PS8601.S435 H47 2021 | DDC C813/.6—dc23

Cover illustration and book design by Kelly Hill
Illustration based on a Getty image by visoook

Printed in Canada

10 9 8 7 6 5 4 3 2 1

For
Miriam Ganze
and
Christina Fitzpatrick

WEEK ONE

October 12–18, 2015

*L*iz liked getting to the paper early. In the old days, a morning newspaper attracted night owls. Everything from the first inkling of a story in a reporter's mind to the finished newspaper had happened in the building then, and the printing press waited, an immense dragon bating its breath in the building's innards, until it clicked into its ferocious, self-absorbed rumpus at midnight. Writers' deadlines were pushed as late into the evening as possible, and the theatre critic was always seated on the aisle so that when the curtain fell he (and it was always a he) could race back to the paper and write like mad. His review would appear next morning.

Now those primeval times—which had lasted up until a few decades ago—were over, and the Washington edition of the paper was printed at plants in Maryland and Virginia. Deadlines were cruelly early, and next-day reviews were things of the past. The old-timers still showed up for work as late as possible, grumbling at the ungodly hour, but Liz was not an old-timer.

She thought best, organized best and was most herself in the morning. When she arrived in the low-ceilinged, featureless newsroom a few minutes before nine on a Monday in October, heads occasionally popped up over the walls of cubicles like moles in a big, bare field, but it was too early for most people. Liz set down the thermos of strong coffee she brought from home, poured herself a cup and laid out her papers and files for the week ahead. Every day she had to fill a page with a personal essay and its illustration, and on Monday she looked ahead to the whole week, checking for variety in the topics, making sure that the illustration for each day was in hand or solemnly promised, sometimes taking a few stabs at a headline.

The page for Tuesday was in good shape—a piece from a father whose child was transitioning from a boy named Shelby to a girl named Tamara. Gender transitioning was a crowded field now, at least writing about it was, but this essay was fresh, with some hard-earned wryness. It would need only a few trims.

For Wednesday, she had the story of a custody battle. Two gay men doted on their two rescue dogs and when their relationship ended, the fate of the dogs was the most bitterly contested part of their breakup. Written by one of the men, the piece detailed their squabbles about who would get custody of which dog, how visiting rights would be organized and—very important—what kind of time the two dogs, who had been inseparable since they were puppies, would have together. It was honest and occasionally unsparing. Thursday's essay was a funny, borderline-ribald story about a woman who treated herself to a visit to a luxurious bra shop after she weaned her baby. And for Friday, she had a lyrical ode to the pomegranate, timed to their fall arrival in grocery stores.

Recently Liz had run into a former colleague at a party, an editor from the foreign desk now teaching journalism. "You could edit that page with your hands tied behind your back," the man said. It was a grudging compliment to Liz and a slight to her page.

Since My Turn, as the page was called, was not "real journalism," but written by amateurs and—even worse—on personal subjects, she knew many of her colleagues felt the same way. Editing it was less demanding in some ways than her last job, as the education reporter, but Liz liked it. She liked the daunting fact of the bare page that met her every morning, needing an essay that was serious or comic or exceptional in some way, trimmed to the right number of column inches, accompanied by the right illustration, headline and summary. She liked the fact that the page was, inexplicably and annoyingly for her colleagues, one of the most popular in a newspaper heavily freighted with dense political reporting and analysis. She even liked the troupe of dour Eastern European freelance illustrators she had inherited from her predecessor. She didn't have the heart to fire them, although she was always trying to leaven their expressionistic gloom with some defter, lighter talents. Most of all, she liked the powerful writing amateurs could occasionally produce when they were writing about something that was important to them.

Her phone buzzed. *Hey, Mom. All good here, just leaving swim practice. Sorry I went AWOL last week, 2 midterms. They went OK. Have you gotten rid of the creepy poet? xx.*

She smiled. Like Telemachus in *The Odyssey*, Peter loathed his mother's suitors.

Dear Telemachus, nice to hear you did well in the midterms. Re the creepy poet, count your blessings: when the original Telemachus returned with his father to Penelope's house, they had to kill 108 suitors. Nothing like that mob scene here. xx.

She went back to work, trying out a few headlines for tomorrow's essay on Shelby becoming Tamara. Riffing on Shakespeare's line, "A rose by any other name would smell as sweet," she played with, "A son by any other name . . ." No, bad idea. How about "A child by any other name"? No, it was making the name too important. A hed, as the headline was called by journalists, condensed the

Katherine Ashenburg

essence of the piece, ideally with wit or even a pun, and ran tidily across the page's three columns. The summary, or deck, was less demanding, either a synopsis of the content or a teaser ("Like the modern, liberal parents we wanted to be, we had been relaxed about Shelby's interest in dresses and skirts").

The morning passed. Colleagues appeared, inquiring about her weekend, telling her about theirs, settling down to a story they were pursuing, a review they had to write, a piece they had to edit.

Norris Davidson, the managing editor, leaned over Liz's cubicle. He wore his usual look, harried but determined to do the right thing, however grating.

"That piece you ran last week is trending on Twitter."

"Which one?"

"The one . . ." He was having trouble remembering. "Oh yes, the one where the old guy whose wife has died goes back to his hometown for his high school reunion and gets together with the girl he took to the junior prom." He raised an eyebrow and slid his lips to one side. It was an expression that asked, In what world would people prefer to read that kind of stuff rather than Mironowicz's exceptionally sound column comparing Hillary Clinton's and Bernie Sanders' attitudes to trade?

By around 10:30, the homemade muesli with no-fat yogurt Liz ate every morning had left a yawning cavity in her stomach, and she went to the cafeteria for a cinnamon roll. The publisher was standing in the coffee line, with three other suits. Normally he did not deign to eat the cafeteria food, or if he did, he sent his assistant to fetch it, but this morning he was showing a few guests around.

"How's it going, Liz?"

"Fine." She bit back "Mr. Donovan," and the "Sir" that leaped unaccountably to her mind would have been even more ridiculous. So she left her reply hanging. He could call an employee by her first name, but unless they were known to be friends, calling him Seamus would attract attention.

4

He introduced her to the suits. "Liz edits one of our most successful pages." Bravely, he began trying to describe it. As soon as the suits realized she had nothing to do with the politics or business sections, their nods and smiles turned perfunctory. .

"Really? Interesting."

"Yes, I think my wife enjoys that page."

On her way back to her desk, she ran into Filip, one of the Eastern European illustrators, carrying his portfolio. Her ignorance was embarrassing: she thought he was Polish, but now it was too late to ask him. No doubt he was in the building to chat up the newly assigned Spotlight editor, although the idea of the lugubrious Filip chatting anyone up was incongruous.

"Not many essays now," he said to Liz. They both knew that there were exactly the same number as always, five each week, but she nodded.

"I have a big backlog to read," she promised, mealy-mouthed as usual.

She worked on. By lunchtime she was finished with tomorrow's page, sending the essay through to the paginators. For a hed, she had settled on "What's in a Name? Or a Gender? Still the Same Beloved Child." It wasn't witty, but it summed up the piece. Later she would walk over to Don Fowler, the man in charge of operations, and make sure there were no problems. He always looked as if that query meant she was fussing. She could see him across the newsroom, a square, compact guy whose walk looked as if he had just dismounted from a long horse ride. Today he wore his favorite sweatshirt, which said, *Don't Tell My Mother I'm a Journalist. She Thinks I Play Piano in a Whorehouse.*

By two o'clock, Liz was ready to start going through her inbox. As usual, the submissions had mushroomed in the dark and quiet of the weekend, and there were forty more than there had been on Friday. Most of the usual subjects were represented, many of which she mentally categorized as "Blessing in Disguise"—moving reluctantly out of a beloved home and discovering that the new one had advantages; realizing that a handicapped child was a unique treasure; being fired and learning that that was a good thing. On average, Liz chose roughly two of every one hundred submissions for publication. After she had read and dismissed about twenty with her usual dispatch, she came to one simply titled "Submission for My Turn." What made her head break out into a sweat and her heart begin thudding was the name of the sender.

It came from Nicole Szabo in Seattle. Even in the instant commotion roused by that name, out of blind habit Liz skimmed the start of the essay. Something about preparations for Christmas. Nicole Szabo was the woman with whom Liz's ex-husband, Sidney, had had a secret affair during the last few years he was married to Liz. Nicole was now married to Sidney, and she had no idea she was submitting an essay to her husband's ex-wife.

That was one of the strange things about Liz's job. Her name did not appear on the page, and outside the paper and her circle of friends, no one knew—or much cared—who edited My Turn. Often the submissions were full of intimate detail, either because the writers thought—incorrectly—that they could appear with a pseudonym, or because they didn't have the writerly skill to control their revelations. Very occasionally, especially if they were from Seattle, where Liz had been married and lived for eighteen years, she knew the writer. There was the piece from a woman who was hiding her melanoma and expected that the paper would give her a pseudonym so that it could remain a secret. She had lived on Liz's street in Seattle and Liz had no idea she had cancer. Sometimes an essay would give her a whole new way to think about someone she knew. That happened with the affectionate piece a young man wrote about his funny, quirky, tree-hugging mother. The mother had been the most difficult member of Liz's Seattle social circle— sour, paranoid and tirelessly garrulous about her husband's short-comings. Clearly, there was more than one side to Nora Dowbiggan.

But nothing this close to home had ever happened before. Nicole was here, in her inbox. At first Liz felt invaded, although she told herself that Nicole was the one who was exposed, not her. She wanted a towel to dry her sweaty head, and a drink. She wondered if any of the old-timers still kept a bottle in their bottom drawer.

She sent Nicole's offering flying into her NO file and she carried on with her submissions. She paid attention, more or less, and did not look at the NO file. It said very clearly on the My Turn page on the paper's website that only successful essays would be acknowledged. So there was absolutely no need for Editor@MyTurn.com to respond to Nicole Szabo.

By nine o'clock that evening, Liz had eaten dinner with *The New Yorker* propped on the handy little adjustable reading stand she kept at her dining-room table. The current issue had an interesting article about next year's election and what the writer considered a new and disquieting direction in American politics—based on feelings and visceral reactions more than the candidate's platform. Hillary Clinton, who often seemed to arouse instinctive feelings of dislike, and the wing nut Donald Trump, whose erratic pronouncements apparently only increased his ratings, were cases in point. The thesis made sense, but Liz found it hard to concentrate. She did the dishes and put the leftover chicken in a biodegradable baggie in case she decided to take it to the paper for lunch. Boiling water to make herself a pot of herbal tea, she said to herself, Spinsterish. She knew what her tidy little evenings looked like and usually she was fine with that. She doted on her reading stand and the companionable dinnertime reading it made possible, but tonight felt different.

There was a phone message from the poet and a text from a man she had met recently, proposing lunch. Her friend Honey always said men were not serious until they suggested dinner. That was fine with Liz, she was in no hurry. But a woman with a newspaper page to fill every day did not have time to lunch. The new man was an academic, with time to spare. She would get back to the poet and the professor tomorrow. She poured herself a mug of chamomile tea and moved to the living room.

Opening her tablet, she asked herself why she hadn't just erased Nicole's submission instead of sending it to NO. Force of habit? Her conscience insisting that she had to at least read the thing?

She circled the piece with her cursor. Perhaps it contained something shamefully personal, even secret. Nonsense, her sensible self said, this is an essay Nicole is willing to have the country read. It's hardly a private document. Yes, her softer side said, but Nicole had no idea that I was going to have some kind of privileged access to it. Oh, get over yourself and your "privileged access," the hard-nosed Liz said. She knew it wasn't reasonable, but Nice-Liz did feel that reading the essay would give her some knowledge about Nicole that she didn't deserve. Not a fraction as much as she has about you and your marriage, Cynical-Liz countered.

There was no denying that. Of all the times Liz had met Nicole during her clandestine affair with Sidney, one clawed its way into her memory now. "Clawed" was appropriate because it involved kittens. Peter's cat had had six kittens and they were looking for homes for them. One went to Liz's Italian teacher, two to a friend's daughter, and three were left when Sidney said casually one day, "I ran into Nicole Szabo in the butcher's. She'd like to come and choose a kitten for her kids." They settled on Saturday morning, when Sidney would be at Peter's baseball game. Thinking about that now, Liz felt a tiny surge. Coward, she said to Sidney over the years and across the country. You didn't have the guts to be there while your wife and your lover stood over a litter of kittens.

It had been a sunny summer morning, and she had been in the kitchen, ironing her clothes for the coming workweek when Nicole arrived. She offered her coffee, but Nicole said no, she had to pick up her kids from swimming class so she would be quick. Liz continued ironing while Nicole crouched over the reeking tangle of kittens in the cardboard box by the kitchen door. She began talking to the kittens, which was the kind of thing she did. Liz and Sidney had met Nicole when she was an assistant at Peter's daycare, and probably kittens and young children were on the same continuum for her.

Oddly, Liz had a very clear memory of one of the dresses she was ironing that day. Perhaps Nicole commented on it. They must have made some desultory conversation while she chose her kitten. It was a two-piece dress in pale blue and white striped cotton, the skirt straight and the shirt long-sleeved and collarless. She remembered that the cotton was very soft. Somehow she equated the innocence and simplicity of that shirtwaist with her own unsuspicious hospitality. Sure, take my kitten. Oh, and while you're at it, take my husband.

She could not remember what Nicole had worn, probably one of her vaguely folkloric outfits. They went well with her mop of light brown curls and the general air of very slight confusion that made people, especially men, want to help her. Nicole picked a kitten whose face had the shape and markings of a pansy.

"We will call her Pansy," she said.

Liz gave her a shoebox in which to transport the kitten, Nicole thanked her and left. She and Sidney must have had a good laugh or at least a guilty smile over their successful caper. The thought of that sunny kitchen scene still galled Liz. In the midst of the big betrayal, it was the little betrayals that rankled most.

It still rankled, on the rare occasions when she thought of it. But ten years had passed. She had moved to D.C., had a good job (even if the life expectancy of a daily newspaper grew smaller and smaller), excellent friends and an agreeably changing cast of gentlemen callers (even if Peter scorned them). She went to yoga on Tuesday nights with her friend Freya, kept on with her Italian, reread *Middlemarch* every four years, enjoyed a rich and full life. Her friends, especially her married friends, thought that her life was much better single than coupled. Usually, she did not disagree.

Now her chamomile tea was cold, and she moved it over on the coffee table with her foot. As usual, she had left something out of her summary of her fortunate life—her affair with Seamus Donovan, the paper's publisher.

Instead of wondering whether Seamus was part of her good fortune or something more problematic, she decided that she would read Nicole's essay. Just so that she could tell herself she had treated it as she would any submission. She took a sip of the cold tea.

The essay was about the disproportionate work of Christmas in the life of a couple. The writer, that is, the wife—that is, Nicole—began thinking about Christmas at the end of November or the beginning of December, making lists of gifts, parties that needed to be attended or given, decorations, food, family dinners and other compulsory traditions. None of this was fancy, but turning those lists into reality involved much toil on the wife's part. For the husband, Christmas planning started around noon on Christmas Eve. That's when this man, a prince of a guy but a mite disorganized, was suddenly seized with the need to go out and buy expensive presents for everyone on his list (if he had had a list). He went shopping without consulting his wife about the presents she had already bought, and without remembering that she needed his help preparing their annual Christmas Eve dinner for his cousins. This was not conducive to warm holiday feelings on the part of the wife. This year, she was determined to avoid any unfestive sentiments. She had invited her husband out for dinner at their neighborhood bistro, and there they would plan Christmas together. They would draw up lists, assign tasks, and everything from their Christmas carol singing party to the chestnuts she was usually too exhausted to roast on the open fire would be prepared according to their fair and pre-arranged accord.

Well. On the positive side, Liz always needed Christmas pieces. Nicole had submitted it well ahead of time, and Liz tried to edit a handful in advance so that she could have a few days off over the holidays while Peter was home. It wasn't a subject that had been done to death, and in the hands of a better writer the essay would have had a fighting chance. But Nicole wasn't a better writer. Too many passive-aggressive, impersonal sentences, too little color and too few specific examples. Too much energy spent praising the husband for his generosity while she shied away from her resentment. But that wasn't Liz's problem, either as an editor or former wife. She had done her professional duty. Whoever had written this piece, it would not have made the cut.

So Liz's conscience could rest easy. The phone rang, and she saw from the call display that it was the poet. Because his muse visited him late in the evening, it didn't occur to him that other people didn't want to chat at close to eleven. She ignored the call. She would watch an episode of the gory and psychologically troubling Icelandic mystery she was following on Netflix instead.

═══

Two permanent engagements marked Liz's Tuesdays, only one of which—"yoga 7:00 p.m."—went into her agenda. "Seamus 4:00 p.m." never appeared, because leaving a paper trail of an affair with your married boss was not smart. Yoga and Seamus made an awkward combination, but the rest of his week was carved up into innumerable meetings and Chip, Liz's favorite yoga teacher, taught only on Tuesday evenings. The late afternoon with Seamus interfered with the serenity and being-in-the-present that Chip urged on the class. Plus, their rendezvous, at a big, anonymous hotel just over the Virginia border, seemed to demand sexy, scratchy underwear. Liz thought it was the least she could do. When she and Freya met in the changing room at the Y, Freya looked quizzically at the lacy, punishingly wired bra and Y-shaped panties that Liz exchanged for a sports bra and comfortable panties. Even when not at yoga, Liz preferred roomy cotton underpants whose waistband was sensibly

Katherine Ashenburg

positioned at the waist, a less extreme version of the ones worn by the heroine in *Bridget Jones's Diary* that Hugh Grant's character found so kinky. Liz sometimes thought of them as "off-duty" underpants, but that wasn't right. Sex was not a duty, she told herself, and she enjoyed sex with Seamus.

It was time to get tomorrow's essay, about the breakup and the custody of the two dogs, squared away. But she procrastinated, trawling through the wires. She chanced upon a story in an English paper about a woman whose husband told her without warning that he was in love with another woman and planned to leave her. The wife took the news with apparent calm and went to stay with a friend. She returned home later the same day to find her husband and his lover in the living room watching a rugby match. She asked to be introduced, and said she was going to make some tea. When it was made, she returned to the living room and poured a boiling cup on the other woman, who screamed and ran out of the house. The wife followed her, pulling her hair. The other woman required treatment for second-degree burns and surgery for a perforated eardrum.

At the trial, the defence psychiatrist said that the wife was suffering from "adjustment disorder." Adjustment disorder. She'd only had the news for a few hours and her failure to adjust was already a disorder. That was Liz's favorite part, although she also smiled guiltily at the idea of weaponizing the solacing cup of tea.

Now she really had to get to work. For the hed, she forbade herself any punning thoughts of "tail" and "tale," or "dogged." Maybe something simple, like "Not Your Usual Custody Battle"? That wasn't just simple, it was boring. Maybe "When Going to the Dogs Was the Right Thing"? No, "When Going to the Dogs Was the Answer" was more succinct and would fit better. That wasn't great, but she didn't feel inspired. She felt distracted, which she told herself had nothing to do with Nicole's piece festering in the NO file. Probably it was only her usual Tuesday nerves, in advance of her meeting with Seamus.

Honey came by. She was the social trends reporter and was

working on a piece about couples who vehemently disagreed about politics.

"I'm too fragile for the cafeteria's steam trays today," she said. "Too many bickering couples. Let's visit the food trucks."

Leaving the building to lunch in Franklin Square, in front of the paper, was an unusual luxury. Usually they cherry-picked the cafeteria's dejected offerings, and Liz often brought a lunch from home. Washingtonians enjoyed complaining about the square's patchy grass and the homeless people who monopolized its benches, but no one disparaged the canopy of nineteenth-century willow oak trees. Food trucks lined up on K Street and Thirteenth Street, and Liz and Honey headed for their favorites. They met under a linden tree, Liz holding a wobbly paper container of corn fritters and Honey a sizeable portion of chicken parm meatballs over cavatappi. Liz put her fritters down carefully on the bench and looked up "cavatappi" on her phone. "Corkscrew," she reported, looking at the twisty macaroni. "Why didn't I guess that?"

She told Honey about Peter's text.

"Is the poet really creepy?" Honey asked, trying to cut her meatballs without spilling them on her pants.

"No, but he does these long, staring silences that unnerve Peter. And he's not really staring at Peter. As a matter of fact, he barely acknowledges Peter's existence. He's just thinking, but his eyes do tend to fix on Peter."

"So, he's not so bad?" Honey asked.

"He's not really good," Liz said, wishing she had taken more napkins to mop up the cilantro lime sauce on her face. "He has an almost unblemished record of relationships with women who support him. Financially, I mean. I like poetry, or at least I did when I was in college. But that doesn't mean I'm up for paying a poet's bills."

Honey said, "They're just so darn limited, aren't they?" It wasn't clear whether she meant poets or men in general but before Liz could ask, she continued, "Do you have anyone else on the go?"

"Not especially," Liz said. "I met a guy who seems nice, and he's been calling to chat. Teaches history at George Washington."

When it was time to return to work, Honey left the half-finished cavatappi carefully on the bench—an offering for a homeless person.

It was easier for Liz to take a late-afternoon break than it was for Seamus. He had chosen the hotel where they met because it was next to a building with some medical offices. As far as his driver and his assistant knew, Seamus had a regular Tuesday appointment with his physiotherapist (a stubborn problem with his rotator cuff) in the medical building. After his driver dropped him off, he walked through the medical building to its rear doors and, once outside, went to the garden entrance of the hotel. Liz had picked up the key card, since he was more likely to be recognized, and texted him the room number.

Liz had long ceased to find any of this romantic. She had no idea whether Seamus still did, or ever had. Their pattern was unbreakable. There was always a stainless-steel container in the room, mimicking an eighteenth-century wine cooler, with a split of champagne for her and diet ginger ale for him. She didn't like drinking alone, but he insisted. She drank half of one very small glass and left the rest.

There was something affectionate and comfortable about Seamus. At the same time, he was such a picture of burnished financial acumen that she always thought of Dickens' description of Mr. Dombey, who was crisp and glossy, "like new bank notes." When she'd read *Dombey and Son* as an undergraduate, she was amused by Dickens' idea of a man who showered in money. Now, with Seamus—his deep cuffs with quiet gold cufflinks, his discreetly gleaming ties, his year-round faint tan—she recognized that look.

At first they sat in the room's two chairs and sipped their drinks. They talked about the paper in general terms, but Seamus was circumspect. He would only praise, never criticize, a piece—today he mentioned approvingly the editorial about Obama's hopeless attempt to close the Guantánamo Bay prison. He asked about Peter, but because asking about his children seemed to involve their mother, she rarely reciprocated. Seamus was an indulgent father who didn't need to be asked. He always brought her up to speed about his daughters, who were a little younger than Peter. One was musical, the other a more driven student.

She asked him, "Will you stay in McLean for Thanksgiving?"

That seemed a safe compromise between too personal and not personal enough. Seamus lived in the Virginia hunt country, in a house within a large park that had belonged to his wife's family. The park was in the eighteenth-century style, formal and uncompromising, with nothing so common as a flower, just long walkways through acres of manicured grass, bordered by tall chestnut trees and interrupted by the occasional sculpture. The park was open to the public and Liz sometimes walked its chilly length when she knew Seamus and his wife were out of town.

"Yes," he said, not looking entirely happy. "My mother-in-law, who grew up in the house, is coming from Florida, and that can be a bit of a mixed blessing."

"Because she doesn't like to see changes in the house?"

"Her focus is more on the park. She has X-ray vision when it comes to the grass, and she sees evidence of grubs and other pests where we see none. According to her, the milky spore we apply to control them is always too late."

"But surely you have gardeners who are in charge of that."

"Yes, but Mrs. Carmichael believes in hands-on stewardship. And so do I, in theory. I'm just not sure how the park came to be my responsibility. Martha is in charge of the house, so I suppose it's fair. But a childhood in a Dublin row house does not put you on a first-name basis with grasses and their pests."

She marvelled at the natural way he spoke about his wife and his mother-in-law, but he was only answering her question about Thanksgiving. With large parts of their work not available for discussion, they had to fall back on carefully edited anecdotes from their personal life. Seamus did that so blithely she could feel vexed. But as usual, she melted a little at the mention of his childhood.

Then they moved to the bed and had sex. Surprisingly, Seamus lost none of his authority when divested of his cufflinks, tie and the rest of his clothes. Liz felt, as usual, that her lingerie, today classic black laced with Schiaparelli pink ribbons, held his attention for a disappointingly short time, but she still thought she owed it to him. When it was over and they lay facing each other, Seamus always cupped her face with his big paw and said, "Well, then." A bit of his Irish accent, which he had successfully suppressed, resurfaced when he was relaxed. Liz wondered about the "Well, then." It sounded affectionate, but did it also suggest something ticked off on his to-do list?

"And what about your Thanksgiving?" he asked, wrapping his top leg around her.

"Peter will be home, of course, and I think I'll invite friends. My brother is going to his partner's family and they're taking my mother with them."

As they dressed, he did spare a glance at her expensively seductive bra.

"That's pretty," he said, and kissed her one last time.

So it had not been a total waste. Their time together in the room rarely took more than an hour. When she was feeling disaffected, she thought of it as the length of an average visit to the dentist, but today she felt fond of him. Next time she must remember to ask him more about his boyhood.

Once Seamus had met his driver in front of the medical building, she took a cab back to the paper. With her coat on, against her better judgment, she opened her NO file. Why? Nicole's essay could hardly have disappeared, but she had an irresistible desire just to make sure it was still there. It was, and she had done everything that could possibly be done with it. It was time for yoga.

In the yoga room at the Y, Liz positioned her mat so that Freya would not see her thwarted attempts at flexibility or grace. Which was unnecessary because Freya, like Liz, was probably concentrating so hard on her own positions she had no time to observe others.

Chip said, as he did every week, "Don't think about what happened today or what might happen tomorrow. Just be here, in the present. This time is for you." Liz wondered why thinking about today or tomorrow would make this time less for yourself, but she tried to obey.

Lying in savasana, the corpse pose that was their reward for fifty minutes of effortful stretching and twisting, she followed Chip's instructions to sink deeply into the mat and to imagine a bright white light travelling up her body.

"Think of the place you'd most like to be," he said every week, "with the person or people you most like being with."

Usually she imagined being with Peter in a variety of settings, her apartment, the cottage her parents had rented when she was a child, or travelling. But tonight, although it was hardly the place she most wanted to be, she saw herself alone, in the park that belonged to Seamus and his wife. Once you passed the park's wrought-iron entrance gates, the first bend off the main road, to the right, led to the Donovans' house. That was off bounds to the public, but they were free to walk the park every day from 9:00 a.m. to 6:00 p.m. There was something pretentious about an eighteenth-century European garden designed in early twentieth-century America, but it was undeniably beautiful.

Liz pictured herself sitting on the bench just before the turnoff to the house, so that anyone going into the house would see her there. She had the mad idea that, if she didn't have a job, she would sit there every day, especially at times when Seamus's wife would be likely to drive by. She remembered a Roz Chast cartoon of a woman wearing a little pillbox hat and a reefer coat, sitting on a bench surrounded by autumn leaves. The caption read: "Susan D: The woman without a heyday." Liz didn't feel that way—although she wouldn't want to be pinned down about the exact time of her heyday—but the idea of planting herself on the bench reminded her of the stoic, disappointed Susan D.

Why was she indulging herself in this pathetic fantasy, instead of imagining walking on an Italian beach with Peter? She was aware that her affair with Seamus was less than full-blooded, so perhaps this bench-sitting idea, both masochistic and aggressive, was an attempt to add some fizz. But adding some fizz by exhibiting herself to Mrs. Donovan was weird if not sick. In general, she avoided thinking about Seamus's wife. They had been introduced once or twice at newspaper functions, but Liz doubted that Martha Donovan would remember her.

There was something disinhibiting about the sweaty work of yoga followed by the profound relaxation of savasana. She struggled up, into the half-lotus position in which they ended the class. Maybe yoga only once a week was too stimulating. If she tried to fit in a second class, it might normalize things, and she could end these bizarre flights of fancy.

Dear Nicole Szabo:

Thank you for your submission to My Turn. It's an engaging idea, and it held my interest from the beginning. However, it's not quite there yet, and I'm wondering if you are interested in doing some further work? Right now it's too abstract. Readers want concrete, particular details. For example, can you describe more specifically the costly presents your husband has given in recent Christmases? What was the menu for the Christmas Eve dinner for your husband's cousins, and how could your husband have helped with it? Dialogue

or even a small scene is always a good idea, e.g., showing
how your ideas of the holiday diverge from your husband's.
And try to turn some of those passive verbs into active
ones, e.g., not "I was expected to make a holiday dinner for
10 on Christmas Eve," but "My husband expected me to
make, etc." Not "I was given the impression that he was too
busy at the office," but "He gave me the impression, etc."
Sorry to sound like a high school English teacher. But
I'm still using the ideas I got from mine.
Good luck,
Editor@MyTurn

Writing that had required red wine, not chamomile tea. Liz
had come straight home, poured herself a glass from a bottle on
the kitchen counter—she hoped she had opened it within the last
week—and sat down on the couch, still in her yoga clothes, to write.
Now, she looked at her tablet with something like horror. Not just
because the message violated her sense of professional ethics, not
just because she had no intention of ever running the piece, but
most of all because she did not understand why she had written a
reply. But she had, and she told herself that just having written it
was cathartic enough. And she needn't worry about professional
ethics, because there was no question of sending it.

Rather than rereading it, she returned the poet's call. He whined
a bit that his latest grant application had not been successful because
he was neither a woman nor LGBTQ. (Why, Liz asked herself,
could they never entertain the possibility that maybe the application or the proposal or even the work itself was not terribly good?
It was always someone else's fault.) Once he had had his moan, he
broke off the call abruptly, as he was in the full frenzy of creation.
But first he asked, "What about this weekend?"

She disliked these general invitations. "I'm not sure, things
look kind of busy. I'll get back to you."

For a long time Liz had thought, Beware of men who keep their toddler names. Johnnies and Donnies had a disproportionately high incidence of Peter Pan syndrome. The poet was named William, and there was no question of Willie or Billy. He was too serious. He dressed the part, in black clothes so old they verged on rusty brown, and he had a ponytail and one pierced ear, with a small stud. Liz thought she would expand the warning: beware of men whose names are diminutives, who wear ponytails, who have pierced ears.

William did have two virtues, which was why she continued to see him, although at longer and longer intervals. He had a surprising gift for physical comedy. His imitation of Charlie Chaplin slipping on a banana peel was impressive, including the wordless evocation of his bowler hat and umbrella. But his forte was animal imitations, especially chickens. He spread his toes (best done barefoot), humped his neck and moved his head back and forth in one sinuous, continuous action. Liz could have sworn he had grown poultry feet, feathers and a beak, and she howled with laughter no matter how often she saw his waddle. She could overlook a number of character flaws, temporarily, when a man made her laugh out loud. William's second virtue was sex. Normally self-absorbed, he was good in bed. He took his time and he paid close attention to Liz's responses. Even so, sex and funniness did not add up to a passing grade, and she really should stop seeing him.

Next she called Henry, the historian who wanted to have lunch. She had met him at a party at Freya's, who also taught history at George Washington. Liz had a cloudy memory of dry humor and chestnut-colored hair. She could not remember whether there was a beard or not, but if there was she thought it would be trim and discreet. It would not be what she thought of as a "philosopher's beard," straggly and bearing bits of the wearer's last meal, scrambled eggs or shards of tofu. She had once dated a man in the philosophy department.

Henry was at home and he accepted, almost as a novelty, the idea that she did not have time to lunch during the week. Academics produced articles and books at what used to be called a glacial pace, so the task of filling a broadsheet page every day was nearly incomprehensible to them.

"But you probably have several essays or even pages in the bank." Like many professors, he apparently believed in a mythical bank where journalists deposited pieces in advance. This partly explained their prodigious output.

"Nope. We go pretty much day by day."

"Okay, then how about brunch on Sunday?"

"Fine. Let's communicate on Saturday about where and when."

Liz got into bed feeling satisfied. She liked Henry's voice. She was looking forward to spending tomorrow morning with the essay from the woman who had weaned her baby and repaired to the specialist bra shop. And, no matter how weirdly she had done it, she had exorcised Nicole.

Two years after her separation, when Liz was offered a reporting job in D.C., it looked like a fortuitous way to leave Sidney, Nicole and the detritus of her marriage behind. She didn't underestimate the seriousness of uprooting a twelve-year-old boy, but she trusted that it would eventually work out. She found an apartment in a boxy nineteenth-century house on Corcoran Street. Her block, between Sixteenth and Seventeenth Streets, was decidedly not chic, although there were lesser embassies nearby and real estate signs mendaciously advertised "luxury" apartments. But her place had two roomy bedrooms and Seventeenth Street had one of everything she needed— supermarket, dry cleaners, hardware store, liquor store, even a ridiculously overpriced gift shop. It was an easy trip to the paper on the S9 bus, or a half-hour walk if she had the time. When she had wrenched an unhappy and protesting Peter from Seattle to D.C., he scorned a city that mostly used numbers, letters and the names of states for its streets. "Was it too hard for them to think up real names?" he asked sarcastically. She was happy to point out that Corcoran Street had a real name.

She associated her neighbors in the building with aromas. The smell of beer wafted out of the second-floor apartment across the hall from hers. If the two young lobbyists who lived there ate any solid food, they didn't do it in the apartment. On the other hand, Leona, who occupied the whole first floor of the building, ran a soul food catering company from her apartment and occasionally taught a class there. Delicious smells of mustard greens and sweet potato pie often perfumed the entrance hall.

The morning after Liz had written her never-to-be-sent message to Nicole, she smelled black-eyed beans with bacon, one of Leona's specialties. She made her way to the paper through a thin, discouraging rain. The woman next to Liz on the bus was reading an article in *Express* about the Republicans' latest presidential hopeful, Ben Carson. Well, at least Carson seems sane, Liz thought, compared to Donald Trump, with whom he was neck and neck in the polls. The bus smelled of damp wool, and Liz felt jumpy. It's exhilaration, she told herself. You dealt with the Nicole eruption.

In her cubicle, she found the piece about the expedition to the bra store as funny as she remembered it, which was always a relief. The new mother, dismayed by newly shrunken breasts decorated with a circle of puckers, showed up at the bra boutique wearing a pre-pregnancy sports bra that looked like an Ace bandage that had lost its elasticity. The owner of the shop, a cross between a doctor and a dominatrix, ran her eyes over the wilted sports bra. Her expression communicated, "Clearly, you haven't a clue about your correct size, so I won't flatter you by asking what you think it is." She left the dressing room without a word and returned with several bras in a size the woman was sure was wrong.

"Just let your breasts fall into the cups," the owner directed the demoralized customer.

This sounded vaguely pornographic but, clumsily, the woman tried to follow orders. The bras fit perfectly. The bra-woman escorted her to the counter and left her with a mixture of diagnosis and prophecy.

"Your right rib cage is higher than your left. That's why you're better off without underwires. Your left breast is bigger than your right one. And those puckers will fade."

Feeling as if no one had ever known her breasts before, the woman left with several wildly expensive bras.

Liz puttered with the hed, determined to avoid "abreast" and concentrating on "support." "Farewell to the Unsupported Life"? "A Support I'd Never Imagined"? She was pulling on her cowlick, always a sign of perplexity, when Honey wheeled an unoccupied chair into her cubicle.

"Can you give me your recipe for the butternut squash you don't have to peel? I'm having twelve for Thanksgiving, including Sol and his wife, and I'm trying to cut down on the prep. I know it's early to think about Thanksgiving, but I want to practice."

Honey was organized. Sol was her ex-husband, and there were always seats for him and his wife at Honey's holiday table.

"You're so evolved," Liz said admiringly. "I could never do that with Sidney and Nicole."

"Well, they live so far away you never had the chance to get used to them as a couple. Besides, you're not really a modern person."

This was a running semi-joke between them, but it was also true. Liz still hadn't figured out the transition when someone with whom you had lived in the greatest intimacy was supposed to become a mere friendly acquaintance. After their separation but before her move to D.C., when Peter went back and forth between his parents, she and Sidney had had to see each other more or less regularly. When that happened, she would be so overcome with rage or sadness or embarrassment, or some combination of those feelings, that often she could barely look at Sidney for the first ten minutes or so. By now, she was a decade and a continent away from those raw, early days. Rage only made infrequent appearances and subsided quickly, which felt to Liz like the sharp peaks on a fever chart. She could go for months without consciously feeling sad, and then something would make her aware that a low-lying level of sorrow was always there, a tactful but apparently permanent substratum. And the initial embarrassment, when she had to speak with or see Sidney or Nicole, was a constant. Did the rareness of her anger mean that she had mostly forgiven Sidney and Nicole? Or did the trace elements of sadness and the perennial awkwardness disqualify her?

Liz wished she understood forgiveness. Whenever she bent her mind to it, or tried to, it skittered away. She couldn't keep hold of it. The philosopher she had dated, the one with the catch-all beard, told her that forgiveness was an absence of resentment about the wrong that had been done to the forgiver. Was that all? That sounded minimal and very doable. Liz didn't think that she resented Sidney or Nicole, exactly. And yet she found it impossible to be natural with two people who had so profoundly changed her life and Peter's, without their consent. So maybe she did resent them.

Honey was close to being the poster girl for no-fault, low-stress divorce, but even she was not entirely a saint. She had given her two dogs the Hebrew names of the significant men in her life—Shlomo for Sol, and Dovid for her boyfriend, Dave. Honey enjoyed watching Sol with Shlomo, who was a high-maintenance dog. Sol didn't realize he was petting his namesake.

"Our marriage ended so long ago," Honey continued, making light of her easy relationship with Sol and his wife. Honey's marriage had ended five years ago, half as long as Liz had been separated from Sidney.

Liz nodded, and Honey shot her a glance. "Are you okay? If my mother were here, she'd say you look a bit peaked."

"I'm fine," Liz said, making a note to send her the squash recipe.

In the early afternoon, Don Fowler gave her his usual benediction, "The page is fine. Go away."

She began ploughing through the new submissions in her queue. Often these days, there were a few pieces written by middle-aged children about their elderly parents. The children fretted that the parents stubbornly refused to take their advice about how to live their last days—how could they shoehorn them out of their over-stuffed and dangerous houses, convince them to go into assisted living, get them to write a living will and, most important, make them accept that they were incompetent and that their children had all the answers? But today there was one that veered from that well-trodden path. It was co-written by an elderly husband and wife, complaining wittily about their worrying, nagging, condescending daughters. The parents were living safely in a way that suited them, if not their children. In their view, they had made complex and satisfying arrangements that included physician-assisted death if the circumstances warranted it, but the children insisted on seeing them as hopeless bunglers.

Liz's first reaction was, please adopt me. Her second was, this is very well written. Her third was the uncomfortable realization that her own mother was overdue for a visit. She moved the piece into her YES file and wrote under the reminder about the recipe for Honey, "Mother."

Liz unlocked the front door of her apartment, hung up her raincoat, left her umbrella to dry in the kitchen, and sat down on the couch. It was upholstered in a heavy off-white cotton that was still in fairly good condition; the parts with incorrigible stains were covered with an old paisley shawl and an afghan knitted by her grandmother. She adjusted the cover-ups. Maybe she should get a cat, or even a dog. A creature to greet her at the end of the day, although she liked coming home to silence and peace, her kingdom uncomplicated by anyone else's wants.

Her living room was a blend of old things, new things and some irresistible objects she had picked up on the street, such as the faux bamboo bookcase and the little greenish-yellow deco vase. Liz could thank her parents for teaching her to keep a keen eye out for things other people had thrown out. She had an older friend, a collector of furniture much more valuable than her clobber, who occasionally exhorted his eclectic belongings, "Now you must all learn to get along." Usually her things did, but tonight they looked shabby and ill-assorted. She couldn't remember ever feeling so dissatisfied with the room. Maybe that's why she felt so restless, because her living room was tired. Or maybe her discontent with the room came from this odd restlessness. Probably she should redecorate, get rid of the old pieces, rely more on the mid-century modern ones. Say goodbye to the citrus and indigo walls—although it had taken her forever to find a blue that was not cold—and turn everything pale and clean.

Thinking of her parents and their magpie ways of collecting furniture reminded her of the "Mother" on her to-do list. Liz was aware that she was among the last people in her generation to resist what she called momification: when she was with her mother she called her "Mom," but to other people she referred to her as her mother, not her mom.

"What next?" she would demand of a bored Peter, who had heard this harangue before. "Will we start celebrating 'Mom's Day' in May? Will people forget what 'mother' even means?" She tried not to allow "mom" in her heds or decks, except when the fit would have been otherwise impossible.

Although Liz's mother had dementia, most of the time she still knew that she was Liz's mother. Maybe that was because the caretakers at her assisted living facility would remind her over and over before a visit, "Agnes, your daughter is coming to see you today." A few times a month, Liz drove to Baltimore, where her mother lived, with a resigned, plodding sense of duty. She stayed longer than she wanted to, but less than she knew she should, and she left feeling a mixture of guilt and giddy freedom. Tomorrow she would organize a visit for Saturday.

Liz picked up her phone to see if she had had a text from Peter. Nothing. And no one else had called or messaged or texted her.

She had written her message to Nicole like one outpouring of breath, it came so rapidly. But she remembered every word. Now she wondered if the reference to her high school English teacher wasn't a false note of friendliness. That made her laugh: the whole thing was false. She didn't need to worry about the concluding touch.

Quickly, before she could think about it, she opened her tablet, found the message to Nicole and pressed the paper airplane icon that meant "Send."

<hr>

Thursday was the first nice day of the week, sunny and with a careless promise of warmth. Trying to pretend that everything was normal, Liz fingered the row of ironed blouses in her closet, looking for one that would make her gray slacks look slightly less humdrum. The phone rang and, unusually, it was Seamus, on the phone he used only to call her. He must have watched some cop show where the police investigated a suspect's or a murder victim's phone, and decided he needed a secret one. Unless he was planning on committing a crime or being murdered, Liz found it unnecessarily dramatic.

"Good morning," she said, clamping the phone in the crook of her neck while she balanced an emerald green blouse and a pale pink one with a retro geometric pattern, vintage 1950s.

He got right to the point, as usual. "Listen, Martha has to be out of town on Sunday. I hoped we could get together."

The speed of her reaction did not surprise her, but the quickness of her excuse did, a little. "Oh, I'm so sorry. I've made arrangements to visit my mother in Baltimore on Sunday. She's expecting me, and I haven't been for quite a while." Seamus didn't know how unlikely it was that Liz's mother could expect anyone days in advance, or when the last time was that Liz had visited.

"What a shame." He did sound disappointed. "Well, I better go."

"See you Tuesday."

"See you Tuesday."

"Oh, just before you go. We just got the news that Helen has gotten a scholarship from the Berklee music summer camp. We're not going to take the scholarship from someone who needs it more, but it shows just how good she is."

She congratulated Seamus and hung up, smiling at his adoring fatherhood. So. She preferred Sunday brunch with Henry the historian, an unknown quantity, to her lover Seamus. Well, surely one of the advantages of an adulterous affair was that it left your weekends free. She returned the blouses to their serried row, and put on a red sweater whose collar and cuffs were discreetly lined with brilliants. It was a little flashy for work, but definitely cheered up the gray slacks.

Walking to work, Liz watched the restaurateurs on Massachusetts Avenue sweeping their entrances. She could feel them itching to unroll their awnings and serve lunch on the sidewalk. A New Englander and not a near-southerner like the D.C. natives, usually she disapproved of such unseasonal activities. It was almost November, she would think, and everyone needed to accept that. But today she felt the pull of a languorous lunch in the sun.

She and Honey arrived at the paper's back door together.

"Did you send me the squash recipe?"

She had completely forgotten it.

"I'm sorry! Last night was crazy. I promise I'll send it today."

"Fine. Is that a new sweater?"

"Not at all. I don't think I've ever worn it to work before."

Honey looked more closely at Liz and the glints around her collar. "You definitely haven't."

At her desk, before she forgot that too, Liz messaged her mother's caretaker, saying she wanted to visit on Saturday and would be there by lunchtime. The illustration for Friday's love letter to the pomegranate had arrived, and Liz opened it warily. She was trying out a new artist, and she prayed, Please, let it be good. It was—a realistic, cross-hatched portrait of the fruit. Such a likeable shape, somewhat like a giant hazelnut, another shape Liz enjoyed. Out of the corner of her eye, she saw her inbox dropping a notch, and a new message appeared.

Dear Editor,

Thank you so much for your speedy and encouraging response—this is very helpful! As you see, I am not a professional writer, and I welcome your advice. I'll work on this, and send it back to you as quickly as I can. Thank you again—this is a big boost!!

I feel strange calling you Editor. Shouldn't I be using your name?

Yours sincerely,
Nicole Szabo

Well, she had only herself to blame. She counted three exclamation points, which was almost restrained. Women seemed to feel obligated to use more and more exclamation points in their correspondence so as not to sound unfriendly. And what in the world would Liz do with a second version? She sent up a silent prayer to the editors' god, whom she had already offended, begging that Nicole would not be able to improve her piece and that she would never resend it.

Driving to Baltimore on Saturday to visit her mother, Liz thought about the Dubroffs, the old couple who had written the piece about their worrywart children. She had emailed them her acceptance on Friday, adding compliments about their sagacity and perspective. She didn't usually bother with things like that, assuming that people knew journalists were always in a rush, but something about the Dubroffs made her . . . want to reassure them? Want them to reassure her? In any case, to be in touch with them, which was unusual for her. Now, in the slow lane on the parkway, she considered their brisk good sense. Maybe the paper should run a regular column written by a senior or pair of seniors. People the age of the Dubroffs were the paper's demographic, although not the demographic it wanted. Older people were not buying enough of anything to satisfy the advertisers. But younger people, who were still significant consumers, were not newspaper readers. So perhaps the elderly columnists could be paired with a columnist from their children's generation, and they could opine back and forth about education, bike lanes, assisted suicide and other matters.

Although her parents had raised their children in Massachusetts, when Liz's father died in his sixties her mother moved to Baltimore. Liz's brother, Greg, and his partner at the time, Robert, and their two boys lived there. Agnes was already showing signs of dementia and after a few years alone in her Baltimore apartment, she needed more help. Haven, the assisted living place where the family had moved her, tried to look homey, but its public rooms were more like a motel—big, splashy upholstery patterns that were ultimately more comforting than bold, with reproductions of lesser-known Impressionist paintings. But better a motel than a hospital, and, fortunately, Haven's prevailing smell of cleaning compounds was rarely complicated by urine or worse smells.

In the private rooms, the residents or their families warmed things up with family pictures, cushions, afghans and whole communities of china figurines. But Agnes was a modernist and even in her diminished state would not tolerate knick-knacks. There were a few severely framed pictures of Liz, Greg and the grandchildren. There was also a photograph of her late husband. When Liz pointed it out, her mother would say, "I don't know him, but he's a good-looking guy."

Agnes had worn the same short bob for half a century: its only change was one of color, as the black paled to an immaculate paper white. Today was not one of her better days. Although she had probably been prepped by her aide, she didn't seem to remember that the woman sitting next to her on the couch was her daughter. She tried to make polite conversation with this unknown woman. Manners, Liz thought. The last thing to go.

There was one moment when Agnes's impersonality dropped away, and she looked at Liz, whom she still did not recognize, more knowingly.

"You're a pretty girl," she said. And then, "But you know that's not enough."

Liz nodded, meaning that she agreed prettiness was not enough. She did not think of herself as pretty: she could look good, and sometimes very good, but she could also look plain and tired, for reasons she could not usually trace.

When she was married, she would say to Sidney during those times, "I've lost my looks again." He would say, "You've only mislaid them."

It was one of their routines.

Agnes and Liz sat side by side on the Danish Modern couch that had come from the family room in Massachusetts. It had never been comfortable, but was small enough for Agnes's room. They watched animal shows on television, or listened to music from her mother's youth in the 1950s. There was a dish of Werther's butterscotch drops on the coffee table, which Agnes sucked slowly. Liz thought, I should be holding her hand. And I should have kissed her less perfunctorily and hugged her when I came in. But she did not, because this plausible-looking woman had stolen her real mother, who was astringent and shy but fiercely attached to her children. This imposter and her deliberate candy-sucking repulsed her, although she tried to hide it.

Watching the Animal Channel, her mother absorbed in lion cubs rolling over each other in the dirt, Liz thought, If only there were a Baby Channel. Agnes would like that. Her brother, who had divorced Robert and remarried since his mother had moved to Baltimore, now had a preschooler. When he brought Poppy to visit, Agnes was delighted. It was as if the little girl stirred her synapses, and she came up with words to describe her that she hadn't used in years—"hilarious," "adorable." But Poppy was not coming today.

Liz tried to interest her mother in a cooking show without success. As the chef overturned small bowls of prepared ingredients into what would become a Bolognese sauce, Agnes reverted to her old sharpness.

"This is no good," she said of the show. "Who did all that chopping?"

Who, indeed? Liz agreed.

On an impulse, she said to her mother, "I can't see where things can go with Seamus."

Agnes was the only person in the world with whom she could talk about Seamus, but she had never done that before. Her mother nodded.

"Is he handsome?" she asked.

Liz shifted impatiently on the couch's meagre padding. Had her mother successfully hidden this obsession with people's looks when she was compos mentis, or was it the result of her dementia?

"In a way," Liz said.

"Does he want your money?"

Liz sighed. Now she was doing the wily old peasant thing, another unpleasant aspect of her "new" personality.

"No."

Agnes thought. "You'll find a way," she said, finally. That sounded like her mother.

Greg dropped in at the end of the visit, kissed his mother with far more affection than Liz could muster, and he and Liz went off for coffee nearby. She asked about Robert and Gabe, Greg's new partner, and his children. He asked about Peter, they commiserated about their mother—Greg always more optimistic than she was—and then it was time to get back on the parkway.

===

On Sunday morning Liz had to decide what to wear. She had resolutely refused to think about brunch with Henry before then. And why had she ever thought it would be more fun to have brunch with a stranger than spending Sunday with easy, familiar Seamus? She stood in front of her closet and wondered how she had come to own so many gray clothes. She ran her hands over various silky blouses and shivered. Freya said when formerly married women started dating again they took to wearing very thin clothes—less material between the world and their bodies. But Liz was not newly single, and she craved the insulating comfort of wool. In the end, she wore the red sweater with the little sparkles again. She didn't feel like trying on more clothes, and she hoped its cheerfulness hid her lack of enthusiasm.

Trying to make her semi-curling hair look deliberate rather than wayward, she thought about academics. They always wanted to hear about journalism, its lightning-fast reactions as well as its slow death, so she was prepared for that. She hoped Henry would not be one of the professors who told her, with an air of originality, that "essay" comes from the French verb *essayer*, to try. Or even that Montaigne was one of his favorite writers.

They were to meet in a Swedish café just off Vermont Avenue, but as she stepped off the bus into rain, a block away from the café,

Liz saw a tallish man with an umbrella. She was almost sure it was Henry, but he was more certain, and said, "Liz."

She said, "I thought it was you," they smiled and he steered her deftly under his umbrella.

The café was called Fika, and as they waited to be shown to a table, Henry said, "*Fika* is the Swedish word for coffee break."

Give him a chance, Liz said to herself. One simple explanation doesn't mean he suffers from male explanatory syndrome.

"Yes," she said. "They invented that word by reversing the syllables in *kaffi*."

Henry looked impressed.

"You *are* well-informed."

"Not really. I'm greedy, and I tend to remember food lore."

Fika's talking point was a wall that was covered in opened, overlapping paperback books, like a thickly padded quilt of books. They both hoped to sit next to the book wall, perhaps thinking they could resort to its pages if conversation failed ("Oh look, here is *The Chocolate War*. Was it required reading in your middle school?"), but the café was full and they sat closer to the center of the room. After all the dread, the real Henry came as a relief. There was no beard, and his sweater was clean. He didn't mention the source of the word "essay," nor Montaigne. He seemed to know why the paper was so thin, so she didn't have to go over that sorry story. He had obviously looked at the last few My Turn pages, and asked how much editing she did. Very little, she answered, thinking guiltily of the huge exception that was Nicole. What were the most popular topics?

"In descending order, 'my mother,' 'my operation,' 'my pet.'"

He smiled. "I could never write about my mother, I don't have a pet and have only had a completely unremarkable appendectomy. But what about the story of going online to meet people? Surely you must get a lot of those."

"Yes, but nothing like the big three."

They began talking about dating sites, with the tacit understanding that they both had used them. Liz had only ventured there twice before deciding that they compounded the awfulness of dating.

Henry said, "I've thought about writing an anti-ad for them. Like, 'I find long walks on the towpath completely boring, I wouldn't dream of going to Kramerbooks late at night to browse, and I have absolutely no interest in the quaint bed-and-breakfasts in Harpers Ferry.'"

Liz laughed. She did like walking along the towpath, but there was no need to mention that now.

She said, "You forgot the Adams Memorial."

The statue in Rock Creek Cemetery that Henry Adams had commissioned in memory of his young wife, Clover, was a favorite romantic pilgrimage. Dissing it should qualify for the wet-blanket personality he was adopting.

But his mobile face softened instantly. "I guess so. But that is genuinely sad. And that she killed herself with the cyanide she used to develop her photographs . . ." He looked down at his menu.

Liz stood corrected. But she liked him for that.

"And what is your curmudgeon looking for in a partner?"

"Well, that's the easy thing about satire. You can concentrate on the negative side and ignore the positive. But what would my curmudgeon want? I guess someone who wanted to go in her own room and read. Or, the essence of togetherness, someone who would read, in silence, with me in the living room."

They both smiled. That sounded like a good time.

Of all dates, the first and last were usually the most onerous. The first one called for a brief, strategic autobiography, like an elevator pitch for yourself. Henry's was well-practiced—a childhood in Chicago, B.A. from Northwestern and Ph.D. from Brown, ten years of marriage followed by fifteen since the divorce, a son and a daughter in their early twenties. He was a social historian, specializing in eighteenth-century France. Right now he was focusing on the role played by white linen shirts in determining a man's status. For example, when Rousseau's garret was robbed, his inventory of stolen goods included forty-five linen shirts, and that was probably an average number for a man trying to make his mark in the world.

He said, "Our work is somewhat similar. We both spend our days sifting through documents about how people lived and felt at a particular time."

She liked that too.

When it came to her own synopsis, he asked a few pointed questions. How had she gotten a job at a newspaper without going to journalism school? (In those halcyon days, luck and timing and some movie reviews for the campus newspaper were enough.) How did Peter get on with his father? (Very well. She did not elaborate. People who said derogatory things about their ex-spouses on the first date were definitely not to be pursued. Any elaboration could come later, if there was a later.) Henry seemed to know how to listen, but Liz knew from experience that good listening did not always outlive the courtship stage.

The first date also involved the question of paying. Would he be a traditionalist or a progressive? She made an attempt to share the bill, but he was definite.

"No, I invited you. You can pay next time."

That sounded like a good idea. The skies had cleared and she walked home, congratulating herself on her decision to see Henry and not Seamus. After all, Tuesday would be here before she knew it.

WEEK TWO

October 19–25, 2015

*T*he paper's management committee had its monthly meeting late on Monday morning. Liz was not in management, and the meeting was supposed to be confidential, but word of the latest disquieting news always spread immediately through the newsroom like a bad smell—the rising cost of newsprint, the falling revenue from ads, the aging subscribers, the unsuccessful competition with online news. Five minutes after the meeting adjourned, Jonathan Gilman crooked an arm over one padded wall of her cubicle. Technically, those dividers, upholstered in a dingy oatmeal fabric, were called baffles. It was one of Liz's favorite little-used words.

Gilman was almost slavering over the latest bad news.

"This is what it's like, working in a twilight industry," he said, looking happily doleful at the bad luck of every single person in the newsroom, including himself. Too bad he lives in a culture without professional mourners, Liz thought. He would have been a natural.

Gilman, who was always referred to by his last name, was a columnist in finance. Small and homely, with hair the color of paprika, he suffered from an apparently permanent head cold. In spite of that and his love of gloom, he was an extraordinarily successful Casanova. Sometimes when he trudged by her cubicle, mentally buffing his bucket of troubles, Liz had the impulse to address the newsroom: "Any woman here who has not slept with Jonathan Gilman, please stand up." She herself had fallen prey to his peculiar charm briefly, but she did not count it as an affair. It had felt more like being an extra in a very large crowd scene. Like most womanizers, she suspected, Gilman rarely discussed his tactics. But once, in an unguarded moment, he said to her, "People are impressed, for good or ill, with all the women I've slept with, but it's only a question of asking. If you ask a hundred women to sleep with you, about seventeen will say yes. And that's a lot more than most men get." He added, "Besides, I look best from very close up."

Now he was sighing over management's failure to read the writing on the wall. "They actually think they can turn this around," he said, "by setting up paywalls or targeted subscriptions. Seriously." An extra dose of contempt in the last word.

"And why are they such bad ideas?"

"Because our pathetic band of aging readers are the only ones who would consider subscribing to avoid a paywall and they aren't enough. Newspaper readers are dying out, and millennials don't know the difference between a blog written by some ignorant gasbag after a few drinks and a reasoned, researched and edited piece of reporting or analysis by an expert. So we're doomed."

After relishing the bad news for a few more minutes, Gilman plodded back to the business section, sowing more pessimism in the fertile soil of the newsroom as he went.

Liz turned back to her email. Damn it, there was another try from Nicole, nestling innocently in her inbox. She had followed Liz's advice like a good student, turning passive sentences into

active ones, trying to transform general statements into more concrete examples, if not scenes. Now it felt like a paint-by-numbers
exercise instead of a vague but lived experience. It still wasn't good
enough. What are you thinking? Liz chided herself in mid-reaction.
You're acting as if this editing exercise were real. God knows what it
is, or why you seem to be persisting in it. And how in the world are
you going to answer this one?

She met the poet for a drink that evening, in a bar with a Korean
name. The food did not seem particularly Korean, mostly fried vegetables, and there were no chairs with backs, only stools. Neither of
these things struck her as promising, but the stool was surprisingly
comfortable and she ordered a Brussels sprout salad, which was
very good. William never talked much about his poetry. He touched
fairly briefly on the unappreciative climate for poetry in general
and his in particular, but his favorite topic was his irritable bowel
syndrome. Although his poetry was abstract and often opaque, at
least to Liz, when it came to his gastric problems he was earthy
and graphic.

"IBS sufferers have both constipation and diarrhea," he said,
taking a swallow of his whiskey, "but I'd welcome more constipation. My thing is diarrhea."

Liz looked neutral, a balancing act between disgust and encouragement.

He went on about his diarrhea, its warning signs, its consis-
tency, the cramps that accompanied it. He drank more whiskey. Liz
knew almost nothing about IBS, but she was willing to bet whiskey
was contraindicated. The daughter of a pharmacist and a nurse,
she was no stranger to clinical dinner talk, but William was testing
her limits.

"'Bowel' is a funny word," she said, moving her plate and the
conversation sideways. She had lost her taste for Brussels sprouts.
"It used to mean compassion, heart or pity."

She couldn't have said where that piece of information came from, probably some eighteenth-century novel. She could not remember the plot from a novel she had read last week, but the things she had read as a teenager or in her twenties stayed with her.

William's interests were unpredictable.

"Yes. The Greeks and Hebrews thought the internal organs were the source of various emotions. The Greeks believed strong feelings, like love and anger, sprang from the bowels, but the Hebrews thought that they were the seat of softer emotions, like charity, mercy and compassion. Have a look." On his phone, he looked up "bowel" in the Oxford English Dictionary, and read an entry from 1832: "'I am a man who can feel for my neighbors. I have bowels—yes, I have bowels.'"

Was it time to re-evaluate William? She need not have worried, because he moved seamlessly from the softer emotions to his ongoing diarrhea.

"Last week, I don't know what it was—too much coffee, drink, depression about the fate of the new manuscript—but I had the runs for almost thirty-six hours."

As he continued, she signaled the waiter for the bill. Well, she had invited him, out of pity (the bowels again) as usual. He paid the tip, as usual, acting as if it were a singular piece of munificence, and then suggested that he could go with her to her apartment. It was unspoken but agreed between them that his basement apartment was beyond the pale. They did sometimes have sex, but less and less often. And tonight's recital about his malady was an anti-aphrodisiac.

"No, I'm sorry, William. I'm dead tired and I have to get up early in the morning."

On Metro on the way home, Liz thought about William's abundant shortcomings. And about Henry, who seemed a much better bet, but was now rousing her usual misgivings and escape plans. God, she hated dating. Her father had sent her off to college with a little brown glass bottle of Paregoric, for stomach upsets, which she rarely had. She remembered taking a swig from the bottle before more than one date, in the hope that it was a magical way to stop dreading the evening. She used to say she got married right out of college so that she could stop dating. Now here she was in her late forties, condemned to date again.

That was something else she could hold against Sidney. In the first months after their separation, suddenly thin and tragic-eyed, she veered between numbness and despair, with the occasional baffling, short-lived streak of euphoria. The self-consciousness that came with dating was not the most horrid thing in her new life, and she plunged in, testing again and again whether anyone could find her lovable.

What remained of her old life was Peter and her job as an arts editor at the Seattle paper. About six months after Sidney left, editing a review of a concert of music by Venetian composers, she came across one of Venice's nicknames, La Serenissima. The Most Serene One. She could not resist that. She did not have to be the most serene, but she craved a measure of serenity.

Peter stayed with Sidney for a week, and she went to Venice, her first exercise in travelling alone as a single woman. Men, she found, were everywhere and almost comically willing. She wasn't sure if they were willing for anything other than sex, but they materialized out of the Venetian stonework and were transparently available.

One night she listened to a band on the Piazza San Marco and at the end of the concert, a young Italian man approached her. Did she enjoy the concert? Where was she from? Liz's Italian was only at the beginning stages so they had almost no language in common but somehow with gestures, smiles and some Esperanto-like words managed a fragmentary conversation. He was an architect from Verona. They went to a coffee bar and, although it seemed unlikely, he told her he was in love with her. At least that's what Liz thought he was saying. To explain to him that he was making a mistake and that she was considerably older than he was, she ransacked the Italian dictionary she carried and managed to compose a sentence. "*Ho un figlio.*" "I have a son." But perhaps she hadn't really said that, because whatever she said apparently made her more alluring than ever, and he began kissing her. Which was not a good idea, and after another frantic dive into the small, square Penguin dictionary, she added, "*Dieci anni.*" As if the fact that her *figlio* was ten years old would conclusively quench the architect's passion. When it only fanned the flames, she said goodnight hurriedly and ran out into Venice's spiderweb of dark alleys. No matter which way she went, she always ended up at a canal, and she remembered Robert Benchley's postcard from Venice, "The streets are filled with water. Please advise." The young man pursued her for a while, until he gave up. Finally she found her way back to her hotel. In the morning, in her bag she found the book he had been reading. She had offered to carry it when they set out walking. It was an Italian translation of *Jonathan Livingston Seagull.* That should have been warning enough.

The architect was a random pickup, but Domenico, whom she met a day or two later, came vaguely recommended. When the Seattle paper's music critic heard she was going to Venice, he said that she could always look up his acquaintance, the music critic for *La Stampa*. Introductory emails followed, and she arranged to meet Domenico one evening under the equestrian statue in the Campo Santi Giovanni e Paolo.

Domenico was several steps up from the architect. He seemed to be closer to her age, the book he was reading as he leaned against the statue had fine print on tissue-thin pages and was definitely not *Jonathan Livingston Seagull*, and he spoke an English that only wobbled occasionally. He told her, soon after they began walking to a restaurant just off the campo, that she "looked fresh from the gymnasium." But she gathered that he was complimenting her, not on being sweaty and well-exercised, but on being so youthful that she looked like a student in a *ginnasio*, the classical high school. In person, Domenico was, if not round, definitely rounding, a short, balding man in a brown suit in spite of the summer heat. Over pizza, talking about Italy's tardy entry into the sexual revolution, he assured her gravely that at that very moment more people were having sex in Italy than in any other place in the world. That might have given her pause, but he was also charming and knowledgeable.

He lived with his widowed mother in the family apartment, and he suggested going there for a drink. She agreed, because she wanted to see the interior of a Venetian apartment and because she assumed she would meet his mother. But she never saw anything of the apartment, which was large and dark, and she only glimpsed Mama scuttling out of sight at the end of a long corridor. Mama clearly had her orders when Domenico brought friends home.

He left Liz on the rooftop, surrounded by a chain-link fence, while he went off to prepare drinks. When he returned, she thought, Oh dear. In his brown critic's suit, Domenico was at the edge of plausibility, physically speaking. But now he had changed into what he apparently regarded as seduction clothes—a two-piece outfit made of white fishnet and red polyester. The mostly fishnet top ended halfway up his ribs, leaving a generous expanse of hairy tummy between it and the red shorts. Did men ever look at themselves in the mirror, or could nothing shake their supreme confidence in their appeal? And could someone bottle that confidence in some diluted form, so that she could take a dropperful?

After a few swallows of Cinzano, Domenico began his advance, which included several unmerry chases around the chain-link fence. After saying No in various styles—at first apologetically, then kindly, then kindly but firmly—Liz finally had to say it sharply. Then he became sullen, and she left abruptly, lying that she knew her way back to her hotel.

Just before she left Venice for home, she had dinner with a colleague and his twin sons. Neither Derek nor the twins were very interested in Venice, but Derek felt that a trip to Europe was what you did with twelve-year-old boys who lived with their mother most of the year. The four of them had a companionable dinner—that is, she and Derek were companionable and the boys were cheerfully occupied in devouring their pasta. They were staying in the same hotel, and once the twins were stowed away in the room they were sharing with their father, Derek invited himself to her room, where he assumed that they would go to bed. With two boys pillow-fighting across the hall, who might interrupt them at any minute? With Derek living with his newish girlfriend in Seattle? With a casually collegial relationship at the paper, but nothing more? Her refusal seemed to surprise him, and he pouted briefly and intimated that she had been leading him on. Then he returned to his normal self and they had a farewell drink on her tiny balcony.

As a result of that trip to Venice, Liz decided two things. One was that she should keep on studying Italian. The other was that she could not fathom men. Their sexual attraction was so reliable that it felt impersonal—no, it was impersonal—and seemed to have no connection with any consequences. Her urbane divorce lawyer, who enjoyed talking like Mickey Spillane, said of his fellow men that they "followed their pants around town." Maybe that was especially true when the man or the woman, or both, were away on vacation. After her week in Venice, Liz would not have said that she felt lovable, but she did feel desirable. Which put her in a very large category and occasionally was bothersome. Perhaps you had to be desirable first so that, later, you could become lovable. Perhaps. She and Sidney had had a courtship that now seemed old-fashioned in its slowness: they had almost been in love by the time they went to bed.

The decision to study Italian had endured. She could read *Oggi* or *Gente*, the gossipy magazines that had big pictures. She could talk badly and sometimes understand what Italians said in answer to her questions. Her idea about men had also endured, but it rarely disturbed her anymore. Gradually in the ten years since Venice, Liz had found, if not serenity, a kind of calmness around the relationship between desirability and lovableness. A calmness that was more theoretical than actual since she had rarely managed to bring the two together.

━━━

At work on Wednesday, Liz couldn't make up her mind about a submission she thought of as "the pedophile piece." It was written by a man who had served a short prison sentence for posting a plan for seducing children on an internet porn site. He had claimed it was pure fantasy, but the jury had decided otherwise. He had done his time, retired from his responsible government job only a little earlier than he had planned, and was now defending porn sites and associated chat rooms as part of free speech. Wisely, he made it clear that porn involving real children was properly illegal: he only chatted and wrote about it. He also minimized the possibility that consuming porn led to action. He was defending fantasy, impure and simple, he wrote, referring to scholarly articles that indicated a very low correlation between watching porn and acting upon it. On the contrary, he added, interacting with porn was a way for people who were sexually attracted to children to keep their predilection within allowable bounds. He wrote well.

Clearly, he had a messianic zeal about the subject, and looked forward to seeing his name in print. He was probably at least a little unbalanced. Many people would object to it, but as her mother used to say, "It's a point of view," and one not often read in the paper. It pushed the envelope, and for some reason Liz felt more willing than usual to do that. She would put it in the paper quickly, before she changed her mind. The illustration for a piece she had planned for next Monday was going to be late, so that needed to be postponed. The new illustrator, the one who had done the fine pomegranate, said she worked quickly, so Liz would send the porn piece to her after the town hall.

"Town hall" was the folksy name for an address by the publisher to the editorial staff. The staff had gathered in the center of the newsroom, and Seamus arrived punctually at ten, looking as if he had had a particularly bracing bath in dollars. He began talking about the challenges facing journalism in the twenty-first century. The paper's solution, he said, was not the newest technological bells and whistles but, in spite of that, he spent a few minutes dwelling proudly on all the different state-of-the-art delivery systems and the cornucopia of apps available to the paper's readers. Then, remembering the plot, he said, "But it's not about the choice between print, android, Instagram, mobile—it's about the reader, and getting him the news where he wants it. The reader comes first."

This was all predictable, if more properly addressed to the readers than the staff, and his audience looked predictably skeptical. It was a group where almost everyone, including the white-haired man who edited the chess and birding columns, thought of himself as an investigative journalist, so cynicism was their default reaction.

"We cover government and policy," Seamus continued, changing tack, "that's in our genes. But we never neglect the human face of these big-picture ideas. We track people's real, everyday lives and the emotions that follow from policy."

More scornful looks from the audience. When had the paper ever given a toss for the emotions of everyday life? Real people and their feelings were most reliably found in My Turn, but that hardly ranked high in the paper's pecking order. Liz looked at her lap. She felt sorry for Seamus. Maybe if he had worn a suit whose tailoring was less expensively self-effacing, he would have been more convincing.

Seamus's tailoring was the first thing that had interested her about him. They had met as part of yet another panel about the future of newspapers, this one put on by Georgetown's journalism program. Seamus was the paper's CFO at the time and since he had nothing to do with editorial, their paths had never crossed. At the reception afterward, Seamus stood talking with a small group, his back to her. His jacket seemed to be a natural extension of his shoulders, as if they had secreted a layer of the finest wool, and its impeccably calculated double vents announced a certain willingness to misbehave. By the time he became publisher, their affair was about six months old. The promotion made things tricky, but since their relationship was a secret and was already established and because Seamus planned to be hands-off where editorial was concerned, they were not really worried.

Her thoughts wandered to Seamus's secret phone, and she wondered if he had really bought it to communicate with her. Maybe it predated her by one or two or several women. If a third of the stories people at the paper told about Seamus were true, he had a long history of extramarital affairs. Far from troubling Liz, she found that reassuring. It meant he was not inclined to leave his wife, and although it was not thrilling to think of herself as one in a line of efficient safety valves, she preferred that to the possibility of breaking up a marriage. That prospect horrified her.

Now she turned her attention from Seamus-the-lover back to Seamus-the-publisher, who was looking forward to a redesign early in the new year. In spite of the sullenness pasted on the faces of his audience, he affected to believe they were equally enthusiastic. Sheets would be posted next week so that people could sign up for committees on different aspects of the redesign.

When the meeting was thrown open to questions, Gilman, as usual, led the charge. What about the constantly falling revenues? What about the competition from cable and online news? Wasn't the redesign a smokescreen for significant layoffs? Hadn't they just had a redesign? Seamus's answers were as smoothly tailored as his suit, although less self-effacing. Yes, these were worrying times, but he was confident they would prevail.

Liz and Gilman fell in step as the staff returned to their cubicles. An intern who was rumored to be involved with Gilman passed them, sending him a smile and a feathery little wave of her fingers. She was working on the foreign desk this month. Gilman nodded at her briskly. He didn't encourage public speculation about his amours.

"When did Donovan ever tell us the truth, anyway?" he complained to Liz.

She knew he didn't expect an answer. All right-thinking people, he was convinced, agreed about the publisher.

On Thursday evening she was going out with a group of women who met irregularly for dinner. They included Liz's downstairs neighbor, Leona, an editor in the paper's national section named Madeleine, a business writer named Jane, Jane's sister Sally who was a lawyer, and the two Anns. One was really Anne, called Brown Anne in the group because she was a brunette. She taught French in a high school, where her red-headed friend, called Red Ann, was a guidance counsellor. Liz didn't much feel like going, but they hadn't met for a few months, and she had no good excuse. Besides, it would be better than staying home and brooding about how to respond to Nicole's second draft.

When they had first gotten together, the women had talked loosely about forming a book club. But Jane had said, "So-called book clubs talk about the book for five minutes, ten minutes max. Then they go back to talking about what interests them. So why don't we skip the book part and go straight to conversation?"

They considered potluck dinners, rotating among their houses, but the two Anns urged a no-cooking, no-cleanup policy. When someone suggested just wine and nibbles in their houses, Leona raised the specter of "snack escalation," where the nibbles would magically grow more and more elaborate until they might as well be cooking dinner. The majority nodded: they knew themselves. Plus, they didn't want this to be a busman's holiday for Leona. So they met in various restaurants.

Tonight's restaurant was Italian and after they placed their orders, Jane said to Brown Anne and Liz, "You two should have ordered in Italian."

Liz and Brown Anne had met in their Italian class.

"Great idea," Liz said, nodding at their waiter, who was Asian.

It came out a little more acidic than Liz had intended, and Madeleine gave her an appraising look.

Liz had most in common with Madeleine and Jane because they worked at the paper. She spent the most time with Brown Anne, at their Italian class. And Leona, of course, lived in her building. Sally and Red Ann were more peripheral, but she liked them too. Sally was clever and enjoyed conversations more political and heated than their typically amiable chit-chat. Red Ann loved to laugh, although tonight she was subdued, probably because she was newly single.

Some groups of women spent their first minutes together in a gushing burst of how-lucky-we-are-to-have-such-great-friends, but these women wasted no time on that kind of burble. They talked about their work, their colleagues, their children if they had them (three did), their romantic entanglements if they had them (two had boyfriends and Red Ann had recently broken up with her girl-friend), books they were reading, Thanksgiving plans and the general state of the world. That inevitably included Hillary Clinton.

Knowing she was starting something, Sally asked, "So, is that why she's put up with Bill's affairs all these years, so she could run for president?"

Madeleine said, to no one's surprise, "How can you say that?" She thought the sun rose and set on Hillary, which was unusual adulation for a politician from a journalist.

At the same time, Brown Anne, a romantic, asked, "Has it ever occurred to you that she loves him?"

They divided between those who wanted to consider if and how long you could love an incorrigible philanderer, and those who wanted to discuss Hillary as a politician. Sometimes the two groups overlapped.

"I've never forgiven them for that shot on the White House lawn boarding the helicopter to Camp David at the time of the impeachment and Monica Lewinsky," Leona said. "The phony way they stage-managed the whole thing and inserted their teenaged daughter between them to show that they were a supposedly happy family. Please."

"In fairness to Hillary," Sally said, "that was choreographed by Bill's people and not Hillary's."

"And although it looks very cynical to us, and I'm sure it was," Liz said, "maybe it gave Chelsea some comfort to walk between her parents holding their hands."

That set them off again, arguing whether or not Chelsea knew she was a pawn, and if that mattered.

Leona, Sally and Liz enjoyed scandalizing their friends by discussing Hillary's tactics as if she were a normal politician and not a gift from the gods.

After listing some of Hillary's compromises and corner-cutting, Sally summed up their position: "Angela Merkel she isn't."

Another firestorm, which only ended because they had been this way before and knew each other's positions. Naturally, they were planning to vote for Hillary once she got the nomination.

Liz noticed that as they progressed through their forties, husbands (Jane and Sally were married) might be mentioned in passing but were rarely the focus of any discussion. Sex, even more rarely.

Jane asked Liz, "What's up with the creepy poet?"

Poor William, Liz thought. Peter's insult had caught on. "Not much," she said.

"He's not a bad guy," Leona said. She had a soft spot for him because he had once helped her carry out some big trays of canapés.

They drank red wine, more liberally if they were travelling on Metro, and agreed that the pappardelle were better than the gnocchi. They perused the dessert menu seriously, but only the two Anns surrendered.

"Let's share a pannacotta," Brown Anne suggested.

"No," Red Ann said, "they're too small. We'll have two, please."

Liz was glad to see that Ann's appetite had survived her breakup. They parted just before ten, chiming in on top of each other that it had been fun, and that everyone was just too busy. They hoped they could find another date that suited them all before Christmas.

It had been a good evening, in spite of Liz's reluctance. Leona was going to spend the night at her boyfriend's in Brookland, and Liz and Madeleine rode on the same Metro line for a while. They chatted casually about how thin the paper was looking, and about Gilman—was he pursuing the intern or was she pursuing him? Madeleine, who lived with her boyfriend, applied a little lipstick and looked over her hair before her stop. Liz was surprised that she took such care, until she reminded herself of her Tuesday lingerie.

Left by herself, Liz's thoughts turned to Nicole. Until ten days ago, Nicole had been like a dress skulking at the outmost edge of her closet, something she forgot for months on end, that was probably hopelessly out of fashion and not worth the trouble of trying on. Now, since the arrival of her damn submission, the dress that was Nicole was the first thing she saw when she opened her closet door. It probably glowed in the dark. Would Liz never be done with this? The thought of traipsing once more through the rigmarole of their relationship made her weary.

No, that was an evasion: Nicole made her feel defenceless, an old reaction. When she had discovered Sidney and Nicole's affair, the women pushing strollers around Seattle suddenly became charged with menace in Liz's imagination. Nicole's children were small at the time and they had met through Peter's daycare, so Liz associated her with very young children and their mothers. Nicole had hurt her, without warning or provocation, so it was possible that these friendly looking mothers doing errands or heading for the park might do something similar. The world, or Liz's world anyway, was not the mostly benevolent place she had imagined it to be, and never would be again. Or was that only the pathetic way an un-modern person looked at these things?

At the same time, Liz had another feeling. Having Nicole settle down in her inbox was distressing, but there was something undeniably illicit and exciting about it too. As if Liz wanted to know a kitten better, and was bringing out a ball of yarn.

At home, she tried to pretend everything was as usual, searching unsuccessfully in the fridge for something that she could bring for lunch the next day, flossing her teeth with a thoroughness that was almost punitive. Then, feeling she had started a machine and did not know how to stop it, she wrote,

> *Dear Nicole Szabo:*
> *Thanks for this second draft. I still think there's something distant about your piece. It needs something more specific, something to which the reader could relate. Maybe you should move ahead in time, and describe the dinner with your husband where you two plan Christmas? That might give the reader some insight into the household dynamic.*
> *Just a thought.*
> *Editor@MyTurn*

Maybe that would end it. The worrying thing was that Liz wasn't sure she wanted to end it.

——

Late on Friday afternoon, the inbox on her screen moved up a notch.

Dear Editor,

Thanks so much for your patience with me. Writing about the planning dinner sounds like a good idea, but it didn't happen. My husband decided we didn't really need to make a plan—I just need to scale down my expectations for the holiday and not make such a big fuss. That's how he put it! So I'm not sure where that leaves me with the essay—or with Christmas.

All the best,

Nicole

Dear Nicole,

Your husband sounds like a glass-half-empty kind of guy. Sometimes when confronted with a more optimistic person, that kind of character can feel that they aren't being listened to, or that no one understands them. And that just roots their negativity even deeper. I don't know, but I wonder if you've thought about expressing the negative side of the question, for once. It might just destabilize him to hear you say, "Well, Christmas is never going to be a good holiday for us, and maybe we just need to accept that." Or, "Christmas for most people is just a yearly gift package of dashed expectations. Why should ours be any different?" You might be surprised at his reaction.

Editor@MyTurn

Now she had really done it. She had left the charade of editing and moved into the charade of couples therapy. When someone went adrift with a particularly obtuse argument, Jonathan Gilman would say scornfully, "Your point?" Liz asked herself, Your motive? Was she really trying to help Nicole and Sidney's marriage? Or was she trying to indicate to Nicole that Sidney was unredeemable? Or was there something else, something subterranean working its way through her inbox?

WEEK THREE
===

October 26–November 1, 2015

For the pedophile piece, the new artist, whose name was Fern, had proposed two ideas. One showed a man sitting on a park bench, his back to the viewer. He was extending his hand to a little girl, whose face Fern had smudged beyond recognition. The other was more abstract—a high-walled garden maze with a child at the center. But none of the paths, presumably porn fantasies, ever led to the child, who stayed safe. Liz chose the first option: it was clearer and less optimistic.

She was good, this Fern, and Liz wrote her an email saying so. Fern answered, "Thank you. I have to confess that illustrating this piece made me feel slightly queasy. I wasn't sure that this guy deserved a hearing. But I guess that's why I'm an illustrator and not an editor!" Liz stared at that for a minute or two. Apparently she had done something rather risky and, for those who knew her, uncharacteristic. Well, then, so be it. She wasn't sure where her decision had come from, but she had no wish to second-guess herself.

The piece appeared in the paper on Monday, and Liz was prepared for the half-dozen or so howls of "contemptible" and "despicable" from readers. One dismayed subscriber asked, "Whose side are you on, anyway?" The Letters to the Editor editor chose that one to print. The unexpected came later in the morning, when Liz bumped into the managing editor on the stairs. Norris inclined his head toward the landing, meaning he wanted a word.

"Liz," he began. "The publisher."

Seamus almost never commented on her page.

"The publisher is not happy with today's My Turn. He said to the editor-in-chief, 'This is not the Weimar Republic.'"

Sometimes Seamus's allusions took her by surprise. Not that she thought that he was unintelligent or ignorant, but this must be the kind of reference on which the Dublin Jesuits reared their students.

"Okay, thanks for passing it on."

The communication chain was typical: Seamus complained to the reclusive editor-in-chief, who almost never left his office, and it was Norris who had to speak with her. She knew Seamus would not mention it tomorrow.

———

Seamus fell asleep in Liz's arms, which rarely happened. He might close his eyes for less than five minutes after sex, but not to sleep. And yet here he was, his breathing changing just enough for Liz to notice. She ran her fingers over his perfectly cut hair, the black just starting to gray. As a teenager, she couldn't bear it when her boyfriends showed up with a haircut. They suddenly looked so vulnerable, and the bare space around their ears broke her heart. She could hardly wait for it to grow in and mentally averted her eyes until it did.

Now she asked, "How often do you get your hair cut?"

Seamus's eyes flew open, as if he had done something shameful. Which from some points of view he had, but not by falling asleep.

"Why do you ask?"

"Because it always looks exactly the same. It never seems either to grow or to get cut."

He smiled, presumably because that was the effect he wanted. "Once a week."

He looked so innocently pleased with himself that she clasped him tighter for a moment.

"Did you have any serious girlfriends before you got married?"

"Why do you ask?"

"That's the second time you've asked that."

"Because it's the second time you've asked something unexpected."

She supposed it was, at least about the girlfriends. Perhaps remembering her holiday in Venice, or trading biographies with Henry had set her on that track. She was always looking for safe topics she could use with Seamus.

"Well, I just wondered . . . about your romantic life before you married."

He shifted out of her arms and up onto an elbow. "Naturally, I had some serious girlfriends, in university and once I was working. I didn't marry until I was thirty."

He looked ever so slightly displeased, and she put a placating hand on his bicep and smiled at him. "You look as if I'm impugning your manhood. I'm sure you had lots of girls. I just like to hear your stories."

He kissed her, and said, "Sweetheart." He called her sweetheart when he felt he had been abrupt. "It's just that I have to get back to the paper. We have a budget meeting about the cost of covering the primaries." That was more than he normally said about his work. "I wish we could spend more time together, and I could tell you all about my misspent youth. That was too bad you were busy the Sunday before last." Remembering why she had been busy and looking slightly conscience-stricken, he asked, "But how is your mother?"

"Her memory is worse and worse, but she doesn't seem actively unhappy. Maybe it's her lifelong stoicism."

Watching Seamus knot today's club tie—oblique stripes of midnight blue and dull bronze—Liz thought what a perfect bubble they had created for these Tuesday afternoons. His displeasure about the pedophile piece seemed to exist in another universe. And so did her reaction to his displeasure—except that she didn't seem to have a reaction. His disapproval interested her as little as the angry messages from readers, and she wondered a little at that.

Changing the subject, at least in her own mind, she asked, "Speaking of the primaries, what do you think of Hillary's chances?" This was not asking for insider knowledge of the editorial board's thinking, she told herself, just raising a subject that engaged most of the country. But before Seamus could answer, she added, "Do you notice how Hillary Clinton is always 'Hillary,' Donald Trump is always 'Trump' and Bernie Sanders is very often 'Bernie Sanders'? Why don't we call her 'Clinton'?"

"You know why," said Seamus, checking for his phone. "Because that would confuse her with her husband."

He was not a wholehearted fan of Bill Clinton.

"Right. What a shame she was pressured to start using his name when he ran for president."

"On the contrary, some people think that is a huge advantage for her." Liz was getting the feeling that Seamus was not a wholehearted fan of Hillary either.

She repeated, "But what do you think of her chances?"

"It all depends on whether or not people decide she is electable."

Which was not an answer, and there was that word Liz kept hearing—electable. It seemed that it was used more for women candidates than men. Liz didn't have an opinion on whether or not

Hillary had made a deal with the devil and stayed with Bill for a better shot at the presidency. But how sad if she had and it proved to be a miscalculation. That would be the worst of two worlds, staying with a philandering husband for reasons of ambition and then being judged guilty by association.

"Did you notice what I did with my wallet?"

"'To support your wallet in its service,'" Liz said, "'you should set aside a place for it to rest.'"

Seamus looked dumbfounded. "What in the world are you talking about?"

"I was just quoting Marie Kondo. A joke."

"Is she in editorial?"

While she explained who Marie Kondo was, Seamus located his wallet, as well as his cashmere scarf. He didn't seem to be attending to the idea of a neatness guru. At the door, he threw his scarf over Liz's head and pulled her in to be kissed. "Next Tuesday," he said, touching her cheek, before he released her. After he left, she collected her coat and bag, still thinking about electability and remembering Brown Anne's question about Hillary and Bill, "Has it ever occurred to you that she loves him?" Liz could understand taking a husband back after one transgression: she had been anxious to do that, but Sidney had been too much in love with Nicole to consider it. Serial philandering was something different. Did you tell yourself each time your partner strayed that it would be the last time? Or discipline yourself to ignore it?

That evening, a woman in Liz's yoga class wore a T-shirt that said, *I'm Only Here for the Savasana.* Liz was lying in corpse pose and wondering how many times she would have to wash her newest seductress bra before its prickly lace softened. Although most people who did yoga agreed with the woman in the T-shirt, Liz had read that these last ten or fifteen minutes were the most difficult part of your practice. You had to be completely relaxed and alert at the same time, banishing distracting thoughts and following the teacher's prompts.

Chip was saying, "Think of someone who needs your love," and Liz turned her thoughts to revenge.

Last week, after she read the newspaper story about the woman who poured tea on her rival, Liz had googled "scorned wife revenge" and found a midden of ingenious acts of vengeance. In one, an Australian woman found pictures on her husband's phone of him having sex with another woman. After he left his wife, she printed the pictures and took them to the volunteer firefighters' hall, formerly the center of their social life. Knowing that her husband was inside with his lover, socializing with all her former friends, she put the incriminating pictures under the windshields of all the cars in the parking lot. The wife recalled, "I slept like a baby that night."

Liz thought back to the first year after Sidney had left, wondering how vengeful she had felt. She had wished for Nicole's unhappiness but only as a side effect, in that she desperately wanted Sidney to return to her. Any signs that he was happy in his new life choked her with grief and some anger, but she only wanted him to be unhappy enough to come home.

Still, she marvelled at the clever women she read about on the revenge sites. Some of their ideas were mildly amusing, like the woman who sold all her live-in boyfriend's possessions in a garage sale, posting a big sign, *Ex-Boyfriend a Cheater. Everything Must Go.* Others were more audacious. She read about a man who was in the habit of begetting children. One of his ex-girlfriends had a bumper sticker made that read, *Honk if Darren Davis Fathered Your Child.* Sometimes the simplest measures produced the most devastating results. A wife discovered that her husband was sexting an ex-girlfriend. She swapped the ex-girlfriend's number in his phone with that of his boss.

Liz saw herself sucking on these stories the way her mother sucked on Werther's butterscotch drops. She ordered herself, Only *one* a day. Was her bogus new relationship with Nicole on its way to becoming another one of these payback stories? She didn't think so. It might make things simpler if it were.

=====

On Thursday, Liz surprised herself by inviting the Dubroffs for coffee or tea. Normally, she had no contact with My Turn writers that was not strictly business, but something about the Dubroffs, or her own state of mind, overrode that. They lived not far from her, and they agreed to meet at Teaism on Sunday, after their usual tour of the Dupont Circle Farmers Market.

As she turned off Connecticut onto R Street, Liz saw a gray-haired couple with full backpacks and cotton bags climbing the stairs to Teaism's door. By now, she wished she'd never had this goofy idea, but she was in for it now. She thought it would be tactful to let the Dubroffs catch their breath before she accosted them, but by the time she entered they were nowhere to be seen. Guessing at the source of her confusion, a waiter pointed to the wooden staircase. The Dubroffs were not at all out of breath and had secured a table on the second floor overlooking the street. Jana was tall and sturdy, with pewter-colored hair in a smart cut that was longer at the sides than the back. Michael was slightly less tall, also sturdy, and his hair was curly. He insisted on going down to the first floor to get their tea.

"His back isn't as fussy as mine," Jana said. "Occupational hazard."

To Liz's inquiring look, she explained that they were retired dentists, and dentistry was hard on the back.

While they waited for Michael, the two women made small talk, agreeing that Teaism, in its Zen determination not to be cozy, with its bare wooden floors, rigid chairs and scuffed tables, ended up being cozy. The master cabinet on the first floor, with scores of glass drawers holding varieties of loose tea, was its raison d'être, and there was no coffee on the premises.

Michael returned, with pots of jasmine, Keemun and something called black peony, where the tea opened like blossoms when steeped.

"Their catalogue is like lyric poetry," Michael said, putting two salty oat cookies "to share" in the middle of the table.

Liz wondered how three people would divide two cookies, until Jana put one on her saucer and one on Liz's.

"That's Michael's idea of sharing," she said. "He's always watching his boyish figure."

"The good news," Michael announced, deadpan, "is that Teaism has eliminated the use of high-fructose corn syrup."

"Whew," Jana said. "How did you find out?"

"There's a poster downstairs, next to the one with all the nutritional information about the menu—which things are soy-free, non-GMO, gluten-free, et cetera."

They settled down to exchanging biographies. The Dubroffs' three bossy daughters lived, respectively, in Virginia, Chicago and Seattle. The Seattle daughter, who was less condescending than her sisters, taught economics at the University of Washington.

"My ex-husband is an economist in Seattle, too," Liz said. "But he works for the government. In trade policy."

Sometimes, when you said the words "ex-husband" or "divorce," people in the Dubroffs' generation gave you a penetrating look, as if they hoped to discover what you had done wrong. But the Dubroffs were too enlightened for that. Their Chicago daughter was divorced, and they knew all about custody arrangements and blended families.

They asked Liz if the paper would support Hillary Clinton's campaign for the nomination, and when that might happen. She tried answering in generalities, but soon had to confess that she was probably one of the least politically informed people at the paper. She was not inspired by men, and now some women, cutting deals in back rooms and often willing to barter away their supposedly cherished ideals for votes.

"I do marvel," she said, "in an abstract way, at the granular detail with which the political reporters and columnists write about these things. And I always mean to read the whole article, but I almost never get beyond the third or fourth paragraph."

The Dubroffs found that hard to believe, and looked disappointed: How could she work in a place so filled with brilliant political writers and not share their interests?

"Well, I enjoy my colleagues," she said. "They're bright and fast and can be funny, even when they're talking politics. And they have plenty of company in their wonkishness, so they don't need me. I like to think I bring some balance to the paper."

She said the last with a smile, to show she was only half-serious.

Liz wanted to hear about their lives. She heard a whisper of an accent in Jana's excellent English, but she could not place it. The pair had met in dental school in Baltimore. Jana had begun her career as a dentist in her native Czechoslovakia, as it then was, but when she immigrated she needed to do a qualifying year in school, learning the latest Western practices. Michael's father was a Baltimore dentist, and the highlight of their courtship, they told Liz, was sneaking into his office every Sunday.

"Not so we could have sex," Jana said.

"How can you say that?" Michael asked. "It was very erotic for me."

They laughed and explained, talking on top of each other and correcting the other's version, that on those stealthy Sunday afternoons Michael gradually removed all of Jana's Communist-era fillings and replaced them with state-of-the-art American ones.

"I guess it did have an element of foreplay," Jana conceded.

"More than that for me," Michael said, taking the last crumbles of his wife's oat cookie. "I still get a thrill thinking of your little mouth opened so trustingly to my father's drill. And the gentle way I tamped the beautiful new fillings. The fact that it was illegal—since I was a student—made it even sexier."

Jana pinged her hand at him in a way that indicated he was both touching and very silly. Liz was charmed. She could not imagine her parents talking about their sex life, virtual or not, either before or during their marriage. Jana and Michael were more sophisticated, but they also reminded Liz of her parents. Both couples leavened their solid values with flexibility, one of their values being a respect for others' opinions. Probably Agnes was more flexible than Liz's father, who obscured his resistance to change with tenderness. She told the Dubroffs about her father's fatal heart attack, and about Agnes's Alzheimer's.

"So you are an orphan," Michael said. "Plus, now you have another child."

Liz's eyes stung. That about summed it up, except that she was neglecting her new child. She missed her parents.

The Dubroffs had to get their food home before going to a matinee, and they parted with resolutions to get together again. Liz left more pleased than disconcerted by her unusual overture, telling herself, Don't overthink this.

In and around the Dubroffs and Henry and her mother (who needed another visit), Nicole still preoccupied her. She was like a centripetal force that drew everything back to Liz's murky, confused center and long-buried feelings about shame and loss and resentment and forgiveness. Especially forgiveness. Unpredictably, Liz found herself considering Seamus and Martha along with Nicole and Sidney. When it came to Martha, she was as guilty as Nicole and Sidney. And if her affair with Seamus ever came to light, chances were that Martha would suffer many of the sorrows that had visited Liz. Why had that not bothered her?

She stopped in at Kramerbooks, where usually she went straight to fiction, followed by biography and memoir. She did that now, but nothing called to her. Moving past psychology, she drifted into self-help. Honey called these books, whose covers were dimensional and their content not overly nuanced, "bumpy-cover books," but

Liz was feeling more curious than superior. She walked slowly through subsections on self-care, anxiety, depression, body image and bereavement, including pet bereavement. Then she found a shelf devoted to forgiveness. The bumpy images on these covers ran to trees, flowers, sunrises, butterflies and hearts, sometimes on their own, sometimes in people's hands. Their titles—in very large print, as were the authors' names—included *28 Days to Total Forgiveness*, *Slow Forgiveness* and *The Only Forgiveness Toolkit You'll Ever Need*. Feeling as if these books might be just what she wanted, Liz ran her hands over the covers as if she were reading Braille. Finally she took *Forgiveness Is a Gift You Give Yourself* to the counter, trying to squelch the feeling that she was buying a particularly reprehensible form of pornography.

WEEK FOUR

November 2–8, 2015

Since Henry had paid for their brunch and said she could pay next time, Liz felt duty-bound to ensure that there was a next time. Plus, she liked his nut-brown eyes, his interested listening face and his skill at sheltering two people under an umbrella, a useful talent in D.C. She had suggested a few dates for supper, but between her yoga and Italian class and the evening seminar he taught, they hadn't yet found a convenient night.

Wednesday morning, on Metro, she read a text from Henry: *Very strong piece today. When can I see you?* She had to admit it was sweet of him to keep tabs on My Turn. Surely not normal reading for a historian, even a social historian. Maybe it was even a little too sweet.

It took a second for her to remember which piece he had just read. Oh yes, the story of a woman who lived in a remote part of West Virginia and decided that if she wanted to continue enjoying such things as leather shoes, roast chicken and pets, she should share some responsibility for the killing that made those pleasures possible. Because she and her family lived several hours from the nearest vet, normally when one of their animals needed to be put down her competent husband did the job. But when their cat was hit by a car, with no hope of recovery and was suffering, the writer, flushed with her new mission, had tried to drown it herself. She bungled it, badly, and her husband had had to step in and end the cat's suffering. Painfully contrite and realizing that "amends could not be made," the writer concluded that she would do it again, but properly next time. The piece was almost Raymond Carver–like in its shapely, tempered admission of failure, and the illustration, a burlap sack with a few telltale bulges, was good too.

Her phone pinged again and, unusually, it was from Honey. She might comment on the day's My Turn when they ran into each other in the newsroom, but Liz couldn't remember her ever reacting with a text. *When did you start walking on the wild side, my friend? First the pedophile and now this slap in the face to animal lovers everywhere. I know, I know, our mission is to afflict the comfortable, but this is a new direction for My Turn. What's up? Is everything okay?*

Liz's first, top-of-the-head response was that Honey was overreacting. And she did have those two dogs. Later, when it became clear just how appallingly insensitive many readers considered this piece, Liz had to admit to herself that deep in a corner she rarely visited, she was not really surprised. But she was tired of being careful.

The woman in the next cubicle, who edited the Opinion section, half-stood to see over her baffle when Liz arrived. She gave Liz a furtive look, then quickly hid in her screen. She was an odd duck who generally avoided much contact, so Liz was not concerned. Then she saw her email, with subject lines that ranged from "Disgraceful piece!" to "What were you thinking!" and "Why print the pitiful details of a cat's drowning, gulps and all?" The angry responses filled screen after screen. So far, Henry was a minority of one.

She could feel Margaret, the woman in the next cubicle, listening to the silence, so she said, "Lots of reaction to My Turn today."

Margaret said, "You made a mistake."

Right after the morning meeting of the section heads, which she did not attend, Liz got a message from the managing editor, saying, *When you have a minute, come and see me.*

She could feel the eyes of the newsroom on her as she walked over to his office, a glass cube where everyone could watch but not hear their colleagues' dealings with management. Norris sat under a framed sign—the keystone of his management style—that said, *What Part of 'No' Don't You Understand?* He looked unhappy, but no more so than usual.

"Quite a tempest this morning," he said.

"So it seems."

"You know, gratuitous provocation is not part of our mandate. This is the second time in two weeks."

"Neither one was gratuitous or provocative. This morning's was a good essay by a woman who made a mistake on her way to a goal, and regrets the way it turned out, but not the goal."

"What kind of person tries to drown a cat in 2015? That's near-criminal stupidity, if not plain malice."

"As you know from the essay"—she decided to assume that Norris had actually read the piece rather than just the outrage around it—"it certainly wasn't malice. She was caught up in her quest to do the dirty work involved in having a pet, but she hadn't done her homework."

"But why didn't she just take the cat to a vet?"

So he hadn't read the essay.

"Because she was on a DIY mission, however misguided. Because she lives in the West Virginia backcountry and it's a long trip to a vet. Maybe most important, because she lives in a culture where sick animals aren't always disposed of by professionals. I'd be willing to bet that more than ninety percent of those angry emails were written by city people on intimate terms with their vet."

"So why do you think so many readers are so upset?" He knew the answer, but this was his way of prolonging the discussion.

"Because it's not comfortable to read about a creature in pain," she said patiently. "That's the reasonable answer. Beyond that, animal lovers sometimes seem to care more about animals in pain than humans. But the page isn't supposed to make readers comfortable all the time. I don't have to tell you that."

Norris picked up a piece of paper on which he had made some notes, then put it down.

"Okay. But the publisher has had a very unpleasant call from some very offended friends. They are appalled that we would publish such a thing, and they want to see the guidelines for My Turn." At that, he gave a grim half-smile, the idea of the paper having "guidelines" was so quaint. "So I want you to write to them. And I'll have a look at it before you send it." Before she could protest, at least at having to show it to him before she sent it, he tore off the top strip of the paper with the notes and handed it to her. "Their email. Name of Dubroff."

Oh dear. Now she did feel uncomfortable, not because she had done anything wrong, but because she saw herself through the Dubroffs' eyes. She couldn't remember if they had mentioned having a pet. Not that you needed a pet, apparently, to be infuriated by the essay. And how like them not to have mentioned that they were friends of Seamus.

Dear Jana and Michael,

I am so sorry that today's My Turn has upset you.

Let me try to explain how I choose the essays for that page. Some of them are fine statements of perennial subjects, while others are original, provocative, unpredictable. I often disagree with them, and sometimes I even disapprove of them, but as a person and not as an editor. As an editor, I choose pieces that may occasionally make readers rethink some assumptions or challenge some long-held beliefs. That was one of the things I liked about your essay, that it

overturned conventional expectations. I think of all the
essays for My Turn as eyewitness accounts from one life or
one sensibility, and that's why I value them.

The woman who wrote this one had the courage to look
at some things many of us try to avoid, and to try and
redress some of the balance. She made a mistake in how she
went about it, and she acknowledges that. Reading about
the cat's struggles was distressing, but that was a necessary
part of this story.

Again, I value your judgment and your wisdom, and I
enjoyed our time together at Teaism. I'm doubly sorry this
has caused you discomfort, and I hope it won't affect our
relationship.

Yours truly,
Liz

Except for some twinges about Jana and Michael, Liz stayed
calm as the emails and tweets mounted during the day. Feeling that
Peter might understand her choice, she sent him a nonchalant text
with the news that apparently she had miscalculated the tolerance
of her readers.

Once he had read the piece online, Peter responded. *Mom?*
Hello? Do you remember Mickey Mouse playing the sorcerer's appren-
tice in Fantasia? *How after he magicked the broom to wash the floor*
for him, he couldn't stop it and the place was flooding? Starting with
last week's piece by the guy who lusts after kids, you seem to have found
the magic formula for really freaking out your readers. Maybe now
you should look for the instructions on how to turn the thing off.

She almost smiled at that one. She had had a similar thought
early in her correspondence with Nicole, when it felt as if she had
started a machine and couldn't find the off switch. She should
think harder about what she was doing with Nicole, as well as at the
paper. At least the Nicole drama compelled her—was that good or

bad?—but her beloved job was strangely not worrying her. Today's commotion felt rather as if someone who looked like her and was unaccountably doing her job had blundered, at least in the eyes of many readers. Liz remained unconvinced that that woman had made a bad decision. Abstractly, she understood what the fuss was about, but personally she couldn't summon up the energy to care.

Late in the afternoon, Henry texted her again, asking about a drink after her Italian class. He had to attend a guest lecture but could meet her any time after nine. Brown Anne was willing, and they met at a bar near George Washington. By then Liz was done talking about "the cat piece," as everyone called the essay, but Henry was not.

"How many emails did you get?"

"I didn't count, but more than fifty."

"How many were positive?"

"Positive? None. People don't usually write unless they have a complaint. What did surprise me was that there were many more readers upset about the cat than about the piece I recently ran by the pedophile."

The waiter came by to ask about refills, but they shook their heads.

Henry asked, "Did anyone complain about the cod?"

"What cod?" Anne asked.

"Do you remember, at the beginning of the piece, the woman recalled that the only killing she had done in her past was when she had fished for a living in her twenties."

"Right," Anne said. "I forgot that. She writes about the pity she would feel when she cut a cod's throat."

"'The heavy, elegant cod,'" Henry quoted. He looked at Liz and repeated, "Did anyone complain about the cod?"

"No. No one mentioned the cod."

"Apparently the pain of some animals is more acceptable than others," Henry said.

Liz knew it wasn't a perfect analogy. People were going to eat the cod, which made its pain more generally acceptable, and the pain was brief. But Henry was on her side. Thank you for noticing that, Liz thought, but she did not say it.

Anne sent her a text later that night: *Like him*, followed by a smiley face. Liz wasn't sure if it was a comment or an order.

———

Next morning, there was an email from Nicole in Liz's inbox.

Dear My Turn Editor,

I'm sorry I haven't gotten back to you sooner. My husband has been super-busy, so I didn't have a chance to have the conversation you suggested—where I took a negative position—until yesterday. I have to admit that his response was quite a surprise. Your guess about how he would react was prophetic! He seemed to find it completely normal when I said that I didn't really enjoy Christmas either. In a way, although it was phony on my side, we had a more friendly talk about Christmas than usual. He went on to mention a few things about our Christmas that he doesn't enjoy. The one that hurt my feelings was something I do with my kids, making and decorating gingerbread men, on one of the last days before Christmas. Some we hang on the tree and some we attach to the ribbon on wrapped presents. He said it messes up the kitchen terribly—which it does—and then there's a panicky cleanup. He also said he didn't like our store-bought Christmas stockings. His son had one that was knitted by his grandmother. Well, my kids like their store-bought stockings, and no one here knits, so what am I supposed to do about that?

I'm still not sure where this leaves my essay. It's all getting complicated. And as for joining him in his negativity, it feels

*like band-aid surgery. I don't think pretending to be something
I'm not—a pessimist—is going to work in the long run.*

*But you have been so kind and patient. Thank you!
Maybe in a few days, I'll see a way to turn all this into an essay.*

All the best,

Nicole

Nicole was right: it was getting complicated. Liz had always
thought that men were less attached to traditions and other senti-
mental details in the predictable way that she and, apparently,
Nicole were. Maybe that left men free to head out for a new love,
while women needed trinkets and other inducements to stay and
raise the children. Liz thought Sidney had left without a glance at
any of their little customs or beloved objects. But now, according to
Nicole, he missed Peter's knitted stocking.

Dear Nicole Szabo,

*You're right, it wouldn't work to play the pessimist
constantly. But it might help to keep your husband company
in his doldrums—just a bit, as an opening gambit. He
might feel less alone, and that someone finally sees the world
as he does. It could be a good start to get him talking. You
saw how he opened up. . . .*

*There are some people who take the most trivial
criticism as an all-out attack. Maybe that describes your
husband. People like that must be especially hard to talk
with about a problem, and it sounds as if you definitely
made some headway.*

*And I wouldn't worry about the essay. Not everything
in life can be or should be written about, and maybe this is
one of those things. I'd just let it rest for a while, at least.*

Yours sincerely,

Editor@MyTurn.com

While she was at it, why didn't she just hang out a shingle that said, *Liz Morin, Who Failed at Her Marriage, Gives Free Relationship Counselling*? And now she'd crossed yet another frontier. She'd written not as an editor, but as a friend. A friend? That was ridiculous, but there was no denying she'd written as a confidant.

She did get a little kick out of the disingenuousness of writing that people like Sidney "must be" difficult to discuss problems with. But really, the only good thing about that message was that it encouraged Nicole to forget about writing for My Turn. That was the hope, anyway.

On Friday, a new message arrived.

> *Dear Editor,*
>   *Thanks again for your reassurance—I'm going to keep thinking how I can make this piece work.*
>   *And I shouldn't say this, but you hit the nail on the head about my husband. Any criticism, no matter how small, looks like total disapproval to him. I've been struggling with that for a long time.*
>   *All the best,*
>   *Nicole Szabo*

That had worked well, Liz thought sarcastically. No matter what she did, this woman insisted on beavering away at her writing. Well, whose fault was that? As for Sidney's hypersensitivity to criticism, she tipped her hat mentally to Nicole. Not in camaraderie, but it was undeniable that they had taken turns paddling in the same kayak. Liz wondered if Nicole traced her husband's touchiness to the same source she did. Sidney had come a poor second in his mother's love. She adored his older brother, a golden boy in her eyes if not in other people's. Sidney had arrived too soon, a scant year after his brother, and his mother resented him for interrupting her honeymoon with her firstborn. As the brothers grew up, neither one was remarkably superior to the other in brains, looks, athletic ability or character, but Mrs. Thayer remained infatuated with the elder and aggrieved by the younger. Her relatively rare visits to Seattle—it was so much more comfortable staying in Adam's lovely house in his separate guest suite—included long soliloquies about challenges Adam had successfully met in his career, marks of recognition from his admiring colleagues and the reflected glory of life with Adam that his wife and children enjoyed. Now that Peter was old enough to send his own thank yous for Christmas and birthday presents, Liz was no longer in contact with Mrs. Thayer and she may well have seen the end of Sidney's first marriage as one more sign of his inferiority. Imagining Nicole sitting at their walnut table—Sidney had kept the dining room furniture—and having to listen to Mrs. Thayer's windy praises of darling Adam did not make Liz at all unhappy.

Just before she left work on Friday, Liz sent an email to Henry, inviting him to Thanksgiving dinner. She would have Peter and his college friend Leo, who was going to be staying with them while he did some research at the Library of Congress. Red Ann and her little girl, Dani, were coming. Red Ann must be feeling bereft about her separation from Maureen. (Liz would not miss Maureen. She had always seemed either inscrutable or sullen, but there was no accounting for your friends' taste in partners.) Also Freya and her husband, Paul. Their daughter went to college in California, and was not making the frantic trip home. Everybody involved agreed that was sensible, but Liz knew Freya and Paul would miss her. And rounding out the guest list, the new neighbor at the end of the street, who had a little boy who looked roughly Dani's age. She hoped the children would play, or at least watch a movie she would ask Peter to choose.

She would make the squash that required no peeling, and the glazed carrots with coriander and cumin she had been bringing to potlucks all fall to general acclaim. She did not know Henry well enough to trust him to bring a pie from a good pastry shop, as opposed to any old store-bought pie, so when he asked what he could bring, she would say wine. It was going to be fine.

Or Liz hoped it would be. She felt a twinge of foreboding when she invited Henry, because in the past when she had asked a gentleman caller to a dinner party, very often it turned out to be the kiss of death. It was strange, because the invitation always went with what felt like positive feelings. She was, after all, introducing the man to part of her circle. Showing him that not only did she know how to cook, she did cook, and was doing it at least partly for him. But in the aftermath of the dinner, it often seemed that she had unconsciously written the man off before the invitation. The invitation turned out to be a way of saying to him, "Look at my big, full life. Don't imagine you could have an important role here." It was different in Henry's case, she told herself, because she genuinely liked him. And maybe she was giving him a little reward for noticing the cod in the cat essay. Still, all too often in the past, her hospitable efforts backfired. She would look around the welcoming, candle-lit oval of her table, with her friends talking and laughing, and silently address the man in question: "I like everybody here more than you."

But that was not going to happen this time. Because, she repeated to herself, she liked Henry. So she was going to stop worrying about it.

He accepted her invitation at once, writing, "You won't want to pass up the chance to taste my well-regarded apple pie. Either double crust or with a crumb topping. Which would you like?" She wouldn't have pegged him for a baker. She asked for a double crust.

WEEK FIVE

November 9–15, 2015

*L*iz went to her Tuesday assignation with Seamus knowing what she had to do. The fact that he had objected to her choice of essays twice in the past two weeks added a coincidental scrap of awkwardness, but that was a mere detail. The only thing she was uncertain about was whether her announcement should come before, after or instead of sex. As soon as Seamus entered the room, she had her answer: there would be no more sex.

Seamus took off his scarf and coat and hung them in the closet. They were both tidy that way. After he had kissed her and they took their usual chairs, his arm moved to the wine cooler, but she stopped him.

"Not today. But thank you."

Liz could see he understood that she meant it, and that more was coming.

"Seamus. I'm sorry, but this isn't going to go on. Today is our last time here."

Apparently he heard "here" as the most important word. "Do you want to meet somewhere else?"

"I said that wrong. I meant that we aren't going to go on."

He looked perplexed, as if he had been shown some poor quarterly results. She knew that was unfair, but the only other time she had seen that disappointed face had been at a town hall when Gilman had confronted him with low numbers.

"But why?"

"Because you have a wife."

A surprise.

"But you have never mentioned Martha."

"Do you think that means I never thought about her?"

"Is it really Martha? Nothing to do with my objections to your page?"

"No, of course not. You always behaved perfectly properly and within your rights at the paper."

"I note the past tense."

"Yes. It is the past."

Liz had been tiptoeing around the idea, if you could call it an idea, for a few weeks, but the actual decision had come last Friday, almost literally from the heavens. The Casa Italiana, where Liz and Brown Anne took Italian, occasionally showed movies on Friday nights, and they had been to see *Divorce Italian Style*. It had been raining all day, but it was over by the time Liz dropped Anne off. The moon lit up the blue-black sky, and mounds of cumulus clouds moved across it. They struck her as accusing. They chided her. Looking up at them, she could only agree with their assessment. This is all wrong with Seamus. I'm just doing to Martha what was done to me, taking advantage of her ignorance and helping myself to what isn't mine. She had always known that the affair was indefensible but Seamus's reputation as a philanderer had eased her conscience, as if being one of his many women made her affair unimportant. She couldn't think that anymore. And there was something else, something she couldn't put her finger on, that was making her affair with Seamus impossible. Something connected to Nicole's reappearance.

She and Seamus left the hotel, separately, after about fifteen minutes. Although he was usually quick on his feet, he looked too genuinely taken aback to plead his case or even question her more thoroughly. They kissed goodbye tentatively, like something between old friends and old lovers.

Once she got into bed that night, feeling half-sad but only half, she patted the book on her night table. She hadn't yet cracked the spine of *Forgiveness Is a Gift You Give Yourself.* But she would, soon.

=====

At nine-thirty the next night, Liz was thinking about getting ready for bed when her phone trilled. It was Seamus calling from his secret phone. Damn.

"Liz," he said.

"Seamus, I don't want to talk on this phone or any phone—"

"Liz," he interrupted. "I've told Martha. And I'm leaving. I'll find a place to stay for the time being, preferably not too far from you."

Her reaction was similar to the one she'd had when she found Nicole's essay in her inbox. After a second or two in which numbness overlaid consternation, her underarms prickled with sweat and her heart began galloping.

"Seamus, that's completely impossible. That's the last thing I want."

But he was too excited, too full of pride and guilt at what he had done, to listen. He was in his car, in the city, and he had to explain. She agreed to meet him at a dim, slightly seedy coffee place on Seventeenth Street.

When she arrived, Seamus was already sitting at a table against the far wall. Although at first glance he was as well turned out as ever, something was askew. He gave the impression that if, for instance, he turned his head, the back of his hair might be uncombed. Or if he shot his cuffs, one cufflink might be missing. He talked rapidly and kept trying to cover her hand on the table with his big warm one. She took hers away, and put it in her lap.

She had felt so confident that Seamus would never leave his wife, no matter how many affairs he had. This was a man who probably always had somebody on the side, and, as far as she knew, it had never threatened his twenty-five-year-old marriage. But Liz had not factored in one thing, which became clear during their coffee. While she insisted that it was over and that his leaving Martha was the very last thing in the world that she wanted, and he insisted that he loved only her and his marriage had been dead for a long time and now they were free, she saw what had escaped her. It was a question of timing. His younger daughter had gone away to college that September. Seamus, the infatuated father, had an empty nest. He could tell himself that he had stayed with Martha only to bring up their children, and as of September he had fulfilled that obligation.

"The girls will be fine," he repeated. "They are fine. They'll be worried at first and probably mad at me for a little, but Martha will stay on in the house, and they'll be okay."

She could only repeat that it was over, wherever he lived, with or without Martha.

"But you told me the problem was Martha." He was too besotted to be irritated with her, but he had taken her seriously. Hadn't he solved the problem?

"I'm sorry, Seamus. That turned out not to be the whole reason. Once I ended it, I saw it was right for other reasons. And I could never found a relationship on the ruins of your marriage."

"Well, we can talk about that later. I don't really understand what you're saying, but right now I'm just telling you that I am going to woo you back." He said this fondly and confidently, like a successful businessman, but with a bit of a hectic flush underneath the calm.

Liz went home in a tizzy. My God, she thought, sitting on the couch in her coat, why don't I have a cat? Petting one now might lower my blood pressure. Wildly, she thought of calling Henry but some saving part of her knew she was too upset.

The phone rang from a private number and she picked it up. As soon as she said hello, she knew it was Martha.

"Is this Liz?"

"Yes."

"You should be ashamed of yourself. Do you also shoplift? Do you pick pockets? Cheat at cards?"

All she could say was, "I'm sorry."

"Or did you think this would get you a promotion at work?"

She said again, "I'm sorry. I never meant for this to happen." Although that didn't absolve her from the need to feel sorry.

Martha hung up, and then so did she.

——

On Thursday morning, Henry sent her a text. *I have two tickets for a concert at the Phillips Collection tonight. Sorry for the last-minute invitation, but the colleague I usually go with is sick. It's a string trio, playing Mozart, Schubert and Leonard Bernstein. If that interests you, we could get a bite to eat before or after, depending on your schedule.*

It did interest her, not least because she hoped it would be a distraction from the Seamus imbroglio. She preferred to meet him at the Phillips and go out for supper afterward, and she reminded him that it was her turn to pay.

Not counting their hurried drink last week, this was the second date. The second date meant that they liked each other enough to see each other again, and Liz was working on convincing herself that that should diminish her shyness, rather than increase it. The second date was also the time when the man's obsessions or unresolved issues could become obvious. He might sound philosophical, if regretful, about the end of his marriage in the obligatory résumé on the first date. But not infrequently, if he returned to it on the second date, the story took on blame, self-pity, justification and other unattractive emotions. It strongly suggested that he was too absorbed in the past to take on the present. Liz doubted that would be Henry's problem, as his marriage was fifteen years in the past. And that could be a related problem, because why had he waited so long before reconnecting? She knew this was a case of the pot calling the kettle black, and she was not going to dwell on that.

If she was overthinking Henry, she knew she was underthinking Seamus. Probably that was guilt, especially the vague worry that she had been using him for something and suddenly he was no longer useful. So far she could not say more than that.

That evening, spotting Henry at the gallery's entrance looking fresh and happy to see her made her feel fresh and happy. His square face had a transparency that, so far, she found appealing. They made their way from the coat check up the stairs to the handful of Phillips family rooms left untouched in the gallery's modifications and enlargements. The small-scale rooms, with fireplaces, wood panelling and window seats, made a reassuring bridge into the modern art that followed. Liz and Henry were headed for the largest and grandest of the original rooms, the Music Room. Its dark oak walls, Ionic columns and coffered ceiling did not sound intimate, and yet they were, especially when filled, like tonight, with music lovers.

Henry led the way to his usual seats, and Liz wondered briefly whether the colleague he usually went with was a man or a woman. She opened her program. There was indeed a piece by Schubert, as Henry had promised, but he hadn't told her it was the Arpeggione

Sonata. He couldn't have known that the Arpeggione was one of a very small collection of pieces that instantly transported her to the most painful period of her separation from Sidney. The other two were Clementi's Piano Sonatina in C Major, which Peter had been practicing in the first months of the separation, and Carl Orff's "Street Song," which Peter's Orff class performed at a concert that spring attended by both his miserable parents. The Arpeggione had come into her life from a friend to whom she complained that she could not read. She had lost all powers of concentration. The friend thought she might be able to listen to music, and sent her a CD of the Schubert. She was right, and Liz spent hours listening to the sonata's quietly noodling, sometimes almost wheedling, melody. It was modest but sustaining, like a piece of folk music that Schubert had embellished. She had not listened to it for years. She could not imagine choosing to listen to it. But here it came.

Henry pointed to it in the program and asked, "Do you know about the Arpeggione?" Nice. He hadn't just assumed that she wouldn't know and jumped in to mansplain.

"You mean, that it was composed for a new instrument, the arpeggione, that quickly became obsolete?"

"Yes. I always forget exactly what the arpeggione was."

Together they read in the program that it was like a guitar you played with a bow. Tonight, as usual, it would be played by a cellist with piano accompaniment.

After the Mozart and before the intermission, a tall cellist and a medium-size pianist took their places at the front. Henry whispered to her, "Have you noticed that cellists are usually tall? I guess to accord with their instrument." She smiled, as if hearing the Arpeggione would be a pleasant, normal experience. When it began, Liz saw herself lying on the couch in their Seattle living room—her living room, as it was by then—with one arm crooked over her forehead. Peter must have been asleep in his room. Perhaps she had lit a fire: making a fire had been one of her new accomplishments as a single woman. Sidney had been in charge of fires. Oddly, none of the music that took her back to that time echoed the jagged, frightened emotions that frequently overtook her then. "Street Song" had an innocent, cumulative energy. The Clementi was briskly joyful. And the Arpeggione was self-effacing in a way she almost thought of as domestic. Perhaps that had given her some hope for the future. Not that it was easy to listen to, even now.

When it was over, Liz stood up cautiously on legs that felt spindly.

Henry asked, "Did you like it?"

"Very much."

Then he looked at her. "Really? Are you okay?"

"Yes. Perfectly."

She gave him what she hoped was a normal-looking smile, and turned toward the aisle. And now she saw that Jana and Michael Dubroff were about to pass their row, on their way out to the lobby. They had not responded to her message. She was sufficiently caught up in old feelings that seeing them wasn't going to upset her any more than she already was, so she insisted on catching their eyes.

"Hello. How nice to see you here."

They nodded and murmured something civil but noncommittal, and she motioned to Henry to follow her, as she pursued them into the lobby.

"Jana and Michael Dubroff, I'd like you to meet Henry Matson."

They all shook hands, and Henry asked if one or both of them were journalists.

"No," Michael said and they made as if to go.

But Liz was determined. "Henry is a subscriber to the chamber music series. Are you?"

No, they weren't. They had come because they were particularly fond of the Bernstein, Jana said, as if Liz was dragging something shameful out of them. They were looking forward to it. And then they really were gone.

Henry went off to buy a cookie, and he shared it with Liz. Their first intimacy, which pleased her.

"Friends of yours?"

"No." She explained that they were the couple who had written to the publisher about their angry reaction to the cat piece.

"Oh, well," he said. "Animal lovers."

But she could not dismiss them so easily. Even though she barely knew them, the Dubroffs were a loss.

Afterward they went to La Tomate, an Italian bistro on Connecticut Avenue. Not an adventurous choice, but Liz felt that Italian bistros were soothing. After the Arpeggione and the Dubroffs, that seemed reasonable. She ordered the fettucine con funghi: mushrooms she also found soothing. Henry considered the ravioli filled with squash but remembered that it was often too sweet. He settled on penne with sausage and leeks.

Once the waiter had left them with wine, Henry said, "I'm sorry about that couple."

"Thank you. What is unfortunate about it is that I liked them so much. Obviously, I underestimated how obnoxious that essay would be to lots of people."

"But you don't regret publishing it, do you?"

She had to think about that. Except for the Dubroffs, she wasn't concerned about all the outrage. The Dubroffs were a thorn in her side, but it was only a personal thorn.

"No, I don't."

"Good. Because I'll say it again, it was an excellent piece."

They spent most of their time amplifying the facts they already knew about each other. Henry's daughter was in her first year of law school, a surprise because she had seemed to be headed for a career in science. But she wasn't going to be a fat-cat, corporate lawyer, he assured Liz, although it sounded as if he were really reassuring himself. His daughter was interested in immigration law. And his son was taking a gap year between his second and third years in college.

"Not his first gap year, either," Henry said, but he did not sound too worried. "He's a perfectionist, and he just has to learn that there's no such thing as a perfect college, or a perfect major, or perfect professors. He'll find his way."

Liz hoped this wasn't another instance of a man being sanguine so that he didn't have to concern himself with a possible problem. Henry asked about Peter, and, trying not to sound smug, she talked about how close they had become since they had moved to D.C.

"Which is why it's good that he's away at college. And I can already feel some of those bonds loosening."

"Which is normal," Henry said.

"Yes, it's normal," she said, with less conviction.

She asked him if he'd ever been seriously involved with anyone since his marriage.

"I've had some semi-serious involvements with seriously nice women," he said. "But they never quite gelled. And you?"

No, she had not. And she didn't know why.

"It gets easier to do without, the longer it goes on, do you find?" Henry asked and she nodded.

The bill having been paid, she looked around the nearly deserted restaurant to remember where she had hung her coat. Henry put his hand on her arm to waylay her.

"Just while we're still sitting, what was wrong with the Arpeggione?"

She didn't answer immediately.

"Could be none of my business. But you looked stricken at the end."

She explained, briefly.

His hand was still on her arm. He was giving her the benefit of his level, kind gaze. "I'm sorry. It wasn't the best concert to bring you to."

"Don't look at it that way. It's time I started hearing the piece for itself, not for its associations. And it's beautiful."

He walked her home, saying that he had time and would continue north to Adams Morgan, where he lived. Between street lights on R Street, he backed her firmly into a linden tree and kissed her. He was a good height for her, tall but not too tall. His lips were soft, but not too soft.

When she was thoroughly kissed, he said, "I did that now so that you wouldn't have to stress about whether or not I would kiss you at your door."

She said, "You think of everything."

===

Liz spent Friday afternoon reading submissions. There was one by a man about his stay in an Airbnb that had been his childhood home. The situation was promising, but it was one of those essays where the situation was everything: the writer hadn't done anything exceptional with it. She put it in the MAYBE file. Someone wrote about the discovery of a half-brother, via ancestry.com. It was deft, but unfortunately she had just run a less good piece on the same subject, so, with regret, it went into NO.

There was a wonderful lament for the bed bath, of all things, by a visiting nurse. The bed bath had just been delisted from the services covered by many insurance companies, and the nurse wrote regretfully about all the things she had learned about her patients while bathing them. In addition to non-verbal information about skin and general well-being, the quiet, deliberate protocol of the bath prompted people to confide things they had not planned to divulge. The piece was a beauty, and she transferred it to YES.

Then she read an essay by a man about his constantly unfaithful wife. When her first few affairs had come to light, the wife begged for forgiveness in tears and promised it would never happen again. By now, after a dozen years of marriage, there were no more promises. Each of them understood that this would continue as long as the marriage continued. And leaving it was unthinkable for the husband. He loved her too much to imagine life without her. The wife no longer apologized, or only rarely, but he forgave, he wrote, over and over. He would take whatever he could have of her.

The wife told him, "With the others, it's sex. I won't say 'just sex,' because sex matters a lot to me. But you're the only one where I have both love and sex."

"The combo platter," he said.

"Yes," she said.

The essay was remarkable in the way it balanced on the knife-edge between hopelessness and a poised stoicism. Liz wrote to the man that she would like to publish it, and waited for him to respond that he would need to use a pseudonym. Which he did, immediately, and she rehearsed her justification for denying the pseudonym—that part of the power of My Turn was the willingness of people to write about very personal things using their real names. He wrote back, asking if they could talk on the phone. She sighed. It was closing in on six, and she wanted to go home, but she agreed.

His voice was confident. "Do you really never let anyone use a pseudonym?"

"Once about every eighteen months or so, when someone is writing about an absolutely dreadful situation, like being raped by her father, yes, I would agree to a pseudonym. I understand that you're writing about something very delicate, but it's not in the same category."

"So you're telling me I have no choice."

"You have a choice," Liz said, "whether to use your own name, or not to publish the piece."

He was going to opt not to publish it, which was too bad, because the piece was good. But, as editors sometimes said cynically to other editors, writers are like buses: there's always another one coming along.

He said, as she expected, "Even if I were willing to expose myself, there is another person involved here."

It was the usual back-and-forth, which happened at least a few times each year (why did people never read the webpage, which spelled out the rules clearly?) but today Liz thought, abruptly, Why the hell are you being so rigid? You're cutting off your nose to spite your face. It didn't mean that pseudonyms had become acceptable, but there was something special about this writer's voice. Or this subject. She was going to make an exception. She told Paolo de Santis, for that was the name that would not appear in the paper, that she would agree to a pseudonym.

She sent the piece out to Filip, because it had been a while since he had had something to illustrate, with a note that said, "Please, no combo platter."

Just as Liz was putting on her coat, an email from Sidney dropped into her inbox. That was alarming, but there was no mention of Nicole. He was coming to D.C. for a conference on globalization, and suggested they might have dinner on Sunday. This happened every so often, but not so often that she felt at ease with him. They arranged to meet at a Greek restaurant near Sidney's hotel in Foggy Bottom. His conference began early on Monday so it wouldn't be a long dinner, he wrote, as if to forestall her hopes of having a leisurely, boozy evening with him. As if.

===

In the restaurant that Sunday, Liz was putting on a good front as usual. But it was still weird to be making small talk with a man who had been her first love, the father of her child, the person who had seen her sitting on the toilet with an unwashed face and unbrushed teeth, or writhing in labor, or teaching Peter to blow kisses and say "Dada," or hurling a teapot at him in the last days before he moved out. (She regretted that: it was a Brown Betty and she had never had another that poured so well.) And now this same man, sitting across the tiny table and trying to decide between lamb loin and dolmades, was having similarly intimate experiences with someone who had worked at Peter's daycare.

While he fretted over the menu, surreptitiously Liz checked out his girth. Sidney moved back and forth between brawny and beefy. The first was broad-shouldered and well-made, the second more slack and available. Liz found both of them attractive. Beginning soon after he left, she had a recurring dream in which she sat in the back seat of Sidney's car while he drove, running her hands over his shoulders and back, as if he were a security blanket she could not do without. She still had that dream, although rarely. Tonight he was at the brawny end of his spectrum, and he wore rimless glasses Liz had not seen before. They looked fashionable, so perhaps Nicole had picked them out.

Liz husbanded her one glass of red wine carefully, as did Sidney. She wanted to avoid anger, however suppressed, and, even worse, nostalgia mixed with disinhibition. As usual, Sidney seemed more relaxed than she was. He talked for a while about the unlikelihood of Bernie Sanders inspiring a leftist movement that stretched beyond young men. Then, as he always did, he caught her up to date on his family and his college roommates. The latter struck her as a far-fetched subject, since she hadn't seen any of these men for more than twenty years. It made sense in a way, because Nicole had never known them and Sidney had no one else who might take an interest in Sweeney's heart problems or Ron's move to Texas. Still, it nettled her. He never asked about *her* college friends. Other than inquiring about her mother, he never asked about her family or about her life.

Normally she accepted that as part of the self-absorption package that was Sidney, or at least Sidney post-divorce, but tonight it irritated her more than usual. Which was foolish, because his lack of interest in her was making her correspondence with Nicole possible—he neither knew nor particularly cared what her current job at the paper was, probably thought she was still the education reporter. So he wasn't likely to blow her cover. He did want to hear about the paper's falling fortunes, because he enjoyed bleak economic news. Just as he was beginning to question her about that, she interrupted.

"You know, I really don't understand why you want to have dinner with me. Or lunch or coffee or anything. Because you just tell me your news, and you never ask me anything about myself. If you're that uninterested in me, I can't see the point in getting together."

He looked horrified. This was not how their pretense of formerly married cordiality worked. Liz was also taken aback by her outburst. It felt as if she had deposited an outhouse smell right in the middle of their table. But, unusually, she was able to return Sidney's gaze, and she waited.

Finally, he said, "I don't ask about you because I'm afraid of hurting you."

Did he really think that if he asked her how she was, she would suddenly remember that she was a "lone lorn creetur," as the widow Mrs. Gummidge always called herself in *David Copperfield*? Was the rejected wife doomed to a lifetime of news about his college roommates in order to spare her hurt feelings?

Liz laughed. "I don't think you need to worry about that."

Sidney was good at following directions.

"Okay, then. Are you happy?"

That was bold, but she had asked for it.

"I'm not sure that's a useful question. But I am . . . interested. I mean, I'm curious about a lot of things, and maybe that's as good as happiness."

That was so pretentious she was mortified. Why did Sidney bring out the fatuous prig in her? Now they sat silent, as if they had exhausted their small stock of intimacy.

To cover her regret, she asked, "Do you have any special plans for Christmas?" Shameless, but he would never know the reason for her question.

Instead of looking relieved that she was leaving dangerous ground, Sidney's face dulled and fell. You could see that in ten years he might have jowls.

"No, not really."

"A nice quiet time with Andrew and Tamsin." Nicole's children.

"Yes, I guess." Now he looked thoroughly miserable and, without meaning to, she had cracked his shell.

"To tell you the truth," he said, "I don't like Christmas, and I don't like thinking about Christmas."

"Because?"

"Because Peter always spends it with you. I miss him. And I'm not complaining, and I know that it's completely fair that he's with you because, well, you know. . . ."

Of course. Because she was a lone lorn creetur and Sidney had a new partner and a new family. Christmas with Peter was a tradition so hallowed she no longer thought about it. But Sidney's response, which came as a surprise although she might have guessed it, put Nicole's Christmas dilemma in a new light.

"Well, you know," she said slowly, thinking out loud, "we could talk about that. Not Christmas Day, that would be hard, but Peter could go out to Seattle a few days afterward, maybe spend New Year's with you. . . ."

She was promising too much, faced with a man who was powerless to take back what he never wanted to say. Peter would never agree to New Year's in Seattle, he had kept in touch with almost none of his boyhood friends. She had better step back from that precipice. Uncertainly at first, she shifted to talking about Peter in general. The conversation was desultory because Peter seemed happy enough at the moment. They had more to talk about when there were problems.

Katherine Ashenburg

Sidney asked if he had a girlfriend.

"I haven't heard about anyone since he and Melissa—or was it Melinda?—broke up." Privately, she wondered if Peter had had relatively few girlfriends, at least as far as she knew, because he worried that he was like his father. "But I'm not sure boys confide in their parents about things like that. Did you?"

They smiled, remembering Sidney's rather forbidding parents. They moved to one of Sidney's favorite worries, that a B.A. in philosophy would not make Peter a good job prospect. She went into reassurance mode, talking about the possibility of graduate school in his minor, political science, as well as all the businesses that valued employees who knew how to think. He listened, perhaps because he thought she was still the education reporter.

Liz was sitting with her back to the rest of the restaurant, and as she talked she saw Sidney looking affably at someone he saw approaching their table.

Before she was quite as close as she should have been to avoid the nearby tables overhearing, the person approaching said brusquely to Sidney, "Are you married too?"

Martha Donovan was a tall blonde, with brown eyes as thickly lashed as an anemone. They gave her well-cut face a welcome vulnerability. In its extreme simplicity and expensiveness, her dark pantsuit echoed Seamus's irreproachable tailoring. But she loosened up the effect with a necklace of large, unmatched African beads.

"I said, are you married too?"

Looking dumfounded, Sidney could only nod. Two men at the table next to them were all attention.

"Well, don't turn your back on her," Martha said, indicating Liz. "She's not to be trusted."

Martha blinked her huge lashes, and just for a second her armor slipped. Then she turned away and joined the woman who was waiting for her at the door.

Well, Liz thought, this unassuming little dinner is turning out to be more than Sidney had bargained for. First, his normally well-behaved ex-wife pulls him out onto thin conversational ice, and now this alarming stranger. This time it was Sidney who stayed silent, waiting.

"Yes, well, sorry about that," she said finally. She couldn't think of anything to say but the truth. "I had been seeing her husband, but that's over now."

"Right."

She knew that he would never ask for more details. Ashamed, she remembered the story of Jesus and the woman whose adultery could be punished with stoning. When the Pharisees pressed him to condemn her, Jesus said, "Let him who is without sin cast the first stone." Her parents had been fervent atheists, but when Liz was about ten, she had begged to accompany her friend Meg to Sunday school. Random memories of those earnest but jolly mornings in the Presbyterian church hall occasionally returned. She couldn't imagine how the Sunday school teacher had explained adultery, but obviously the story had stuck. Not that Liz was casting stones in great numbers anymore, but she had to admit that she occasionally lobbed one in Sidney's direction. Now she had definitely lost her stoning rights.

WEEK SIX

November 16–22, 2015

*L*iz thought of her former lover as "Seamus in exile." Only his driver knew that the publisher was no longer living in McLean, and discretion was tightly woven into his job description. Gilman had a formidable nose for scandal, and his silence on the subject reassured Liz that Seamus's secret was safe. As usual she rarely saw him at work, but even the rapid, middle-distance glimpses she caught—heading for the boardroom or touring important visitors around the newsroom—showed her a man infinitesimally off his stride. His cuffs looked the tiniest bit shorter, although that was impossible, and even the stripes on his tie seemed to glimmer less confidently. But no one else would have noticed.

Coming out of the ladies' room that Tuesday, a week since their breakup, she heard someone behind her.

"Liz?"

Even the interrogative lift in his voice betrayed the new, humbled Seamus. She turned and faced him.

"Liz, we have to talk. I have some things to say, and you can't freeze me out like this. And I want to understand your side of things. . . ."

She was dismayed that he would risk being overheard. Anyone could step out of the ladies' or the men's rooms or the supply cabinet or float up on the escalator and find the publisher in an intense moment with the My Turn editor.

"Seamus, I'm so sorry. We've gone over and over what little we have to say. I honestly think you'd feel better if you stopped trying to see me or talk to me."

His face said, You don't know what you're talking about.

She could only repeat, "I'm sorry."

At the end of the day, there was another message from Nicole.

Dear Editor,

Maybe you're right, not everything that happens to us can be written about. And I'm feeling more and more that my "holiday problem" just isn't going to shape up into an essay. But you've gotten me interested in writing, which I never thought I could do. I wasn't any good at it in school, and I never got over that. But you've given me confidence!

So I had a stab at another piece—something I've always felt guilty about. I need to let it sit a few more hours, but will send it soon. Let me know, please, how it strikes you. And thanks again.

All the best,
Nicole Szabo

For your own twisted reasons, Liz thought—and who knows what those reasons are?—you've created someone who thinks she might be a writer. But underneath Liz's disapproval of herself was a more excited feeling. "Something I've always felt guilty about . . ."

Was Nicole going to write about her affair with Sidney? Liz raced home from yoga and pretended to tidy, while she listened hard for the bell that told her she had a new message. After more than a dozen new submissions sent her racing to the computer, Nicole's essay landed at nearly eleven o'clock. Liz's finger trembled slightly as she opened the file. But the story Nicole had chosen to tell was not about Sidney. Instead it was a fairly banal account of a high school girlfriend of hers who had had a crush on Nicole's older brother. She asked Nicole to let her brother know that she liked him, which she hoped would jump-start a romance. For some reason that she didn't explain, Nicole was not keen on her girlfriend getting together with her brother. She never passed on the message, although she told her friend she had. When the friend heard nothing from the brother, she naturally assumed that her interest was not reciprocated.

And you feel guilty about *that*, Liz said balefully to the orderly lines of type. *That* makes you ashamed. Really. Not a family coming apart, not a child whose parents were suddenly leading separate lives in separate houses, not a wife who . . . whatever. But a teenage romance that didn't happen. Of course, lying to her friend was not good, but surely it paled when compared to what had happened to Liz and Peter.

There, Liz addressed Nicole mentally. *That's* what you should feel guilty about.

This new submission had torn it. I'm done with this stupid charade, Liz thought. Contemptuously, she whispered her latest Italian expression, "*Non ne vale la pena*"—"It's not worth the trouble." Italian was a good language, she had found, for sarcasm and scorn, best said with a curled lip. She didn't know how to curl her lip, but she would work on it.

She felt restless. Her clean and ordered apartment gave off its annoying, self-pitying "no one cares about me" air. A bath with Epsom salts normally raised her spirits—she preferred bubble bath, but good-quality bubble bath was old school and hard to find—although not tonight. Feeling wide awake, she unfolded her neatly made bed. The books on her night table included her undergraduate paperback of Gerard Manley Hopkins' poetry, and an equally slim London Times anthology of poems from the Renaissance to the twentieth century. She had bought it in a second-hand bookshop on her first trip to England, with Sidney. Liz admired the two books' demure, wallpaper-like covers. She made regular resolutions to read a poem every night, but was usually too tired.

The poetry books shared the night table with a new stack. Buying *Forgiveness Is a Gift You Give Yourself* had turned out to be the thin edge of a rapidly broadening wedge. Since then, she had returned to Kramerbooks twice and bought two more books on forgiveness. She no longer skulked through the self-help section, but treated it as a normal part of a bookstore. A few months ago, her superego would have demanded of Liz as she paid for a new forgiveness book, "What in the wide world are you planning to do with that thing?" Now her superego had apparently left on vacation. All three of her manuals had optimistic, soft-focus covers and provided worksheets with daily exercises, and two included audio downloads. There were so many references to toolkits that Liz imagined a forgiveness tool belt laden with worksheets, meditations, mantras ("I reject the negative") and journals. She was not good at exercises, meditation or tools other than the occasional hammer, and so far she had only skimmed the books selectively. But occasionally she changed the order of the pile and patted it, hoping that if she slept near the books, something like osmosis would occur and she would absorb some of their lessons. Tonight she put *Journaling Your Way to Peace and Forgiveness* on top of the stack. Right now forgiveness was not high on her agenda, but peace sounded like a good idea.

=

Walking home from work the next day, Liz detoured onto P Street at Dupont Circle to look into Second Story Books. Maybe on their teeming shelves of second-hand books she would find some older ones on forgiveness, without all the gimmicks. Perhaps, who knew, there was an out-of-print classic in this genre. Pushing open the door, she was assailed by Second Story's unmistakable aroma of thousands of pages impregnated with cigarette smoke, coffee, beer and fingerprints—variously greasy, perspiring and dry. The poet worked there for a few hours a week, regretting mightily that he had to ring up other people's bad choices in books. Liz thought she knew his schedule and avoided going there at those times. But there was William at the front desk, and it was too late to back out. He had seen her.

"So," he intoned by way of greeting. "What brings you here?"

"Oh, nothing really. Just browsing."

He was in one of his staring moods.

To unlock his eyes, Liz asked, nodding at the book opened face down on his desk, "What are you reading?"

Reluctantly, as if he did not want to give the battered paperback more undeserved publicity, he said, "It's an anthology of post-war Polish poets. Szymborska, Herbert, Milosz, Zagajewski. People like that. You know."

Liz did not know, but she was pretty sure William was not interested in her knowledge of post-war Polish poets.

"Are you enjoying it?"

He sighed. Praising other poets did not come easily, but sometimes it had to be done. "Some of it is brilliant, absolutely brilliant. Of course, writing in Polish is a big advantage. If I wrote in Polish, I'd be much better known. And their stuff is pretty damn gloomy."

William's poetry, insofar as Liz could understand it, was not exactly overburdened with laughs, but everything was relative.

Just as Liz was planning her exit, a voice behind her said, "William! How lovely to find you here."

The speaker was an ash-blonde woman, perhaps in her mid-fifties. Liz suspected that a significant amount of self-care, to borrow a term she had learned from the self-help section at Kramerbooks, had gone into her healthy, natural looks. Even "work," as people called cosmetic surgery, might have been involved. Her style could be described as artistic, but once you noticed the fine leather piping around her cape and what almost looked like bespoke jeans, it was clear that her bohemian casualness came with a high price tag.

"I'm so glad you're reading that," the woman said, indicating William's Polish anthology. "Do you like Baranczak as much as I do?"

Transferring his stare from Liz to her, William made no attempt to answer that impossible question.

"But I'm so sorry, I'm interrupting," she said, turning to Liz. "I'm Claudia."

"And I'm Liz."

"Do you write poetry, too?"

"No. I do try to read it, but not the way you two do."

"Well, we're very lucky," Claudia said, adjusting her cape and smiling at William. "William has made a few guest appearances at a poetry circle I belong to. Just amateurs reading poetry, and trying to write it. He's been invaluable." Her smile deepened and became more confiding. "And so inspirational."

Liz tried to guess what William being invaluable and inspirational would look like.

"And while I have you here," Claudia said, retrieving her phone from her patchwork leather bag, "could we just settle on the date for the next poetry circle? Sorry again, Liz, but William can be hard to pin down. We could do it either on December third or the tenth. Later than that would be too close to Christmas. At my house, of course."

William indicated that the third would be preferable. Claudia turned to Liz. "He's so modest that not enough people know about his poetry. I'm hoping to get together an evening to launch some of his latest work, and introduce him to some people who might be helpful to him. I'll get your email from William and send you an invitation."

Claudia picked up William's book and began looking for some of her favorite Baranczak poems. Liz thanked her and said goodbye. She had to pick up her textbook and homework at the apartment before her Italian class at seven thirty. Heading out into what was now an inhospitable, slushy evening, she thought, With patrons like Claudia, no wonder William only has to work a few hours a week at Second Story. She wondered if Claudia had seen his chicken imitation, or if that was in her future.

The classes at the Casa Italiana were housed in a nondescript office building on G Street. But once past the panelled door, you entered Italy. The espresso and biscotti in the diminutive café, the posters of neorealist films in the classrooms and the chairs in the lounge—mid-century Fornasetti knock-offs—were stylish incentives. They promised the center's students that if they persisted with the two confusingly similar past tenses, the many-tentacled subjunctive and the maddening placement of pronouns, this *dolce vita* could be theirs.

Liz and Brown Anne arrived just in time for their Advanced Intermediate class. In the hall, before they rounded the corner to the classrooms, the door to the director's office opened and Seamus and Signora Venturi, the director, stepped out. Astonished, Liz had just enough presence of mind to realize that it would be a mistake to pretend to Brown Anne that she did not recognize her publisher.

"Anne Schneider. Seamus Donovan."

Anne, who had never heard of him, nodded. Seamus, who might have had a dim memory of Liz's friend who was also taking Italian, nodded. Signora Venturi smiled in a proprietary kind of way. She usually wore dark sweater sets and pencil skirts, like an Antonioni heroine from a 1960s film, but sometimes appeared in a suit that was severe and drastically asymmetrical. Tonight was one of her asymmetrical evenings, which probably meant she had an event after the Casa closed.

She said to Seamus, "If you'll just come this way," and they went into another room.

Quick-eyed Anne whispered as they walked down the corridor, "When was the last time you saw a man wearing cufflinks? Who is he, anyway?"

In class, Liz found it impossible to concentrate on hypothetical sentences and the ensuing subjunctive. (If you were just meeting that man, would you have found him attractive? If that man had not been married, would you have had an affair with him?) She begged off coffee with Anne afterward and went straight home.

She was ready when the phone rang.

"What the hell were you doing there? Does the word 'stalking' mean anything to you?"

"I'm not stalking you. I always admired the way you persevere with your Italian, and I thought it would be fun to brush up on mine."

"Brush up?" This was the first she had heard that he had any Italian.

"Well, I had just a bit one summer when I was in school. But not enough."

"Not enough for what?"

"To place in Advanced Intermediate. Signora Venturi gave me a test."

She could hear her mother saying, "He has a lot of gall," with a heavy emphasis on "gall." But Liz found the idea of Seamus invading her Italian class more worrying than that, even creepy. She wondered if he was coming unhinged, just a little.

She also wondered, more and more, why she had gotten involved with a married man in the first place. The reason was like something glimpsed in a dense fog, advancing and retreating, on the edge of being recognizable but always frustratingly elusive. And she had ended it so precipitously. She seemed to be making a specialty of rash decisions lately, but she stood by this one.

"Seamus, I can't say it any more plainly. Your hare-brained schemes to crash my Italian class or run into me in my neighborhood won't do any good. It is over. O-V-E-R. How can I make you see that?"

"Couldn't we talk about this one more time?"

"I don't have anything more to say." Then, she could not resist: "What level did you place in?"

She knew he would tell the truth.

"Beginners."

———

On Thursday, Liz and Honey went for a walk in Foggy Bottom. Although Honey was shorter, she had a long, brisk stride and Liz worked to keep up with her.

Honey said, "I hear Donovan is sniffing out someone in advertising."

"What do you mean? I mean, who do you mean?" Liz asked.

"Do you know the curly-headed one, not too tall and kind of new? I think she has the university and private school accounts. She wears sleeveless dresses a lot."

Liz shook her head.

"Well, it doesn't matter," Honey said. "But Donovan's on the prowl again." She paused for a few beats. "Listen, I want to ask you for a favor."

"Okay."

"I want you to come to a cuddle party with me."

"You what? What is a cuddle party? Does Dave know?"

"Ha ha," Honey said. "It's for a story. Do you remember reading about those evenings where strangers could get together—"

It was coming back to Liz now. "And pay for cuddling, but cuddling that doesn't get erotic?"

Honey nodded.

"But wasn't that a long time ago, around the start of the century? Why is that a story now?"

That was the question, posed as skeptically and aggressively as possible, that reporters faced at story meetings: "Tell me why this is a story NOW?"

"Because people are piggybacking on the cuddle party model, which is non-sexual and mutual, to introduce things that are more like 'soft escort' services, where the customers are all men and the cuddle-providers, who end up doing a lot more than cuddling, are all women. And the original cuddlers are up in arms, insofar as such gentle types can take up arms. But behind that hard-news story, I want to write a feature about the fact that these parties, that sound so New Age and needy and even babyish—they usually end with what they call a 'puppy pile'—are still with us after a dozen or so years. And not just with us, they're expanding. No doubt social media and its isolating effects will turn out to be one of the culprits, but whatever the causes, cuddle parties are happening all over the map. They're in Australia, Sweden, Denmark, Germany, Hungary, Ireland, Canada, all over the U.S.—"

"Cold countries or Protestant ones, or both," Liz interrupted.

"—and there's a very active group in D.C.," Honey continued, ignoring Liz's interjection. "There's a party near Thomas Circle tomorrow night, and I'm going. And I want you there with me."

"No, Honey, I couldn't possibly. Cuddling with strangers, that's just icky. Why do you want me to come?"

"Because with two of us there, the piece will be richer. Obviously. Sometimes I wonder if you're just masquerading as a journalist."

Liz had heard that before.

"But you're getting paid for this, and I'm not. And I couldn't snuggle strangers or do any of the weird things they do, you know that. I'd rather have a root canal."

"You don't *have* to do anything. Everybody gets asked if they're willing to have a back rub or their feet massaged or whatever and you can say 'No.' Their literature says something like 'We celebrate 'No' because it shows the person is doing self-care.'"

"'Doing self-care.' Oh God, Honey. We won't be able to keep our faces straight."

"Good, so you're coming. I'll send you the address. Meet me there tomorrow at six forty. The doors lock at seven."

"That's a joke, right? About the doors locking?"

"No, they do, but not for sinister reasons—because the person in charge, who is a trained cuddle party facilitator, goes through an introduction about all the rules and no one can be part of it without agreeing to them."

"But suppose I have a panic attack, and have to leave?" Liz had never had a panic attack.

"Then you'll tell the facilitator and she or he will call a cuddle lifeguard, who's in charge of the cuddlers' safety. He'll escort you out. Maybe, if the group is big enough, the lifeguard will have a cuddle caddy, who assists him."

"You know all the lingo. Cuddle lifeguard. Cuddle caddy. For God's sake."

"And bring your jammies. And if you have a special stuffed animal or blanket, bring that too."

Liz walked home, thinking about her niece Poppy. When she was three, she had announced haughtily when Liz tried to hug her, "I only snuggle with my daddies." Probably her daycare had been teaching them that they owned their bodies, and it sounded like a good MO. Liz tried to remember snuggling with her parents, but failed to come up with any memories. Probably she had, but more with her father, she guessed.

At home, she went straight to her nightwear drawer. Various unappetizing choices were tightly rolled into sausages, following Marie Kondo's plan. Liz was not a slavish Kondo disciple, but storing her clothes in one layer of rolls rather than flat layers was a brilliant idea. No more messing up the whole drawer when you wanted the sweater at the bottom of a pile. But nothing here was right for a cuddle party: nightgowns were out by definition, so was her collection of tired, oversized T-shirts, and there was a lone pair of pajamas whose dispirited waistband could not be trusted to stay on her waist during an evening of even moderately enthusiastic cuddling.

The next day, she stopped off before work at Nordstrom Rack. In the Intimate Apparel section, she headed for the flannel pajamas. Most of them were overrun with cozy-looking bears or sleepy bunnies, the kind of pajamas Poppy would wear. As a matter of fact, the cuddle party sounded ideal for a preschooler, except that Poppy had her boundaries in place more firmly than the adult cuddlers. Liz bought the pajamas with the sleepy bunnies, which at least came in navy as well as pastels.

====

After three days of silence from Nicole, an email arrived on Friday afternoon.

> *Dear Editor, I'm sorry to bother you, but you're usually so prompt. I haven't heard from you about my essay. If you haven't received it, please let me know.*
> *Thank you.*

Liz responded, *No, this doesn't work for me.*

Nicole wrote back, *You sound so different. Have I done something wrong?*

Yes, Liz thought. You have.

At 6:40 that evening, Liz met Honey at a yoga studio that the cuddle organization had rented. As directed, Liz brought with her the bunny pajamas, an absence of scent (apparently, many cuddlers were allergic) and a pseudonym (Eliza). Over the next quarter hour, eight men and seven women paid their thirty dollars, filled in their name tags and changed into pajamas. Liz gave herself a brief once-over in the women's changing room mirror: wearing a bra under her pajamas gave them a more alert and public look than usual. In the studio, the group gravitated toward the snack tray but once they got there, the celery sticks and ranch dip were mostly left undisturbed. Their flickers of conversation concentrated on transportation— how they hoped to beat the holiday stampede if they were leaving town next week for Thanksgiving or how they had travelled to the yoga studio, by Metro or car. And if the latter, how impossible the parking had been. Some of the cuddlers were very attractive, others not. In total, their looks were probably average or slightly above average. They ranged from late twenties to sixties, appeared variously shy, keen or impassive, and they were all white.

Their facilitator, Nancy, was a welcoming social worker type, just maternal enough to reassure but not rouse anxiety. She went through the philosophy of the cuddling party—"a playful space where people connect through non-erotic touch"—and the rules. You must always ask permission, and no means no. No touching in the areas covered by a fairly modest bathing suit, two-piece for women, trunks for men. Nancy had a few suggestions.

"Most people look forward to spooning, but that is an advanced position. You might be better to start by staring into each other's eyes, holding hands, simple moves like that for a while. If you become aroused," Nancy continued with superb neutrality, "don't worry. You can adjust your position gradually, not in a panicky way. Trust me, it won't last."

Everybody laughed nervously, especially the men.

Nancy predicted that after two hours of "cuddle mingle," many of them would find themselves in a state of "cuddle intoxication," which came with an almost overwhelming sense of connection. Liz had avoided meeting Honey's eyes at the mention of cuddle intoxication and now, as Nancy asked for volunteers to role-play asking for permission and refusing, Liz ignored the look on Honey's face that said, "Do it!" She was going to take as limited a role in this amiable weirdness as possible. A friendly-looking man and probably the youngest woman there obliged. Then it was time to go around the circle and have participants tell the group why they had come.

Liz thought, Oh no. Here comes the embarrassment. But people talked very naturally, mostly, about the circumstances that had left them without enough touch in their lives. They were widowed or divorced, too timid to date, had a physical problem that was only vaguely described. One woman said matter-of-factly that her cat had died. Many of them repeated Nancy's regret that they lived in a culture where it was hard to disconnect physical contact from sex. A few referred to the shallowness of their "touch tank," a term Liz connected with special containers for petting fish in aquariums. Peter had loved touch tanks. Two men and one woman retreated to science, saying they wanted to stimulate oxytocin, the so-called "cuddle hormone" that supposedly lowered your blood pressure. Honey, a.k.a. Marian, was surprisingly minimalist and inarticulate, speaking barely above a whisper. Reporters hate being part of the story, Liz remembered.

Then it was her turn.

"My name is Eliza," she began as if this were an AA meeting. She had planned to say something bland that echoed the others, but now she said, "I'm not exactly sure why I'm here, but something in my life is missing. And it's not sex. So I thought maybe tonight would give me a clue." Her voice wobbled at the end, and people nodded at her sympathetically. One man gave her a thumbs-up. Honey looked astonished. She thinks I'm giving an Oscar-worthy performance, Liz thought.

When everyone had spoken and agreed to the terms, the cuddle mingle could start. Liz thought of the line in *Where the Wild Things Are*, "Let the wild rumpus start!" Only there was no wild rumpus. People seemed to find the celery sticks and dip more interesting than they had before, and there was some conversation about oxytocin and whether cuddling could really lower stress and make sleep and social life easier. Finally, a woman approached a man, and they lay down on one of the mats spread around the room. They chose a fairly inconspicuous one near the wall, faced each other and ran their hands over the other's arms while they looked into each other's eyes. Liz thought locking eyes with someone was more intimate than all the back rubs in the world, and she hoped she would not have to do that. Slowly, other people, some giggling from embarrassment, others silent, began rubbing backs, letting their feet be massaged, manoeuvring themselves into hugging circles that stretched to four. Honey was in one of those circles, looking as if she wanted to die.

Liz was frozen against the wall. A woman, perhaps in her fifties, came up and asked if she wanted to hug.

"Yes," Liz lied.

The woman took her hand, firmly, and led her to a mat, where a man was lying.

"Mike wants to join us, is that okay?"

Liz lied again, and the woman, whose name was Patricia, became the filling in a hug sandwich. They kept it loose so Patricia, who was small and kept her head at the level of their shoulders, could breathe. Liz's own breathing was shallow at first, but she found things easier when she took deep breaths.

Patricia's body was as firm as her hand-holding, and Mike's was soft, with what used to be called love handles.

Liz tried to ignore them, out of politeness, but Mike said, "Go ahead and hold onto them, if you want to. That's what they're there for."

So she ran her free hand up and down his back, stopping regularly to cup, gently, one of his rolls. She found they fit perfectly into her hand. Mike began playing with her hair, winding it behind her right ear and then investigating all the complications of her ear with curious, careful fingers. It seemed as if he had never encountered an ear before. Liz found this irresistibly restful. She closed her eyes and thought, A stranger is massaging my ear and hair and I'm wearing my bra under my pajamas, and I'm having a good time. There wasn't all that much for Patricia to do and Liz worried about that, but she seemed content. Every once in a while, Liz would detach her arm from Mike's spongy back and pat Patricia's wiry forearm.

After what seemed like a short time, one of the cuddle lifeguards rang a bell. That happened every fifteen minutes and meant you could stay with what you were doing, but were encouraged to change things up. Liz wished they did that at parties: it was an inspired improvement on the phony "I'm just going to get another drink and I'll be right back" way of exiting a conversation. In a way she hated to leave Patricia and Mike: they were lovely people and she was so fond of them. But she was getting the idea that setting out for pastures new would also be rewarding. The three of them smiled at each other, Mike gave her hair a last smooth-down, and they went their separate ways.

After that, there was no stopping Liz. She seemed to have developed an internal engine, one might call it a cuddle motor, that kept running. She did group snuggles where the members turned and regrouped frequently. She did one-to-one hand holding that progressed to hugging, and she did face-caressing. After a shaky start, she did not find eyeballing her partner in these last two positions as saccharine as she had feared. She even did a threesome of spooning.

After a few minutes, the middle spooner whispered, "And don't forget, you two, this is an advanced position."

They all chuckled, smugly, and wriggled in for a tighter spoon.

Honey detached her from a shoulder-massaging conga line and led her to an alcove. To blend in, they stood nose to nose, holding each other's hands, which was peculiar enough. In real life, they hugged when one of them was setting out for a vacation, but that was the extent of their usual embracing.

"Whoa," Honey whispered. "Down, girl. Don't feel you need to be part of every grouping, I mean groping. Ha ha. People will start to get suspicious."

Liz was affronted by the word "groping." Didn't Honey see that that was not the point here? As for arousing suspicions, the cuddlers were too high on touch, if not oxytocin, to be skeptical. Before she could protest, an older man with a neatly trimmed beard approached and asked if they wanted to be part of a mini-pile.

"It's not the big puppy pile we'll have at the end," he said. "This one is more intimate."

He seemed to be a regular.

Honey said, "Maybe later," and drifted off.

Liz said, "Yes, thank you," because a man she had had her eye on was already in the pile. There was nothing remarkable about this man except his mouth, whose upper lip was a distinct Cupid's bow. Right now he was on the bottom layer of a five-person pile, where apparently the point was to clamber over each other, try to balance on a shifting hill of bodies and fail, laughing. It wasn't Liz's favorite, being more about good-natured scrambling than gentle touch— she imagined Poppy would enjoy it—but she stuck with it until the lifeguard rang his bell.

Then, trying to sound casual, she asked the Cupid's bow man, whose name was Andy, "Would you like to hug?"

Andy agreed, and they moved to a smaller mat. He was warm from all the scrambling, and his biceps were impressive. Liz liked the warmth and wasn't sure about the biceps. They hugged in silence. He fondled her shoulder with the arm he had circled around her neck and kept his other hand on her spine at waist level. She put one hand on his chest and breathed in his faintly soapy—but as unscented as possible—neck. Every once in a while she looked up to make sure that he wasn't bored, and he smiled at her.

When she couldn't resist any longer—and what did she have to lose?—she asked, "Would you mind if I touched your mouth?"

Andy did not mind. Softly, she traced his Cupid's bow. It was so like Sidney's, the only delicate thing in his craggy face. She used to tease him about having the mouth of a starlet. Andy stopped fondling her shoulder and held her without moving. It felt to Liz as if she had been wanting to touch a Cupid's bow mouth for a very long time. Maybe ten years. When the bell rang, her eyes were wet and she burrowed her head in Andy's chest so he would not see, but he produced a handkerchief from his sweatpants and dried her eyes.

After two hours of cuddle-mingling, a lifeguard led them in a closing ceremony. They were encouraged to nod and smile at all the people with whom they had snuggled. Liz aimed a smile at Mike and Patricia, and then at Andy. She hoped her smiles looked mate-y, until her eyes threatened to fill again and she looked away. If they were happy with their experience, the lifeguard urged them to go on the website and contribute a "cuddlemonial." Then came the puppy pile, an anticlimax as far as Liz was concerned, but it was clearly a crowd-pleaser. Afterward, as the people headed in and out of the changing rooms, several were showing pictures of their dogs on their phones to fellow cuddlers. There must have been more dog-chat than Liz had heard. She saw a few exchanging contact information. She had no impulse in that direction. The evening had been more than enough.

In the cab, Honey said, "I'm sorry I sneered at your journalistic nose, Lois Lane. I take it all back. You were awesome."

Liz didn't bother telling Honey that she hadn't been acting in the service of journalistic excellence.

"I didn't see anyone with a stuffed animal, did you?" Honey asked, making notes.

"What?" Liz was remembering the carving of Andy's lip and the way it felt to touch it. Sidney's starlet mouth. "No, I don't think I did."

"I can't wait to use the word 'cuddlemonial' and see it in the database," Honey gloated. "I'm sure it will be its first appearance."

Inserting a word for the first time in the paper's database was an honor mostly reserved for science and technology reporters.

"Liz? Are you okay? Liz? Don't tell me you're cuddle intoxicated."

Honey thought that was funny. Liz smiled at her.

"Let's debrief tomorrow, you look kind of beat," Honey said. "Or you can send me your notes and we can talk later. I can't thank you enough, Liz. I owe you."

Honey got out first, and Liz leaned her head back on the cab's dubious upholstery and closed her eyes. Tracing Andy's Cupid's bow mouth had been bittersweet, but right now the sweet side was edging out the bitter. She was done with Nicole, finally. There were probably some loose threads to tidy up with Seamus, but she had made the right decision there too. Next week was Thanksgiving and she was looking forward, a little tentatively, to seeing Henry at her table.

WEEK SEVEN

November 23–28, 2015

The problem with the holiday turkey-stuffing-gravy-mashed-potato-etc. dinner was that it was the most complicated meal of the year, and you only did it twice a year so you forgot how to pull it off. Christmas was marginally easier than Thanksgiving because you were only a month out of practice, but after that you forgot for the next eleven months. How to keep the turkey hot while it rested long enough to carve gracefully, accompanied by the other dishes—all hot—was a Rubik's cube Liz rarely solved. Then she seethed at the table, picking miserably at the room-temperature turkey or the too-salty gravy. But this year, she had plenty of cooks. Freya and Paul were bringing Prosecco and some finger food for the living room. Red Ann insisted on making the squash, which she could then reheat in Liz's microwave. Better that than outsourcing the mashed potatoes, which never reheated evenly. Kara, the new neighbor, was making her grandmother's cranberry sauce and a salad "without too much kale." Everyone was tired of kale. And of course, Henry was bringing two double-crust apple pies. Liz had a fresh container of vanilla ice cream in the freezer for them. By the time dessert came around, the kitchen would be a shambles and whipping cream would be beyond her.

Kara did not eat gluten and Dani, Red Ann's little girl, did not eat anything with a face. Peter's friend Leo was allergic to shellfish. Had Liz remembered to tell Freya and Paul to avoid pastry and shellfish in their hors d'oeuvres? She doubted there would be shellfish because, although not a strict vegetarian, Paul was happier not eating flesh. She woke in the night counting the vegetable dishes for the vegetarians—the honey-glazed carrots, the squash, mashed potatoes, salad. And for the last year or so, although Liz did not approve, the stuffing had also been vegetarian. Peter was adamant that cooking it inside the turkey encouraged salmonella, so now they roasted it in a pan, which dried it out. Liz fell back asleep and dreamed of trying to fit in all the pans in her oven: for the turkey, carrots and stuffing. It wouldn't work, plus the carrots had to cook at a higher temperature than the turkey. So the carrots would have to roast ahead of time, then be reheated at the last minute.

Peter and Leo arrived home on Wednesday evening, in Leo's car, and Peter told his friend there would be no sleeping in: they would be put to work. On Thursday morning, looking virtuous, they pulled out the leaf in the dining table and began setting the table. The papier-mâché turkey Peter had made in art class in sixth grade came out once a year and went in the center. Peter was past being embarrassed by this childish relic, but every year he said, "I can't believe you moved this from Seattle."

Leo teased him: "I didn't realize you were a sculptor. Why are you wasting your time in philosophy?"

Liz stopped Leo from putting the dessert forks to the left of the plate.

"There's no right or wrong, but we put them at the top of the plate, like this."

Peter half-rolled his eyes, wordlessly asking, Can you ever give your control-freakishness a rest?

The control freak in her thought that the people bringing the hors d'oeuvres should arrive promptly. But Freya and Paul, usually so conscientious, were nowhere to be seen and here was Henry, balancing pies, making his way up the walk.

Peter said, "Mom, chill. No one is going to starve here. Have a glass of wine."

"But Paul and Freya are bringing the Prosecco."

Indicating by the way he managed the corkscrew that his mother was beyond help, Peter began opening a bottle of red wine.

Henry put the whipping cream he had brought in the fridge, and found an obscure place on the already crowded counter for the pies and his mini-mixer. He took a small bowl from Liz's cupboard and put it, with the beaters, in the fridge, for faster whipping. Then he shook Peter's hand—they had not met before—and accepted a glass of wine.

Freya and Paul arrived, with apologies. The cheese straws had taken longer than usual to bake to their golden, buttery best. They also brought tapenade, which worried Liz slightly. It often contained anchovies, and she was pretty sure anchovies had faces. But Dani ate several cheese straws and showed no interest in the tapenade. Kara avoided the cheese straws and enjoyed the tapenade on endives. By now everyone had arrived and Liz's normally pale cheeks were pink with directing people where to put their coats and their food, thanking them for their contributions and being thanked for her hospitality. It was, as more than one person remarked, Thanksgiving.

The meal turned out better than usual. Although he rarely ate turkey, Paul revealed an unexpected gift for making gravy, Liz's Achilles heel. His gravy was dark and hot, with a richness that came in layers. The turkey was also hot, because Red Ann had inherited her Scottish mother's conviction that the turkey must rest under a tartan blanket once it came out of the oven. She brought a Black Watch lap robe and swaddled the foil-wrapped turkey. Whether or not it was a Scottish miracle, it worked. The mashed potatoes were almost hot. Only the carrots were not, and their flavour suffered the least from being lukewarm.

Kara's son, Ned, and Dani were happy to watch *How to Train Your Dragon*, and happy to be called to the table. Liz had deliberately not made a seating plan, so as to look relaxed. That resulted in the two children, their mothers and Henry sitting at the opposite end of the table from Liz. It turned out Kara had gone to the high school where Ann was a guidance counsellor, so the women had plenty to talk about. Kara was a software designer, and Henry talked to her about that. And he could not praise Kara's grandmother's cranberry sauce enough. "It's the raisins and the pecans. They raise it to a level I never thought cranberry sauce could reach."

Liz looked at her guests fondly. She wondered if Kara had been married to Ned's father, and what had happened to him. She watched Henry enjoying the cranberry sauce. Of course, he would not spend the night. The two of them had not progressed beyond that first kiss, but even if they had, Peter and Leo were staying at the apartment and Liz always gave Peter fair warning when he was about to meet a gentleman caller at the breakfast table. But she liked the way Henry's nose twitched ever so slightly when someone said something interesting.

It was impossible to have Thanksgiving that year without talking about "the Trump column," as everyone called Chris Cillizza's recent piece. In it, he told Washington to wake up and smell the coffee: in spite of Trump's hideous and uncensored opinions— perhaps because of them—this bizarre contender was not going away. Peter retrieved the paper and read his startling conclusion. "It's time to accept this reality: Donald Trump is and will continue to be a major player in the GOP nomination fight and, yes, could even wind up as the Republican standard-bearer next fall." Even though everyone had read it, it was still bewildering and depressing. Peter and Leo were Sanders supporters, and saw Trump's success as another sign that the establishment was moribund. Freya said, "But to look on the bright side, if he actually got the nomination, Hillary's win would be a sure thing." Even so, no one looked happy. Perhaps because it was Thanksgiving, they reached a tacit agreement not to talk any more about the election.

Other than that, the conversation was not scintillating, but amiable. They talked about the food, about travel fiascos at past Thanksgivings (in case Freya and Paul were regretting their daughter's decision not to come to D.C.), about a movie only two of them had seen but most had read about, about possible mutual connections, but they did not know each other well enough to venture on more interesting subjects. The adults paid attention (but they hoped not too much attention) to the children and to Peter and Leo.

Henry asked Peter what he was working on.

"I'm just starting the reading for a paper on forgiveness."

Liz looked up from the mashed potatoes she was trying to urge on Ned. He had pushed the meat and veg to the far end of his plate and was lapping up a lake of cranberry sauce with a spoon.

That probably has to do with Sidney, she thought.

"Is forgiveness a philosophical subject?" Red Ann asked. "I would have thought it was psychology."

"Or pastoral counselling," offered Paul. He taught at the divinity school that was associated with American University, although, confusingly, his specialty was how best to live in a godless universe.

"It's for my ethics class," Peter said. "Although there are connections with linguistic philosophy, of course."

Liz thought, "of course?" Was it only a matter of time before Peter realized he was smarter than she was, or had that happened already?

Henry asked, "What are some of the philosophical concerns?"

"Well, for example, who is entitled to forgive. Who has what the philosophers call 'standing.'"

"Doesn't everyone?" Liz asked.

"Not at all."

But before Peter could say more, Paul interrupted. "Someone told me you can't forgive unilaterally. You need the perpetrator to apologize or accept responsibility first. Is that true?"

"I'm just starting the reading," Peter said.

Liz thought, He's had enough of this.

Henry turned to Leo and asked what he was researching at the Library of Congress.

After all the grownups but Kara, who ate only the apple filling because of her gluten problem, had exclaimed over the flakiness of Henry's pastry, Ann asked him what fat he used.

"For me, lard is the best. But I didn't know all the guests and I thought someone might not eat pork, so these are made with butter."

Dani looked at Henry approvingly: pigs had faces.

Freya was loading the dishwasher when Liz came in the kitchen to get the coffee cups.

"He's a paragon," Freya said, slotting in the last dinner plate and considering the salad plates. Although she and Henry were both historians, their department was large and their contacts were minimal. "How many men can go into a stranger's messy kitchen and find what's needed to whip cream without bothering the hostess?"

Liz counted out eight cups. Not everyone would drink coffee or tea, but she hadn't wanted to break into the conversation to ask.

"You know," she said finally, "the pie was very good, but I still think Honeycrisp or Northern Spy are the best pie apples. The McIntoshes in this one break down into something close to applesauce."

Freya gave her a look. "I'll repeat that, Liz. He's a paragon."

"Maybe he's too much of a paragon."

"Are you crazy? You're starting to be one of those people who inspect the underside of furniture to see if it's all perfectly finished before you even look at the top."

Liz said, "Could you help me with the rest of these cups? I can't find the tray."

Freya gave her another look and hugged her quickly before she picked up four cups.

Henry hugged her, too, when they bumped into each other in the hall. Liz was on her way back to the kitchen for the cream and sugar, and Henry must have been returning from the bathroom. His embrace was warmer and longer than Freya's, and when he let her go, he said, "Thank you. I'm having such a good time." Then he kissed her, more comprehensively than he had under the linden tree. Or, more accurately, he began kissing her, because Liz broke away quickly and said, "It's so nice to have you here, I just have to get something. . . ."

He looked confused—had he just been rebuffed?—but made an effort to switch gears. "Can I help?"

"No, no, you just go back to the dining room."

He smiled at her, a little inquiringly.

———

Leo left early the next morning for the Library of Congress. When Peter came down at ten for breakfast, Liz was in the last stages of wiping the counters and the turkey carcass was bubbling away in the soup kettle. Nobody really liked turkey soup, but she always felt obliged to make it.

Peter transferred a hefty square of stuffing into a soup bowl and ladled cranberry sauce on top of it.

"Here, have some gravy with that," Liz said, passing him the saucepan, but he shook his head.

"I see you brought out the shroud again," Peter said, putting the bowl in the microwave and looking around for coffee.

"Did I?" Liz said, surprised. She poured him a mug of coffee. "No, I didn't at all. You're totally wrong."

"Bringing out the shroud" was their expression for Liz cooling on a gentleman caller. In *The Odyssey*, Penelope keeps her suitors at bay by weaving a burial shroud for her father-in-law, claiming she couldn't choose a suitor until the shroud was finished.

"Mom, I know the signs. I saw you dialling down his real kiss into a thanks-for-dinner kiss. You talked to everybody more than to him. If you ever met his eye when he was talking, I missed it."

"You're wrong. I like him. He was seated at the other end of the table. Where he seemed to be getting along fine. And I had a lot to do with the meal, in case you hadn't noticed."

The dig was part of her ongoing project to keep Peter attentive as a host. After a promising start with the first few guests, he tended to enjoy himself and forget his hosting responsibilities.

He shrugged, his cheeks squirrel-like from an immense bite of stuffing. After he swallowed, he said, "Maybe Thanksgiving is your new shroud."

Liz had talked an unenthusiastic but dutiful Peter into going with her to Baltimore to see her mother. The traffic was surprisingly light, as if the world had gotten up early for the Black Friday sales and was already at the malls by the time they set out in late morning.

They used to have their best conversations in the car, where there was no possibility of having to look in each other's eyes.

So Liz asked, "But do you like Henry?"

"What's the point of me liking him or not liking him? You've got your loom out in the middle of the living room and the shroud is growing like crazy. Henry's finished."

She kept her eyes on the road and let him feel her annoyance.

"Okay. He seemed nice enough."

She noted the past tense, and changed the subject.

When they arrived at Haven, they found Greg's partner, Gabe, and their little girl in Agnes's room. Greg had had to work at the last minute, so Gabe and Poppy had come to visit without him. While Poppy was there, Agnes was all smiles. Grandmother and granddaughter played with a set of magnetic paper dolls, and Agnes indulged Poppy's insistence that her paper doll would only wear pink. But as soon as Poppy and Gabe left, she turned cantankerous.

"That was nice of Gabe to bring Poppy," Liz said unwisely.

"I liked the other one better," Agnes said.

She meant Robert, Greg's first husband, but she could not fish out his name. Greg had come out long before Agnes's dementia appeared, and her response had been of a piece with her rational, modernist self. But now that that self made only sporadic visits, she sometimes expressed less progressive views. At times she seemed to have an obstinate pride in what she considered her son's masculinity. At other times, she regretted it. When Greg and Robert were splitting up, she had said with grim satisfaction, "A couple needs a woman, and it's not going to be your brother." Exactly how Robert, an accountant and an ardent father with a passion for ballroom dancing, had failed to fulfill what Agnes considered his feminine role was unclear.

Peter was used to his grandmother's unpredictability. He volunteered to look at old family albums with her, and she agreed. They sat together on the ungiving couch, and Agnes looked as if the people in the albums were interesting enough but she didn't know them.

But every once in a while, she would put her finger on a dog and say, "He was always bringing home dead squirrels. That's the thing with retrievers." Or of a toddler Liz in a shirt checked like a tablecloth, "She loved that shirt. I had to wash it at night while she slept so she could put it on again in the morning."

That night, after Peter and Leo went out to see friends, Liz, wanting a palate-cleanser after the mostly happy intensity of Thanksgiving, opened her favorite revenge site. She read about a scorned wife who hired a mariachi band to play under her husband's lover's bedroom from 4:00 a.m. to 6:00 a.m. on the day the lover was to take her bar exam. She failed the exam. Clever, Liz thought. She couldn't see Nicole taking a bar exam, but the thought of the unstoppable mariachi players and the nerve-racked law student pleased her.

But she also felt a twinge of guilt. As penance, she decided she would give some of the techniques in her forgiveness books another try or, more accurately, a first try. Now, from *The Only Forgiveness Toolkit You'll Ever Need*, she read about an exercise that began with twenty minutes of meditation, followed by five minutes in which she was to focus on the wrong that had been done to her and think good thoughts about the ones who had hurt her. Then came the kicker: "Let those feelings remain in your mind, but separate them from your thoughts." Huh? How in the world did you do that? After that piece of mental juggling, she should say out loud that she welcomed what was good and rejected only what was negative. And finally she would return to her "peaceful place," an image of a place that brought her tranquility. Ordering, "Stop the overthinking and analysis. Your worries and problems are still there, but you have learned how to walk away from them. You're no longer their victim, and your bad feelings will also detach themselves from you," the writer promised that she would see results in her level of forgiveness on the very next day.

That was baffling and had FAILURE written all over it. *The Only Forgiveness Toolkit You'll Ever Need* was not working for her. Wondering again how these books had come to colonize her bedside table, she rearranged them and put *Slow Forgiveness* on top. The title had a gradual, mature promise that calmed her. She tried to imagine Hillary Clinton in the self-help section of Kramerbooks, hoping to read her way to forgiving Bill. It did not seem likely.

Finally, she got into bed to read *The Odyssey*. She thought of *The Odyssey* as a Boys' Own adventure story, but Emily Wilson's new translation was making her more conscious than she had been of Telemachus's relationship with Penelope. She felt sorry for Telemachus. He barely remembered his father, and his capable, clever mother left him feeling unsure and impotent. No wonder he occasionally lashed out at Penelope, ordering her, "Go in and do your work. . . . It is for men to talk, especially me. I am the master." The braggadocio only underlined his weakness.

━━

In the morning, she read an email Henry had sent late in the evening. The subject line was "Black Friday."

> *Dear Liz,*
>
> *Thanks again for a terrific Thanksgiving dinner. I liked your friends, including Freya, whom I usually only see at department meetings. And, of course, Peter. I predict his paper on forgiveness will be interesting.*
>
> *In a meal full of good dishes, the carrots were exceptional. I had already asked for that Ottolenghi book for Christmas, so I will look forward to making honey-roasted carrots.*
>
> *I enjoyed getting to know you a little, Liz, and obviously hoped to know you better. But I'm not bad at reading the writing on the wall. And while a good time was being had by all at your table, I realized that my hopes were pretty one-sided. I should probably take out the "pretty"—they were one-sided.*
>
> *So I'll remember our times together with fondness.*
> *Wishing you all the best,*
> *Henry*

Well. This was not the thank you Liz had expected. Her first thought was that Henry was as mistaken as Peter. Her second thought was that the score was two against one, and maybe she should pay some attention to that. Her third was annoyance: Did either of these supposedly woke men realize that the constant vigilance involved in putting on a Thanksgiving dinner did not make it an ideal time for courting? She would write to Henry and explain that he was quite wrong, but not for a day or so.

WEEK EIGHT

November 29–December 5, 2015

*A*n email from Sidney arrived on Sunday, as unexpected as Henry's but much more serious. It was headed "Sad news." *Liz, I'm sorry to break bad news this way, but Neil died last night of a heart attack. Everyone is in shock, and I don't have any news about the funeral. Or memorial service, more likely. I doubt you'll be able to make it here anyway, but I'll keep you posted. S.*

Sidney was wrong: Liz had every intention of going to Neil's service. Neil had been Sidney's boss in the trade department, and they quickly became friends. Liz got along with Trina, Neil's funny and sometimes abrupt wife, and the two couples went to movies and restaurants and picnicked with their children, although Trina and Neil's girls were older than Peter.

It was a blow when Neil left Trina for a colleague in his department, but he was determined to keep the friendship with Liz and Sidney going. Liz never took to Alice as she had to Trina, and underneath their superficial congeniality both she and Alice were wary. Neil persevered, lunching with Liz alone, emailing her regularly with entries for their list of bizarre or bizarrely appropriate names (Priestly Demolitions, Clytemnestra O'Higgins, Paul Edge for a carpet salesman, Nancy Pulling for a dental surgeon). And when Sidney left Liz, Neil had been a godsend. He understood Sidney's situation too well to demonize or excuse him, and he extended a sympathy to Liz that included countless cups of tea and glasses of wine. What she remembered of those sessions was Neil repeating calmly that, although she could not believe it now, she would feel better in time. And of course, he was right.

Later in the day, Sidney sent the details of the "celebration" of Neil's life, scheduled rather hastily for Tuesday. Neil's older daughter had to leave Seattle on Wednesday for a conference in Tasmania. Liz saw Peter and Leo off, begging them to drive carefully, and arranged to take a few days' leave. There was a young, keen, floating editor who could perform the finishing touches on My Turn, as long as the essays and the illustrations were in hand.

On Monday morning, before she left for the airport, Liz sent Nicole a curt, businesslike response to her last, pleading note. Certainly Nicole hadn't done anything wrong, she wrote, it was just that she accepted a tiny percentage of essays.

As usual, Seattle's tin-colored skies and familiar gloom landed on Liz even before she got in the cab. Was the city forever tinged with the end of her marriage, or was it the New Englander in her, preferring the sunny cold winters of her childhood to this moist, misty heaviness and this endless, smudged palette of grays and greens? Peter thought Seattle's silvery closeness was cozy, so no doubt childhood conditioning was crucial.

She had dozed on the plane, but now on the way to Trina's, where she would stay, she surrendered to unhappy thoughts. First and foremost, of course, was Neil. His death was more than sad and with it, an important link to her married life and her time in Seattle was gone. Then there were Nicole and Sidney, whom she would see at the memorial service. Worrying about meeting them when she should only be thinking about Neil made her feel small and superficial, but there it was. She was small and superficial. And Henry's farewell message, which she had first dismissed as something she would fix, now struck her as yet another demonstration of her failure with men.

=====

On Tuesday, as Liz and Trina approached the government building where the service was to be held, she saw people walking more slowly as they neared the entrance, looking uncertain, as if they still could not quite grasp what they were doing there. Calling a memorial service a celebration worked best, she thought, when the person was full of years and the peaceful, anticipated death was a few weeks or months in the past. Neil's faulty heart had given no warning, and people were still grappling with his premature death. There were no happy greetings of friends and acquaintances who hadn't seen each other for a long while.

Liz and Trina met Trina's daughters, now at the far end of their twenties, at the front door. Inside, the guests were directed to a large, plain room interrupted with square pillars covered with the same tiles that covered the low ceiling. A few baskets of flowers and pictures of Neil arranged on easels by the podium were dwarfed by the room's workaday facelessness. Oddly, the only note of comfort came from the folding chairs, which were thickly padded on the backs and seats. A small solace for the interminable meetings bureaucrats have to sit through, Liz thought.

Once in the hall, the daughters made their way to the front where the family and their stepmother were sitting. Trina and Liz chose seats in the middle. A few people said hello to Liz. Still disgusted with herself, she found it hard to concentrate on anything but where and when Nicole and Sidney would appear. At this point, it seemed to her there were two Nicoles. The lunatic My Turn escapade felt as if it had been taking place on Mars, and yet, Liz's anger toward that Nicole, Nicole-the-writer, still smarted. It seemed curiously unattached to the other Nicole, whose arrival she was dreading. With Nicole-the-writer, Liz had the power. With the other Nicole, Liz was braced for the familiar, tongue-tied discomfort.

The proceedings began before she could locate them. The program was the usual mix of speeches and music, performed by a trio who played everything from Bach to—surprisingly—Lerner and Loewe. The speakers painted a picture of a man who counted the months until Seattle's jazz festival (Trina despised jazz, and Liz did not remember that Neil had liked it), who loved kayaking on Green Lake and gardening with Alice (the Neil Liz knew had hated gardening) and who had become a student of the golden age of the American musical. (Who knew? That explained the Lerner and Loewe and the medley from *Carousel* the trio had played as people took their places.) Apparently the man the speakers remembered today had sprung fully formed into the world in his forties. There was no childhood, no education, no passionate involvement and gradual disenchantment with the labor movement, very little of the Neil his oldest friends had known. Definitely no youthful marriage that had lasted for twenty years. There was only the briefest mention of his daughters and no indication of how they had come to be, perhaps discovered under one of the hostas he had taken to cultivating.

At the end, as people tried to walk solemnly out of the rows of seats to the strains of "Oh, What a Beautiful Mornin'" from *Oklahoma!*, Liz turned to Trina and widened her eyes.

"Well," Trina shrugged, twitching the collar of her gray jacket (not black but not bright either), "the current wife gets to script the funeral."

Her Turn

Liz made her way to the front, to say a few words to Alice. The widow looked everyone in the eye, submitted to their hugs or allowed her hands to be grasped. Later this composure might fray, and she gave the impression that something more pressing than the guests needed her attention, but for the moment she would do her social duty.

"Liz," she said, "you came all this way."

"Of course I did. I'm so sorry. He was a wonderful friend." And with that she moved aside, to make way for the next people in line.

As luck would have it—well, she did have to get it over with—Sidney and Nicole were talking with Trina. She took a glass of Merlot from a tray, knowing it would be syrupy and that she would regret it.

"Hello," she said to the bridegroom of her youth and the woman who, following Trina's logic, would eventually write her out of Sidney's eulogy. At least the occasion meant that she could be unsmiling. No false jolliness.

Sidney nodded. He did look quite shaken.

"I thought the speeches were very good," he said.

"Really? I didn't feel I knew the man they were describing. Of course, you saw much more of him than I did in the past few years."

Sidney seemed confused by that. Honestly, Liz thought, has he forgotten everything about the Neil they had known together? Sometimes it seemed that men lived in an eternal present. But this was a loss for Sidney, and she had sounded churlish.

To make amends, she said, "He had such a gift for companionship."

He gave her a quick look of gratitude.

As always, Liz found Sidney marginally easier to be with than his wife. Nicole stood silent, wearing her usual expression of kindly concern and a bright blue flared jumper. Maybe she thought wearing dark colors to an occasion like this was an outmoded convention. Maybe she was taking "celebration" literally. Liz's in-person

129

interactions with Nicole usually began with a series of mental jerks, in which she saw herself lurching toward Nicole in thickly dramatized neutrality, then fleeing in the opposite direction, then trying again with more moderation. An observer would have seen a woman quietly greeting another woman, her half-rictus of a smile the only giveaway to any strain. As for the hope that Neil's death would give a mature person some perspective on her stale, trivial problem with her ex-husband's wife, Liz had failed yet again at being a mature person. Feeling after feeling folded in on top of each other, and she had trouble disentangling them.

Finally, in the silence that had fallen, Nicole said to her, "You and Neil were so close. I'm sorry."

Liz nodded, trying to look thoughtful. As if any uneasiness she might feel was swallowed up in grief.

A couple Liz recognized approached them. Their daughter, Sarah, had gone to school with Peter.

After Liz and the couple exchanged expressions of surprise and sadness, Davis, the husband, said to Liz, "I haven't seen your byline for a while. Are you still reporting on education?"

She hadn't been the education reporter for more than two years, but people often cast journalists' bylines and assignments in stone. It wouldn't do for Nicole or Sidney to hear about her current job, so she manoeuvred Sarah's parents off into their own little threesome. She was editing a column on social trends, she said vaguely. Davis wanted to hear more, but she redirected the conversation to Sarah and what she was doing. Few parents could resist that, so Liz listened amiably to their stories of Sarah's lacrosse scholarship at Notre Dame, the ways in which the school bent over backwards to accommodate the team, their chances of winning the divisional championship, the coach who seemed to know exactly how far Sarah could be pushed. Between appropriate nods and "Wows," out of the corner of her eye Liz watched the group around Trina, Nicole and Sidney. Trina's older daughter joined them and yielded to a round of hugs. Those poor girls, Liz thought. This is terrible for them. A colleague of Sidney's came up, and after a while the two men were deep in their own conversation. Trina and her daughter hived off, which left Nicole with a woman whom Liz did not recognize.

Telling Sarah's parents that she needed to say hello to someone, she slipped past Nicole and heard her saying, bashfully and confidingly, to the other woman, "Actually, I've started to do a little writing."

Oh no. Aside from the guilt that innocent statement aroused, Liz felt a more selfish anxiety. There probably were a few people in this throng who did know what Liz did at the paper, and if Nicole started talking about My Turn to one of them, the game would be up. Just as Liz swerved away from Nicole, the woman she was talking to looked up.

"Liz!" she called, rather too cheerily for the occasion. "Isn't that you?"

Still not knowing who the woman was but dismayed at the thought of exposure, Liz pretended she hadn't heard and dived into the crowd, which unfortunately was a little thin at that point. She sidled close to the wall until she came to a busier part of the room. Liz and Trina were going out to dinner, with either or both of Trina's daughters if they felt like it. She thought of telling Trina she would just go ahead to the restaurant they had chosen, but now that she had joined the larger throng, she had lost sight of Nicole and the mystery woman.

Feeling like a fool, she watched Trina talking with old friends and accepting condolences, at a decent distance from Alice. What exactly did condolences for a long-divorced husband mean? Both Wife One and Wife Two were behaving with poise and dignity, and Liz doubted she would do as well. She remembered a Washington story of the death of a senator with a long-term wife and a long-term mistress. The two women received mourners at different ends of the funeral parlor, the widow nearer the casket, the mistress nearer the exit. The widow dressed in black with gold jewellery, the mistress in gray with silver jewellery. (That part must be apocryphal, it was too shapely to be true.) After the funeral, they held separate receptions in their two houses. How enlightened, people said.

The room was filled with Sidney's colleagues, and she noticed him chatting animatedly, pink with wine and sorrow. Nicole, on the other hand, was now alone, blessedly so, as far as Liz was concerned. No more talk of her attempts to write. She seemed to have run out of people she knew and her good-natured expression was starting to look a little tired. Liz recognized that face: Sidney has forgotten me, and I have to look as if I'm enjoying myself. A kind person would step over and chat with her. Or a modern person, who would think of her own marriage with Sidney as practically prehistoric and see Nicole as a friendly woman who was much better suited to Sidney than she had been. A person who would say, if reminded of the grief she had felt as Sidney moved from her to Nicole, "Oh, but that was *such* a long time ago." Liz was not feeling particularly kind or modern, but she noted Nicole's face. She knew what she was feeling.

Robin and Lewis, a couple Liz knew slightly, stopped to chat. Robin was a colleague of Sidney and Neil's, and Liz could not dredge up their last names, but she did not need them. They looked approvingly at the widow and the ex-wife playing their decorous parts.

"Very civilized," Robin said, and Lewis nodded in conjugal complacency.

Liz wanted to kick them both. Or maybe she could content herself just by slapping that self-satisfied scrim off Robin's face. She never again wanted to hear the word "civilized" used to compliment people involved in a divorce, at least not people who had young children. (She ignored the fact that Neil and Trina's divorce was not new, and the children were grown up.) There was nothing the least bit civilized about ending a family. And those on the receiving end had no obligation to act "civilized"—hurt, anger and screaming on both sides of slammed doors were perfectly appropriate responses. There. That was Liz's uncool, intemperate and uncivilized reaction. Of course, adultery and divorce were going to continue. They were two hardy perennials, like prejudice and meanness. And like prejudice and meanness, they often involved the suffering of the innocent, like children, and the sometimes only moderately guilty, like the surprised spouse. (Here she sent a mea culpa in Martha Donovan's direction.) Adultery and divorce would persist, and everybody needed to work hard to minimize the damage, but that was no reason to commend them.

"Liz! Liz!"

Oh God, here was that woman again, pulling a reluctant-looking Nicole in her wake. The woman was jabbering on.

"Nicole has just been telling me she's starting to do some journalism, and I suggested she get in touch with you because of course with your experience . . ."

The woman nodded at Robin and Lewis, who seemed to know her and nodded back. Even as Liz's heart juddered terrifyingly around in her chest, she thought, Starting to do some *journalism*? Oh please. What Nicole was trying to do, with, let us be fair, Liz's encouragement, was the furthest thing from journalism. And this woman—wait, Liz was remembering who she might be, wasn't she Neil's PA, whom Liz had barely met, and her hair was different—seemed to think it was perfectly natural for an ex-wife to lend a helping hand to the incumbent. Another vote of support for Robin and Lewis's position on divorce, who were looking on with interest, and another arrow aimed straight at Liz's tattered self-image. "With your experience": did that mean she knew about My Turn or just that Liz was a journalist? But Liz wasn't going to stick around to find out.

This time she couldn't pretend not to have heard, so she said rapidly, "Oh, hi. Thelma. Hi, Thelma. You'll have to excuse me for just a minute. Trina and I are trying to round up her girls, and I need to find Molly before she takes off." And she was gone, but not before she saw Nicole shoot her a look. It lasted only a second, but Liz filed it away to think about later.

Now that she had made a thorough idiot of herself, Liz found Trina and told her she would meet her at the restaurant. By the time she had collected her coat, she decided it was unlikely that Thelma knew about her current job. Liz remembered her vaguely as garrulous, and she could have been further disinhibited by grief—Neil had been a beloved boss. That made Liz feel even more stupid.

Outside, it was raining and Liz had no umbrella. Putting her head down, she shook it as if to dislodge all the conflicting, sad, confusing events of the last few hours. The one that stubbornly refused to leave was the look on Nicole's face as Thelma burbled on about Liz helping Nicole with her writing. The expression was directed at Liz and seemed to ask, What would ever make me come to you for help, and what would ever make you consider giving it? And behind that was a tiny flicker of something that looked conspiratorial, that looked as if she were poking gentle fun at Thelma for barking up a very wrong tree. That look had been almost buddyish, which made Liz feel worst of all.

═══

Just before she'd left for Seattle, Seamus had left Liz a message from his private phone: "Hi Liz, just fair warning. I decided to take the Beginners course after all. Signora Venturi thinks I have an aptitude for Italian, ha ha." An embarrassed but pleased-in-spite-of-himself laugh. "The class also meets on Wednesday evenings, but I promise I won't make any claims on your time during the break. I'll start this week."

So much for Liz's happy, absorbed-in-Italian Wednesday nights, but there was nothing she could do about it. She felt sad for Seamus, although she didn't want to encourage him by showing that, so perhaps this evened the score between them a tiny bit. Feeling as if she had been in Seattle much longer than three days, she had just enough time to drop her suitcase at home before she headed out for the Casa.

Signor Pugliesi, Liz's teacher, got so cheerfully lost in his grammatical mazes that he often forgot to announce the break until late. When he did, the class poured into the hall, the Americans immediately lapsing into English, while the Europeans, especially the Eastern Europeans, carried on in Italian. That's why they are multilingual and we are not, Liz thought every week at the break.

She hoped the Beginners would be back in their classroom before the Advanced Intermediates were released for their break, but when they reached the café, Brown Anne said, "There's your publisher."

Wearing a blue knit shirt, Seamus was chatting with the Beginners' teacher. Liz had almost never seen him without a tie, unless he was naked. Sports clothes didn't suit him as well as a business suit, or nudity, but he was still an agreeable-looking man. Opening what looked like their textbook, he circled something with his hand and looked inquiringly at the teacher. He was more animated than Liz had seen him since the breakup. But why couldn't he have found a hobby outside the Casa Italiana?

"Do you mind just getting me a decaf espresso and bringing it out to the bench by the front door?" she asked Anne. For Italians, decaf espresso missed the point completely, but they accommodated themselves to American taste at the Casa. She added, "I don't feel like socializing with the boss."

Anne nodded. She had a principal who struck her the same way.

———

The piece by the man whose wife had numerous affairs needed very little editing, but Liz had a few questions and possible clarifications. They spoke on the phone late on Thursday afternoon, which he explained was early in his workday. Paolo de Santis, who was soon to appear in the paper as Paul Arnolfi, was a security guard. He had been dyslexic as a boy and learned to read only after he dropped out of school. He worked the night shift in a big government building, and liked his job because it gave him hours and hours to read.

Paolo was amiable but no pushover when it came to the editing. He was not "copy-proud," as editors said of some writers, but he drew a firm line between the negotiable and the non-negotiable. Liz was intrigued. His situation would strike many people as deplorable, but he wore it in a way that, while not lighthearted, was graceful and perhaps even wise. Once they had settled on a final version, Liz realized she wasn't ready to end her contact with him.

Remember the old Liz? she asked herself frostily. The professional Liz? The Liz before she'd responded to Nicole? That Liz didn't make overtures to My Turn writers once the editing was done. This is not a social club, much less a dating service, she told herself. This is your job. But there was no denying she wanted to see Paolo. Not knowing exactly why she wanted to see him only sharpened her wish. Just recall, the disapproving Liz scolded the transgressive Liz, how well that ended with the Dubroffs. But that didn't count, transgressive Liz responded: the cat piece had made that a special circumstance. Disapproving Liz gave in, and suggested to Paolo that they might meet for coffee. He agreed to come to the paper tomorrow afternoon, on his way to work.

===

Waiting for Paolo in the lobby, she looked at its two-story height, sheathed in gray and white marble, through a stranger's eyes. It looked more like a 1930s luxury hotel, a place where Fred Astaire and Ginger Rogers would shortly be tap dancing all over its shiny floor, than a twenty-first-century newspaper. The only sign of its true identity was a screen on the wall that showed the first few pages of that day's paper. Visitors signed in at the massive front desk, also marble, which communicated more gravitas and power than was necessary.

Because Paolo had an Italian name, Liz was looking for someone dark and not terribly tall. But the man who approached her was taller than average, with an easy smile aimed half at her, half at the lobby's grandiosity. Not at all lovelorn or hangdog. Fair-skinned and green-eyed, with close-cut auburn hair, he wore his security staff uniform. He and Liz signed the form at the desk and moved to the gate. Liz pressed her identity card on the reader, and the guard passed Paolo through.

In the cafeteria, neither drank coffee. It was too late in the day for Liz, and she made a pot of mint tea. Paolo needed caffeine, but he drank it in the form of Coke.

"I'm very happy with the way your piece turned out."

"Yes, my wife liked it too."

Liz allowed her face to show something between interest and mild surprise.

"Of course," he said, "I wasn't writing anything we haven't already talked to death."

She supposed not. It was a logical part of this relationship that combined openness with ongoing adventures for his wife and ongoing pain for him. It felt odd to be sitting with a stranger when she knew so much about his personal life. She retreated to something neutral by asking Paolo about the books he read during his shift. They had more than a few favorites in common, although his taste was contemporary and American, and hers tended to slightly older Brits. Right now he was working his way through Cormac McCarthy.

"I'd like to do that," she said, "but I find I'm rereading more and more. That way I know what I'm getting, although a second reading can surprise you too."

He shook his head at her. "You're too young to be doing a lot of rereading," he said, with authority, as though he were a reading consultant. "You need to keep in contact with what's being written now or at least with books new to you, whenever they were written. For every book you reread, you should be reading three, no, four, that are new to you."

She bristled invisibly. Had she asked for counsel about her reading life? And where did he get his magic formula? She disliked unsolicited advice, and yet she felt chastened. So, reading was another area where she was culpably risk-averse. Maybe that was better than her recent inclination to fling herself off every available bridge when it came to her job.

She changed the subject by asking about his schedule.

"I'm asleep in the morning when the kids go to school, but I pick them up in mid-afternoon and spend a few hours with them then. Natalie is home from work by the time I have to leave."

Children had not figured in his essay.

"You have children. How old are they?"

"A boy and a girl, six and ten. So you see," he said, shaking his Coke to see if there was any left, "this is a permanent situation."

"But parents of small children do separate and do divorce. I'm not advocating that, just saying that it happens."

"Yes, but not to us. Natalie, who probably loves me less in some ways than I do her, would never consider splitting up the family. Neither would I."

Paolo had to go to work, so Liz took him to the elevator and they shook hands. Walking down the stairs to her office, Liz thought, He's attractive. A little bossy, but there are surprises there. Interesting that he thinks that his wife "probably" loves him less "in some ways" than he loves her, while the conventional belief would be, "Of *course* she loves him less, otherwise she wouldn't be having all those affairs!" Maybe we make too much of monogamy. She went from that to imagining walking on the towpath with Paolo, and smiled, remembering Henry's satire of the typical D.C. singles ad. What a congenial brunch they had had.

Once she was back at her desk, Gilman made one of his sudden appearances. Resting his arm on her baffle, he said confidentially, "You do realize the paper has its own security service." He had passed her saying goodbye to Paolo.

"Very funny. He's written something for My Turn."

Sotto voce and with relish, Gilman got to his real point. "So. Donovan's wife has kicked him out."

She felt herself turning red. "How do you know that?"

"I have to protect my sources," he said smugly. "I just know. And now he's putting the moves on Melanie Dermot."

That made Liz half-laugh, in spite of her burning face. Melanie Dermot was a political reporter who looked unassuming but made a habit of melodramatic affairs. At least that was her reputation. One of the most theatrical scenes in living memory at the paper had taken place when Melanie was having an affair with a political columnist. One day, the columnist's wife showed up in the newsroom and began berating Melanie loudly. Drawn by the shouting, Liz had gone down to the huddle where the wife was yelling and Melanie stood like an English primrose, looking down resignedly as if this was unpleasant but would have to end soon. The terrified husband had run to the men's room as soon as the shouting started. After a while he recovered some of his courage and returned to the newsroom, where he collected his hoarse wife and took her home.

Gilman was grinning too, perhaps at the same memory. "Don't be surprised if Mrs. Donovan shows up in the newsroom," he said.

Remembering Martha's phone call and her appearance in the Greek restaurant, Liz willed her smile to wane in what she hoped was a natural way.

═══

On Saturday evening, Peter and Liz were Skyping, which rarely worked well. Either the sound was terrible or Liz couldn't get the camera above her rib cage. Technologically, this time was better than most, but Peter was not in a good mood.

He asked briefly about Neil's service and then announced he was planning to come home next weekend. A high school friend would be in town, and Peter needed to do a little work at the Library of Congress.

"How nice. Is it the paper on forgiveness you're coming to research?"

"No. Tufts has plenty of philosophy books." As if she should know that. Grudgingly, he added, "The research is for my politics course. I have to do an oral presentation the last week before the holidays."

"Oh. How's the forgiveness paper going?"

"Okay."

"Do you have a particular thesis?"

"It's more of a survey of the different ideas that philosophers have about it. Kind of showing some of the different aspects that philosophers consider."

His tone indicated he was done with her clueless questioning. Liz nodded at the truculent young man on the screen. If he wanted to talk, he would talk.

Giving in, he said, "For example. As I said at Thanksgiving, do you need the wrongdoer to apologize before you can properly forgive?"

"What does an apology have to do with it?" Liz asked. "Surely you can forgive even if you never see the wrongdoer again. You don't need them to change your heart."

"You may or may not need the apology to forgive, but it makes it more complete," Peter said, sounding more like himself.

"Complete for whom?"

"For the victim and the offender."

She would think about that. "What else?"

"Some philosophers think there are some things that should not be forgiven."

"Like what?"

"Well, for example, say, in the Rwandan Civil War. Your enemies killed your baby and husband and raped your little girl. Some people see forgiving them as disloyalty to your family, or that you were condoning their deeds."

"But that's wrong," Liz said. "At least the condoning part. I'm not sure how I feel about the disloyalty, or possible disloyalty, but forgiving something doesn't mean you think it was right. And it seems cruel not to let someone who was wronged have the consolation of forgiving."

"Forgiving isn't about *you*," Peter said scoldingly and with an air of fatigue. As if her mistake did not surprise him, but obviously needed correction. "Or about consolation. That's the modern, therapeutic understanding of forgiveness. But it isn't a feel-good strategy, it's a gift you give the transgressor. It's not about you," he repeated, as if he knew precisely what she was thinking.

"And do all your philosophers agree about that?"

"They don't all agree that some things shouldn't be forgiven. But the idea that forgiveness is part of some self-help program"—his eyebrows rose and fell briefly to indicate scorn—"is for therapists, not philosophers." Therapists apparently were the lowest of the low.

"So what does forgiveness look like?"

"Do you mean, what is essential about forgiveness?"

"Yes."

"It means you wish no harm to the person who hurt you, and maybe even wish him well."

That jibed with what the bearded philosopher had told her.

"But how do you do it?" Liz asked.

"What do you mean?"

She sensed that his hand was moving to the hang-up icon.

"I mean, how do you forgive?"

"That's not the kind of thing philosophers consider."

"Why not? That's the most important part. Maybe the only part."

She told him about Paolo de Santis, who seemed to have no trouble forgiving.

"Maybe his need for his wife is stronger than his self-respect. You can't forgive out of weakness or need. It has to be with a full sense of what you and the other person deserve. Got to go, Mom. I'm meeting some people."

Well, he was certainly disaffected. It was probably a phase, as her parents used to say of Greg when he was a teenager. Apparently she'd never had phases.

She checked in on her revenge sites for some relief from Peter's priggishness. She preferred the stories from the U.K.: the women spoke crisply and acted with dispatch, while the Americans' revenge was more histrionic and less detailed. Spray-painting "slut" or "cheater" on a car was just not interesting, but she did appreciate a succinct post from Chicago: "My husband had an affair with my best friend. She is bi. So am I. So I got to prove to him that I'm better in bed than he is—she left him for me."

Today she found the story of a woman in Manchester who was putting some clothes in her husband's suitcase for a business trip while he showered. A text came in on his phone, which was lying next to the suitcase, and thinking that it might be about his flight, she read that someone would be greeting him with a sexy welcome when he arrived in New York. During the two weeks he was away, she put their house on the market and sold it. When he returned, he found five young men living there. The wife had left only her husband's treasured guitar and a few pieces of his family furniture in the house, including them in the "fixtures and fittings." Sweet, Liz thought. I like an efficient woman.

Her own efficiency was at a low point. She had meant all week to write to Henry explaining that he had misinterpreted her behavior at Thanksgiving, and why didn't they choose a movie and go to it together? But she hadn't sent that message, and after a while she began to agree with Henry's interpretation. He was probably right, she just wasn't interested.

Her thoughts strayed to Seattle. Every time she remembered Neil's service, the image that surfaced was of Nicole standing against the wall, her genial air not stretching quite enough to cover an underlying loneliness.

WEEK NINE

December 6–13, 2015

*T*he poet had called late on Saturday evening, sounding more energetic than usual.

"Liz, I've got news. Let's go for a walk."

He almost never suggested anything but a drink. She wondered whether the news involved his poetry or his irritable bowel, but she accepted. Not only did William want to walk, he knew exactly where.

"Meet me tomorrow at the L'Enfant Plaza Metro station at two o'clock."

It was an odd place for a walk, mostly distinguished, as far as Liz knew, by a shopping mall and other commercial buildings. She usually saw William in the evening, so in the bright sunshine outside the station, his ponytail and sepulchral black clothes looked more clichéd than usual. But he was ebullient.

"Isn't that space amazing?"

"What space?"

"The station, of course. That huge vault without a single column, the coffered ceiling . . ."

He was so lost in admiration that he seemed unable to finish his sentence.

"They're all the same, you know."

"All what are the same?"

"The Metro stations."

As soon as the words left her mouth, she realized how stupid they sounded. As if he would never have noticed that. It was just that she had never heard anyone express enthusiasm for the Metro stations.

He gave her the look she deserved and said drily, "I'm aware of that. Harry Weese, 1976."

Harry Weese, Liz presumed, had built or designed the stations. Taking her arm and walking her south to Seventh Street at a brisk clip, William told her his news.

"I'm writing a long poem about Brutalist buildings."

"Brutalist buildings."

"Yes, you know, like the station. Like this"—he opened his arms to take in the vast Department of Housing and Urban Development building in front of them—"these big, brawny, concrete beauties."

He pointed out the building's curving X-shape and its proud lack of details except for the endlessly repeated, deeply set windows. Liz was at a loss for words.

Finally, looking out at the bleak plaza that prefaced the bleak building, she said, "I see at least they tried to warm things up with some shade canopies and planters."

"Yes, not everyone liked Breuer's plaza. But all this stuff"—looking contemptuously at the awnings and containers—"compromises his vision."

Then he marched her north and east to the Hubert Humphrey Building, on Independence Avenue, extolling the merits of precast concrete on the way. Unlike regular concrete, he explained, the precast variety was "cured" in molds off-site, before being transported to the building under construction. She was only half-listening, wondering more at William's enthusiasm than paying attention to the content, so she missed the reason why this made it cheaper and safer. William seemed especially fond of this featureless, bunker-like building.

"Look."

He took her up close to one of its massive supports and pointed out the grain of the wooden form in which the concrete had been cured. This odd phenomenon, called "board-formed concrete," was the mark of something ancient and natural left on something modern and industrial. Liz could admire the grain of the tree more than the concrete support.

"And they're called Brutalist because they're kind of graceless and aggressive?" she asked gingerly, realizing by now that she was treading on delicate ground.

"They're called Brutalist from the French for unfinished concrete, *béton brut*. 'Brut' sounds like brutal in English, but in French it means raw or unfinished. Brut champagne just means that it has no added sugar. These buildings were modern, efficient and inexpensive, just what people thought was needed in the nineteen-fifties and sixties. Big architects like I.M. Pei and Marcel Breuer loved the style."

Finally, he took her to the Hirshhorn Museum, which she knew, but not as a piece of Brutalism. Its drum-like smoothness was a relief after the others' belligerent roughness.

She mentioned that, rather timidly, and William said, "It came in for some criticism for that reason. People thought it was too polite, maybe too hidden, to be really Brutalist. But it does have frontality."

Where had he learned all this new vocabulary? Liz would not mention this new development to Peter.

She ventured, "And your poem is a . . . kind of appreciation of Brutalism?"

"More of an elegy. Nobody looked ahead to the day when they would need maintenance—part of their modernity was supposed to be that they needed no care, like drip-dry shirts. Now several are in such bad shape that the structure is compromised. And people, unlike architects, never liked them. They show up regularly on the lists of D.C.'s most hated buildings. So the poem is about the fragility of the apparently strong, about the failure to see that hulking can be beautiful, about mutability. About unpopularity. About death."

As usual, he warmed to the thought of his dark material, but there was something new here. He had never looked happier. Or more appealing. The wind around these buildings that did without landscaping as well as ornament had reddened his cheeks and brightened his eyes. Sex in the afternoon had always seemed the most intimate sex to Liz. It was not the sleepy, semi-conscious coupling of the early morning, nor the late-night, alcohol-fuelled triumph of lust over fatigue. It was deliberate, personal. She would probably regret it, but she took him home.

Later, with William dozing beside her, regret was the last thing on Liz's mind. She cared nothing for Peter's judgmental, conventional views. William looked content, perhaps dreaming of precast concrete. His arm extended on the sheet, with the wrist bent and the hand relaxed, looked like a detail from a Renaissance drawing. He really had a sweet side, with unsuspected depths. Perhaps they could do some travelling, looking at Brutalist buildings in other cities. She reminded herself that she would be footing the bill for any travelling.

William stirred.

Wrapping himself around her, he murmured, "I can see you have a feel for Brutalism. Next time we'll have a long look at the Forrestal Building."

She decided that she would take him to a nicer-than-usual restaurant for dinner.

=

Now that her Tuesdays did not include Seamus, Liz went to yoga in a sports bra that circled her chest in a way that was firm but friendly, and a pair of cotton underpants.

Freya, who had never commented on her come-hither lingerie, said, "You've had an underwear conversion."

"Yes," Liz said, "this saves me having to change for yoga."

Freya nodded, looking studiously neutral.

Tonight's class included the usual mix of serious men, older people trying to keep up and young women who seemed born to do cobra or triangle pose. Their downward dogs reminded Liz of stringed puppets when you abruptly dropped their top half, and their sun salutations were one silken motion that mutated from prayer position through lunges, planks, folds and swan dives. Watching one impossibly supple woman out of the corner of her eye as she struggled with her own plank position, Liz thought of the goddess Calypso trying to keep Odysseus on her island. He longs to return to Ithaca and Penelope, and the goddess says, Fine, go back to that wife you pine for, but you will suffer terribly before you get home. She adds, "And anyway, I know my body is / better than hers is. I am taller too."

Liz wouldn't have guessed that tallness was an advantage for women in eighth-century B.C. Greece—that was interesting. Women comparing their bodies, on the other hand, was an eternal story. She didn't remember it, but she must have judged her body against Nicole's in the bad old days, when she tortured herself trying to figure out what advantage Nicole had over her. As if discovering that, whatever it was—funnier stories, easier orgasms, a more loving temperament—would have made any difference. She did know one thing for sure, though: she was taller than Nicole.

At the end of the class, lying defenceless in corpse pose, her palms open to the ceiling, Liz tried to banish the Arpeggione Sonata. Listening to the plaintive, brave melody meandering through her mind was no doubt forbidden during savasana. Chip said, "Think of someone for whom you feel unconditional love." Instead, she began to count the ways her life was careering off the rails. I'm engaged in a false relationship with my ex-husband's wife, she thought, who doesn't know that I'm her correspondent. My ex-lover has left his wife and thinks he is wooing me back. My former gentleman caller has bowed out. My new about-to-be-friends, the Dubroffs, want nothing to do with me. I seem to be losing my instincts for doing my job. My usually comradely son is verging on surly. My formerly smart mother doesn't know me and I can't love her. Okay, that last was old news, but she added it to round things out. Thinking about Marie Kondo's *The Life-Changing Magic of Tidying Up*, Liz thought, I must be the anti-Kondo. My book would be called *The Life-Wrecking Stupidity of Messing Up Everything*.

She relented and let the Arpeggione back in, although the melody was a one-way ticket to sorrow. Something about its stoic delicacy took her back to forgiveness. One of the hard things about forgiveness was that to do it properly you had to return to some very dark times. And even though the re-entry would be temporary, she dreaded it.

At home, Liz turned to a section about "tapping" in one of her forgiveness books. Tapping used the meridian points of the body to free you from negative emotions. The meridian points were the top of the head, the eyebrow, beside the eye at the edge of the face, under the eye, under the nose, the chin, the collarbone and four inches below the underarm. Before tapping, Liz was to say out loud, "Even though I haven't forgiven Sidney and Nicole, I totally accept myself." Then she was to tap each meridian point five to seven times with two or more fingertips, while saying "my grudge" with each tap. When she was finished tapping, she would rate her resentment on a scale of zero to ten. If she scored herself more than two or three, she was advised to do another round of tapping. This time, she would preface it by saying, "Even though some bad feelings linger, I totally accept myself." Flipping through the pages, she saw that there was no indication what she should do if her resentment scores still refused to budge.

Now Liz was baffled as well as skeptical. What did accepting herself have to do with lingering resentment? And did she even have lingering resentment? She would happily never see or correspond with Nicole again, although she could not say that about Sidney. Seeing him was a complicated, layered business that always brought a measure of discomfort, but it gave her something, too.

═══

Next morning, Norris sent Liz a message: *We need to talk. Come to Douglas's office at 2 p.m.*

Apparently, her most recent miscalculation about what made an acceptable column had landed her in the editor-in-chief's office. Since Douglas generally avoided contact with the staff, she had to take that seriously. Norris would do most of the talking, but the location was its own message.

The essay that had appeared in the paper that morning had been written by a woman defending her husband's battery of guns. Guns, this woman argued with force and some humour, came with masculinity. They were part of a package that included heroism, pissing contests, gallantry, aggression and, yes, occasionally violence. Some men with "issues" (when did we stop having "problems," Liz thought, grinding her teeth, and instead developed "issues?") would turn their aggression and guns against the innocent, even innocent children, as in the recent school shootings. That was horrible, but the writer saw it as a kind of natural disaster that no gun laws would eliminate. The part that had aroused the most furious reaction, at least so far on Twitter, was a description of her husband's arsenal. Stroking and even fondling his rifles and revolvers, their glittering barrels and hammers, their doughty cylinders, the writer compared them to her bracelets and earrings. They accessorized her husband's virility. It was a bravura paragraph, erotic and disturbing.

Liz and Norris settled themselves in the sitting-room end of the office while Douglas shuffled papers on his desk. He had little to work with, as the desk was almost empty, but it was a way for him to ignore them as long as possible. The paintings on the wall were modern but strangely innocent pictures of people riding unicycles in Parisian-looking parks. It was tempting to call them incongruous, but no one knew Douglas well enough to say what would have been congruous with him.

Norris turned to Liz.

"Have you seen Honey Spiegler's feature for Sunday? She went to one of these crazy cuddle parties, you know, where you pay money to hug strangers. She went feeling cynical and suspicious, but the way she lost her inhibitions and just went with the flow . . . it's brilliant. Funny, as you'd expect, but moving, too. And the oddest thing is, you start to feel that these people are pretty normal. Maybe even sensible. It's a shoo-in for a National Journalism Award nomination."

"Great," Liz said. "I'll look forward to reading it."

Norris had nothing more to say and he stared at Douglas's paintings as if trying to understand why people rode unicycles. Liz attempted some small talk about how could it be December 9 already and Christmas only a little more than two weeks away. Norris did not even pretend to be interested.

Finally he said, "Douglas, why don't we start? Let's not wait any longer."

Wait for what? Liz wondered. Sighing, Douglas left his desk. As he walked toward them, the door opened and Seamus entered.

This meant her misdemeanor was even more grave. Now she had three levels of bosses filling up the boxy leather chairs, and the questioning and chastising began. It was all pro forma, as each of the four knew more or less precisely what would be said. She was being needlessly provocative. No, she insisted, she wasn't. It might be a position that rarely appeared in the paper, but that was all the more reason to give it a hearing. She was antagonizing subscribers, Norris countered, and the paper had never needed them more. Before Liz could respond to that, Douglas spoke up, unexpectedly, and noted that the essay was the day's most shared story on the paper's web-site. Seamus and Norris glowered at him for breaking rank.

Other than that, everyone kept to his or her script. The closest thing to a threat came from Norris. If My Turn didn't seem like a good fit for her anymore, he said, of course there were other things she could do. They were always looking, for example, for someone to cover religion. Liz kept a straight face at that one: it was hard to say whether the newsroom considered the religion beat or obituaries the very bottom of the barrel. The point of the meeting had been to let Liz know she was skating on thin ice, and once they judged that message had been given, it was time to adjourn. Norris and Douglas had something to discuss in the hall, and just for a minute she was left alone with Seamus. As she moved to leave, he intercepted her.

"Please, Liz."

He had lowered his publisher mask, exposing the private, love-lorn Seamus. She was shocked again at the need on his face and in his posture, which had lost its alpha-male erectness and inclined toward her, like a supplicant.

"Can't we just have another coffee?"

Reluctantly, she agreed to see him that evening.

After their Italian classes, Liz joined Seamus in the darkest part of the dreary café where they had met when he'd just left home.

"Have a glass of wine," he urged her.

No, thanks, she would have a decaf cappuccino.

Seamus went through the usual routine, which he probably thought of as courting behavior, telling her how much he loved her and, more important because unacknowledged, how much she loved him. Why did some men think they could talk you into loving them? And what would success look like? She imagined suddenly striking her brow and saying, "My goodness, you're right! I do love you, I just hadn't realized it!" Or, "I just forgot!"

Other than the pleading, the conversation was half-hearted. They had never spent much time talking, and Liz wasn't sure what interested Seamus, other than the business of publishing. He read biographies of presidents, generals and captains of industry, and he had a good memory for the classic poems the Jesuits had drilled into him, but she could hardly ask him to recite "Dover Beach." Inquiring about his apartment in Foggy Bottom was not a good idea: he would be stoic, with an undercurrent of melancholy.

She looked at him not drinking his coffee, splaying his square, well-cared-for hands on the table. She felt fond of him in a remote way, as for a cousin she had played with as a child, and was sorry that she had hurt him. Remembering her conversation with the poet in the Korean bar, she thought, I must turn my bowels toward Seamus. I must sympathize with him. Seamus had been a convenient overcoat, and now she had thrown it off. It wasn't only that what he offered her had suddenly become irrelevant: it now felt like an impediment to something she needed to do.

"How are things going with your wife?" Calling her Martha seemed too familiar.

Seamus looked grave, but resolute. "Well, it's a hard time for her. I don't think either of us ever thought it would come to this." He shifted in his chair. "She suspected or maybe even knew about the other women. But they didn't threaten our marriage, until you. I never imagined that I would find anyone so perfect for me."

This was the first time he had ever mentioned other women, but Liz was more intent on discouraging any talk of her perfection. She set her cappuccino down on its saucer so sharply that the foam quivered timidly. "How are the girls?"

"They're furious. Helen isn't speaking to me, and Maggie is, but only to let me know what a terrible person I am."

She nodded. No surprise there.

But Seamus was surprised. "The thing is," he continued, "the only thing I've ever felt proud of is how I've been as a father. Not my work, certainly not my relationship with Martha, nothing except my bringing up the girls. This hurts, but I know it's temporary."

Seamus had never made her angry—there hadn't been enough time in their brief interludes for him to annoy her—but now his serene confidence in his parenting hit a nerve.

"I don't think you've earned the right to be so proud of yourself as a father. One of the chief duties of parenthood is making the other parent as happy as possible. That wasn't high on your list of priorities, to put it mildly. The girls must have suffered from that, even before the separation. And now you've put them in the situation every child dreads."

She hadn't meant to sound so categorical, and she reminded herself that people in glass houses shouldn't throw stones. But his self-satisfaction irked her.

Seamus flinched, and his nostrils flared white for a minute. "The girls never knew anything about the other women. Or about our marriage."

"Of course they did. Kids are brilliant at sensing those things. And now they definitely know."

Seamus murmured something irrefutable about her not knowing his daughters, and signalled for the bill. He insisted on walking her back to her apartment, although she insisted it was not necessary, but he did not attempt to kiss her goodnight.

———

The next day, a letter marked Special Delivery arrived, on thick paper monogrammed with Seamus's initials.

Dear Liz,

I want to let you know that I am dropping 'my suit,' to put it in the Victorian terms you like so much. I will not be bothering you anymore with my attentions. I don't accept your point, but you caught me in a tender place with your remark about my failure as a father. That showed me you don't understand one of the most important things about me, which makes me conclude that ours was not a good match.

I do have good memories of our time together.

And all the best,

Seamus

So, she had succeeded, but by accident. Tarnishing his idea of himself as a father was the thing Seamus could not tolerate—he'd been wounded to the quick. It was unexpected, but Liz stood by her words.

Having Seamus out of the picture was a relief, but Liz could not stop thinking about Paolo. When she had Skyped with Peter, he had dismissed the ease with which Paolo forgave his wife—"You can't forgive out of weakness or need"—but it didn't look like weakness to Liz. Paolo's mixture of acceptance and authority appealed to her. Added to that, she liked his looks, the way his hair curled very slightly around his ears at the back and the almost stylish nonchalance with which he wore his uniform. Subtracted from that, he had small children and was in love with his wife. The math wasn't promising, she saw that, but there was something about his comfort with forgiveness that she found irresistible.

It wasn't easy to get together with Paolo, whose shift began at six after a late afternoon with his children. Weekends, of course, were reserved for his family. She had suggested another late-afternoon meeting on Friday, and fortuitously his children had a playdate. They met at a café near the paper whose atmosphere was hardly more inviting than the cafeteria, but at least it *wasn't* the cafeteria.

It felt very normal to talk with him about Sidney and Nicole. Not the fact that she had been corresponding with Nicole—no one could know that—but the story of Sidney's affair and the end of their marriage. Partly because Liz knew Paolo's situation and partly because of some quality in Paolo himself, it seemed a natural subject for conversation.

As if she were returning to a subject they had talked about many times before, she said, "It's embarrassing to be so maladroit about this, after ten years. Other people seem to get on quite well with their exes, and I seem to be brooding or stewing—those ugly words—when it's ancient history for everyone else."

"That's just the trivialization of adultery," Paolo said.

She didn't know quite what that was, but she had a feeling that she was going to like it. She wished she could put her hand on Paolo's thigh, which was close to hers under the table.

"What does that mean?"

"That's my name for the project we've been in since the sexual revolution, when suddenly everything was permitted and only dolts took monogamy seriously. And even when that first flush of what we called emancipation wore off and people accepted that, no matter how liberated they were, it usually isn't fun when your partner has sex with someone else, there remained this sense that the bad feeling is something to get over as quickly as possible. You're allowed a shortish tantrum, but then you have to be cool about it."

"And so, are you a part of that, of the trivialization of adultery? Is that how you cope with your situation?"

"Not at all. To me, it's serious, it's regrettable, but it's what I have. I don't like it and, in spite of what Natalie says, it feels unstable. Nothing about it is trivial to me."

"Unstable because she may fall in love?"

"Yes."

"There's a line in a play I saw once, but I can't remember which play, where someone says, 'There's a promise in the flesh.' I guess that's what you mean."

"The play is *The Crucible*," he said. "And the line is really, 'There is a promise made in any bed.' But yes, that's what I mean."

Right. Midway through their marriage, she and Sidney had gone to a production of *The Crucible* at Seattle Rep. She sat with that memory for a minute.

Then she said, "It's lonely, with everyone thinking I'm so slow to adjust."

Paolo nodded. "Yes. You're out of step with the times. But there aren't any shortcuts."

Liz went back to the paper, although her page for Monday was ready to go. The essay was by a man who spun and knitted hats, scarves and other mementoes from the fur of dead cats and dogs. He saw his work as healing, and the bereaved pet owners who engaged him agreed. At first the idea sounded wacky, but he made the point that it was no different from the human hair jewellery mourners in earlier times had worn.

In her inbox, she found a new, unusually petulant message from Nicole.

Dear Editor,
We haven't corresponded in some time. I'm wondering whether I should even bother to submit any more essays, if I get another idea. You didn't sound very receptive last time.
Nicole Szabo

Dear Nicole Szabo,
People often submit several essays to My Turn. There is a very low rate of acceptance, so one or two or even five unsuccessful attempts are not out of the ordinary.
editor@MyTurn.com

Liz had no time to brood about Nicole: she needed to buy some groceries. Peter was arriving later that evening and her fridge was a sad little anthology of the distracted single woman's needs, not wants. Yogurt, salad things, brown-around-the-edges hummus. Nothing delicious, or even satisfying. Happily imagining meals for her manly son, she decided that this called for a trip to Costco. The store was its usual overflowing but hyper-organized self and although she told herself, No potted miniature roses, no curried roasted pumpkin seeds, no Dutch sausages, her cart was soon full.

She turned into the seafood aisle and there was Henry—in consultation with her neighbor Kara over smoked salmon. Henry was pushing the cart and Kara was weighing the merits of two frozen slabs. It was too late for Liz to back out of the aisle, and they both greeted her with smiles. "Liz! How are you?" They almost said it in unison.

She mumbled that she was fine, and indicating her cart, she said, "Peter's coming home."

Henry nodded and said, "Yes. That's nice."

She thought his "Yes" was rather odd, but no doubt he felt as embarrassed as she did.

"So I need to get this home and start cooking," she said, reversing her cart with only a moderate amount of clumsiness. Henry and Kara beamed goodbye and went back to the smoked salmon.

Meeting Henry would have flustered her no matter what, but the addition of Kara upped the ante. Kara and Henry. Now that she thought about it, they'd had a lot to talk about at Thanksgiving, even beyond Kara's grandmother's cranberry sauce. Kara might be considered a little young for Henry, and did he really want to start parenting Kara's boy now that his own children were grown up? Well, Liz didn't have to worry about any of that. Henry seemed considerably more intellectual than Kara, but when had that ever been a problem for a man? Liz stifled that bitchy thought. She didn't know Kara well enough to feel that she wasn't the most obvious match for Henry—but she felt it anyway.

Liz always put all the food away as soon as she returned home from grocery shopping. But this evening, after she had put the frozen things in the freezer, she left the rest of the food in bags on the counter for a while. A whiny message from Nicole followed by the encounter with Henry and Kara surely deserved a little pick-me-up. She found what she was looking for on a revenge site. A woman, knowing her husband was planning to spend the evening with his girlfriend, emptied his bottle of conditioner and filled it with hair removal cream. His hair started coming out in chunks during his date.

Peter arrived home about an hour later, overcommitted with friends and too ambitious about what he hoped to achieve in a weekend. That was normal for him, but he always made time for a long, relaxed dinner at home with his mother. This time he hemmed and hawed, wasn't sure if he had time, thought maybe they should just have a quick bite early tomorrow before he went out with friends.

"Okay," Liz said, disappointed. "Whatever works for you."

She had bought veal shanks to make osso buco, one of his favorites. But that deserved a more leisurely evening than Peter was granting her, so she would grill lamb chops with green beans and try out a new recipe for a salad of Brussels sprouts and pomelo.

They sat down before six on Saturday, Liz struggling to put a good face on things. Peter's cowlick, which he had inherited from her, stood up, a flag that he was feeling tired after a long day at the library.

The lamb chops were perfectly done. But when she started to put two on his plate, Peter said, "No thanks."

"No thanks? But you love lamb chops."

He had the grace to look slightly embarrassed. "I'm not eating meat these days. Or hardly ever."

Where was a god who would give her strength?

"These days? Do you mean since Thanksgiving?"

"Well, it started before Thanksgiving, but I didn't want to make a big deal over the holiday. And I concentrated on the vegetables and the stuffing."

Of course. The stuffing that was not allowed to come into contact with the cavity of the turkey. The stuffing that he did not moisten with gravy.

"And why are you doing this, if it's not too much trouble to explain to me?" Bad move. Sarcasm was not useful.

"I started reading this philosopher, Peter Singer, for my ethics course. He's written a lot about animal liberation and the ethics of killing and eating other creatures."

Liz had nothing against vegetarianism. As a matter of fact, she thought vegetarians were probably correct, which is why she avoided thinking too hard about it. She wasn't ready to give up chicken and fish. What irked her was something different: Peter's offhand failure to tell her about his conversion was another sign of his irritable distance.

"Don't worry. This looks great." He helped himself to the green beans and the Brussels sprout salad, but he didn't eat much.

On his way out, he paused at the coffee table. "You're reading Cormac McCarthy? Not your usual cup of tea."

A copy of *All the Pretty Horses* lay on the stack of *New Yorkers* she would never finish. Paolo had said that was the best introduction to his work.

Shrugging into his jacket—he clearly needed a new one but insisted there was nothing wrong with unravelling cuffs and a threadbare collar—Peter said, "As long as we're back here by noon, we could make a quick trip to Haven tomorrow morning."

"Really? I never thought you would have time for that."

"Just because you avoid seeing Agnes, don't assume I feel the same way."

Stung, she said, "I do *not* avoid seeing her!"

Peter continued looping his scarf around his neck and zipping his jacket, as if this required his full attention.

When he opened the door, he turned and said, "Tomorrow morning, then. We should leave before eight-thirty."

She did not understand why he had turned on her.

After she did the dishes and put away most of the food she had prepared, Liz got into bed and reached for *The Odyssey*. Bonding with Cormac McCarthy was turning out to be a slow process. A bloody fight with the Cyclops or a savage encounter with Scylla was just what she wanted. Instead, she read of Telemachus,

> A son whose father is away will suffer
> intensely, if he has no man at home
> to help him.

Her eyes filled with tears. Poor Telemachus. Poor Penelope. And yes, she had to admit, poor Odysseus.

———

At Haven the next morning, Liz and Peter found Agnes drinking coffee in her armchair. When she'd moved in, she had said to the staff, "I don't talk to strangers until I've had my coffee," and they indulged her with room service for breakfast. By lunchtime, she was willing enough to sit with the other residents in the dining room. The staff turned on the television news for her when they brought her breakfast, although she couldn't follow most of it.

Now she greeted Liz by saying, "Turn that thing off."

She was brighter than usual, and Liz thought, I should come more often in the morning. This is probably her best time of day.

Looking at Peter, who had his father's short upper lip and widely spaced eyes, Agnes said, "Sidney was a nice guy. But he never comes to see me now."

Liz said, "Mom, he lives in Seattle."

"And whose fault is that?" Agnes returned sharply.

Which made no sense, because Sidney had lived in Seattle before, during and after their separation, but Agnes meant it as a rebuke. Great, Liz thought. Now her mother, as well as Peter, was blaming her.

Thrown off by Agnes and thinking out loud, she said, "Sidney wishes he saw Peter more often."

"Well, there's Christmas," her mother said.

Liz was opening her mouth to say no, Peter wouldn't want to go at Christmas, but perhaps later in the holiday, when Peter said, as if it were entirely inconsequential, "Yes, I think I will go for Christmas this year."

What had just happened there? Her mother and son had pulled the rug out from under her so smoothly it almost felt rehearsed, except that Agnes was incapable of following a plan. Liz told herself, Don't panic. This is just an impulse, he won't follow up on it. But even the impulse hurt.

The trip home from Baltimore was mostly silent. Peter took off almost immediately to see friends, saying he wasn't sure when he would be home, probably late. Normally, Liz loved a more or less empty weekend, but today she was out of sorts. She walked over to Kramerbooks, although she had sworn off forgiveness manuals until she actually found one that was helpful. Thinking of all the half-finished books at home, she bought nothing.

The bookstore's red-and-black café, with its grotty refusal to charm, suited her mood. She sat down at one of their mid-century kitchenette chairs and ordered fish tacos. With nothing to read, she listened to the conversations around her. The café had a reputation for flirtatious encounters, but all she heard today was earnest chat about courses, maternity leaves, restructured departments and Hillary's plans for affordable childcare. She remembered Henry's mention of the store's open-all-night weekends in his mockery of online dating ads. Maybe that was when all the fun happened, although the thought of chatting up strangers in a bookstore at one or two in the morning sounded dismal.

She wasn't ready to go home, so she walked for a while. On New Hampshire Avenue, on her way home, she passed Heurich House, the mansion of a beer baron. The house was a gloomy exercise in dark stone with bartizans and other faux-medieval trappings, and an entrance fee, but its garden, off Sunderland Place, was open to the public. In December, there were ferns and holly, and a few dahlias still struggled to flower. It was not a manicured garden with a unified design, but an amateur, rather unkempt one with some successful patches and other straggly bits.

Liz sat there for a while on an iron bench, thinking about Peter. This pulling away was part of growing up, she told herself. The main paradox of parenthood is that from the minute your child is born your job is to teach him how to live without you. But all that teaching, from encouraging the baby to grab his spoon and smear carrots all over his face to leaving him to pack his things for college, is fatally attaching for both of you. No doubt she and Peter had been too close since the divorce, so his bid for independence was correspondingly aggressive. The more she thought about it, the idea of his going to Seattle for Christmas acquired a horrible inevitability. It was too cold to sit on the bench for long, so she headed for home.

As usual, the contents of the backpack Peter had arrived with had multiplied all over the living room. Before Liz could read in peace, she needed to tidy his things away, so she gathered the underwear and socks under one arm and the books and papers in the other. She put the clothes on his bed and the books and papers on his desk. Perhaps she should straighten the papers more thoroughly. As she did so, she saw some pages paper-clipped together, with a title on the first page, "Forgiveness: Some Philosophical Questions."

She read it standing up, with a last pair of socks in her hand. It was organized around imaginary cases, people whose stories illustrated various problems with forgiveness. There was Philip, who believed he had forgiven his father for leaving his mother when he was a child. There were two possible problems here. Since a child absolutely needs his father and could not afford to alienate him seriously, could the boy Philip really be said to have forgiven in the way philosophers considered proper—that is, while not condoning the wrong? Had he made a free, rational decision to forgo angry feelings? Or did the needs of a child make forgiveness in that crucial, disinterested sense impossible? (And does that really matter? Liz thought impatiently. If the boy thinks he has forgiven, surely that's enough. He's got a lifetime to learn how to forgive in an adult way.)

The second issue was Philip's inability to forgive his mother for not forgiving his father. Did Philip have "standing" to forgive his mother on behalf of his father, since the wrong she was doing was to his father? Or did he only have "indirect standing"? And why did the mother have to forgive the father? Liz asked the paper. Was it a kind of round robin in which everyone had to forgive everyone, including forgiving people who could not or would not forgive other people? This was beginning to sound like one of the mad dances in *Alice in Wonderland*. Reading further, she learned that the mother's inability to forgive was harming Philip also, so his standing was probably more direct than indirect.

Forgiveness was turning out to be an even busier can of worms than Liz had imagined.

Then she read about a woman named Betsy. Betsy was stuck in being angry at her husband, who had left her for another woman. She was also angry at the woman, although in some ways her feelings about the woman seemed clearer than those for her ex-husband. Unable to see that her own behavior had played a part in the breakdown of the marriage, she made her daughter (yes, in a trans-parent attempt at fictionalizing this story, Peter had given Betsy a daughter) miserable with insulting comments about the girl's father. By now Liz was livid, but not too livid to shout, "I do not!" Betsy's real life was stalled. She went from one inappropriate man to the next, choosing people with whom a real relationship would be impossible. At this point, Peter had the unmitigated chutzpah to use Liz's birthday gift to him, *The Odyssey*. He quoted Telemachus's complaint about his mother,

> She may be clever but she acts on whims!
> She treats unwanted guests with great respect,
> and rudely sends the better ones away.

That was unfair to Penelope, Peter wrote, but was an apt descrip-tion of Betsy's love life. As a result, she relied too much on her daughter for emotional support.

Betsy believed that her inability to "forgive" was the biggest obstacle to her happiness. Peter put the word in quotation marks to indicate that Betsy's understanding of forgiveness was deficient. Unwilling to consider any meaningful relationship with her ex-husband or his wife, Betsy expected that forgiveness—if only she could figure out how to do it—could happen in isolation. She had the vulgar modern belief that its purpose was to benefit the forgiver, whereas the truth was that forgiveness is a free gift given to the offender. Peter quoted some philosopher, "Forgiveness is a moral issue with psychological implications; it is not a psychologi-cal issue with moral undertones." So why, Liz asked Peter mentally, if psychological concerns are a fetid swamp compared to the high moral ground that philosophers inhabit, have you described this woman's problems almost completely in psychological terms? Is your hostility toward her taking you off-topic? Is this a psychology paper or a philosophy paper?

When Peter returned, long past her bedtime, Liz was sitting in the living room, with his paper in front of her on the coffee table. She had brewed caffeinated tea, although she did not need it. Rage would keep her awake for quite some time. Peter looked at her inquiringly while he hung up his jacket, before he noticed the paper.

She nodded at it and said, "Interesting essay."

He paused, but only for a second. "When did you take up snooping?"

Briefly, she considered the teapot sitting innocently on the coffee table. Breaking the Brown Betty during an argument with Sidney had been her single greatest act of violence so far, but that had been ten years ago. She was not going to sacrifice another one. Brown Bettys were increasingly hard to find, and besides, Peter was her son and not her husband. Words were called for, not teapot smashing.

"I was cleaning up the mess you had left in here, and taking it to your desk. You can hardly consider something that will be read by your professor as private."

"Of course it is. It was intended to be read *only* by my professor."

She let that one go.

"What a pathetic person this Betsy must be."

"Mom, for Chrissake, she's a composite. I took things from here and there, to make a few points."

She let that one go, too.

"I don't even know where to start. Maybe the most outrageous charge is that I say insulting things about your father, which I never do."

Peter sat down across from her, folding his long arms and legs deliberately. His whole body communicated, *Let's get this over as quickly as possible. But you won't like it any more than you liked my paper.*

"You don't even realize the tone you use, the rolled eyes when I tell you something he's said or done, the little 'that's typical' asides, the way you can't let a happy memory surface without mentioning that Dad was late for that recital or forgot to pick up the cake for that birthday party. It's all crap, and you don't ever think how it makes me feel. You never had to listen to Agnes saying mean things about your father."

The last was undeniable, but the rest of it was a gross exaggeration.

"And I reject the idea that I make all these bad choices about men, and that it's somehow connected to my failure to forgive."

"I didn't say Betsy's taste in men was connected to her failure to forgive—maybe she thinks that, since she thinks forgiveness is the magic bullet."

"Let's just stop this Betsy nonsense. What makes you think that I'm obsessed with forgiveness?"

"Well for starters, why do you have all those self-help books about it on your night table? Crowding out your old poetry books, which would do you a lot more good."

Why did everyone, or at least Paolo and her son, think she needed reading advice? She said only, "Who's snooping now?"

"Books in plain sight on your night table don't require snooping. Snooping is when you lift the mattress to see what's underneath, or open the shoeboxes on the upper shelf in the closet. As for the men you choose, maybe you should just look at what you're doing. You prefer to be sort of with and sort of not-with the creepy poet instead of being with a nice, smart, *normal* person like Henry. And now I can see that you're getting interested in that weird security guard who wrote about how much he loves his unfaithful wife. Another brilliant idea.

"And I'm not talking just about your taste in men. I get it that you want to push the envelope a bit with My Turn, but don't you see that the pieces you're picking are more and more aggressive? Is this a game of 'catch me if you can'? And why? First that older couple you liked broke off with you because of the cat story, and now you're complaining that your bosses are pissed off. Which is understandable. I always thought your work was the place where you were most together, but now it looks like you're trying to screw up your job too."

The awful thing about this patronizing, overthought, over-embroidered diatribe was that Peter didn't even know the whole story. He had no inkling about Seamus or the Nicole farce, for which she could only be grateful. Somewhere in the roiling feelings he roused was a small voice suggesting she take at least some of this seriously. Not about the part she might have played in the failure of her marriage—that was predictable from a son and beside the point. But perhaps she should think about why so many things in her life were heading south, with a momentum that felt unstoppable. Only, not now. Now she had to stop this.

"You know what?" she began, her finger pointing threateningly and her voice shaking. "I take some of your points. Especially that I never had to live through my parents being unhappy and divorcing, and of course I know that was hard for you. Very hard. And I tried to protect you from as much of that as I could, and your father did too. But at the same time, you've never had to live through what happened to me. I hope nothing remotely like that ever does happen to you, because I love you. But until it does, you don't have a clue what it feels like. *Not a clue.* Do you understand me? You're jesting at scars that never felt a wound. And I don't ever want to hear again, 'Are you still going on about that?' or 'It's been ten years, Mom.' Ever. Again."

Peter paled at her vehemence, and perhaps at what she was saying. Instantly, she retreated.

"On the other hand, I'm your parent and your life shouldn't be burdened by my problems. So, I'm sorry that it has been. That's all I can say. I don't think I'm in as bad shape as it looks to you."

Peter didn't apologize for anything. And Liz wasn't going to bring up the young man named Philip, who either had to or did not have to forgive his mother. She had forgotten how that example ended, and it was too late to start a new disagreement. They said goodnight and goodbye to each other as normally as they could. Peter would take a cab to the airport early in the morning. He had only one more week of school before Christmas, but the week included the oral presentation he had just been researching.

In her bedroom, Liz tried not to look at *Forgiveness Is a Gift You Give Yourself* and the other self-help books. Seeing them through Peter's eyes was too humiliating. She picked up her copy of Hopkins' poems, whose pages fell open easily at her favorites. "As Kingfishers Catch Fire," with its marvellous opening line. "Pied Beauty," for its celebration of "All things counter, original, spare, strange; / Whatever is fickle, freckled (who knows how?)." She'd always thought that poem should be the anthem of freckled people. But the most read, judging from the way the page that held it was threatening to leave the rest of the book, was "The Windhover." The poet, his "heart in hiding," stirs at the sight of the free, glamorous falcon, but he reminds himself that beauty and power also come from other sources. The "sheer plod" of ploughing, for example, exposes the lustrous minerals in the soil, making the earth shine.

No doubt parenting involved a lot of sheer plod before anything shiny appeared. So, probably, did forgiveness. Maybe there was something in sheer plod that was akin to "slow forgiveness"—the real thing, not the self-help title. She really should read poetry more often.

She slept then, and in the early morning she heard Peter close the front door as if from a great distance.

WEEK TEN

December 14–20, 2015

*L*iz ran into Gilman at the paper's back door.

Taking off her mitten to punch in her code, she asked him, "What's new?"

As they went through security and boarded the elevator, he chattered cheerfully about the certainty, as he saw it, that the moribund paper would be operating with a skeleton staff within five years and the majority of the newsroom would have to find jobs in public relations. From there he shifted to Seamus's latest absurdity. In a farewell letter to an editor who was retiring, he had praised him as "someone who never missed an opportunity to see the possibility of brand-building." The paper's brand, presumably.

"Seriously?" Gilman asked, shaking his head at Seamus's failure to see how irrelevant if not insulting that was to a lifelong journalist. "Does he make these things up himself, or does someone who hates him write his stuff for him? I would volunteer, except that whoever does it now is doing a bang-up job."

Listening to Gilman was relaxing because he never expected a reply. But Liz felt a pang of guilt at enjoying his contempt for Seamus, more than she had felt when she was involved with him.

They had reached the corridor in the newsroom where Gilman diverted right to the business section, and Liz to the left.

"See you later," he said and then he stopped. "Oh yeah, I forgot something. Donovan must have put on sackcloth and ashes and walked on his knees out to the family castle, because his wife has taken him back."

Liz laughed in pure relief. Surprise too, but there was no reason to be surprised.

Gilman must have found the laugh excessive, because he asked, "Is it that funny?"

"Just your picture of him on the penitential trek to McLean. I suppose you're going to protect your source and not tell me how you know."

"Calling it a source would be an exaggeration. The happy couple sent out invitations for their annual holiday party to senior management and the board of governors."

———

Liz and Brown Anne arrived early for Italian on Wednesday. Anne had not finished her homework, so they sat in the empty coffee room while she rummaged in her yawning bag for her notebook.

"More of the elusive subjunctive," she grumbled. "Aha." She extracted her notebook. "Okay, I need five sentences that express emotion and need the subjunctive. Give me one."

Liz thought, I'm happy that Seamus has given up on me. She said, "I'm happy that Signor Pugliesi is making us learn this bafflingly subtle form."

"Have a heart," Anne said. "'Bafflingly?' 'Subtle?'"

"You can modify that," Liz said.

Across the hall, Seamus came out of Signora Venturi's office, followed by the director herself. Perhaps he was refining the talent for Italian that Signora Venturi had spotted. More likely, he was paying his bill. Liz had noticed that Signora V. was wearing her dressier, asymmetric outfits more frequently these days, and somehow they looked sexier than before. As Seamus headed for the Beginners' classroom, the director touched his hand. Well, thought Liz, Italians do that.

Two hours later, Liz and Anne opened their umbrellas outside the Casa Italiana.

"*Sono triste che piova sempre mercoledì sera*," Anne said. I am sad that it always rains on Wednesday night.

For all her complaining, her subjunctive was readier than Liz's. It helped that she was a French teacher. As they walked away, Signora V.'s saucy little Fiat sped out of the underground parking, sending up a cresting wave of rain along the driveway.

"There's your publisher," Anne said, dodging the spray and nodding at the broad shoulders and leonine head in the passenger seat.

So it was. Signora V. and Seamus. Liz's mother used to have at least one proverb for every occasion. Nodding to her mentally, Liz thought of the difficulty of leopards changing their spots, of old dogs learning new tricks and of ponies mastering more than one. She wondered how you expressed that in Italian.

═══

Two emails came from Seattle, the first from Neil's ex-wife, Trina.

It's an odd state, life in the wake of Neil's death, and I go for quite a few hours before I remember that he is dead. Then it feels sad, because he was too young. As for me, am I a widow now? Not technically, I guess, and I did my mourning, at least for our life together, when he left. It's the girls who are really grieving, especially Molly.

I ran into Sidney and Nicole at the rerun movie house in Ballard recently. They were seeing that documentary about the complicity of various people before, during and after the crash of 2008. Obviously, Sidney's choice. She seems more like a romantic comedy kind of gal. I had a rather naughty impulse to bring you up, or maybe I just imagine that Sidney feels uncomfortable when you're mentioned in Nicole's presence. I was about to ask them what they thought of that notorious essay you ran about the cat killing—isn't Nicole an animal lover?—but we got interrupted by some friends of Nicole.

Liz's heart pounded. Close call. It was just luck that her identity had stayed a secret for this long, and it was only a matter of time before someone would out her.

The second email, Liz saw with irritation, was from Nicole. She was like one of those children's toys that keep bobbing up no matter how many times you try to squelch it. The irritation was compounded today because, true to her foreboding, Peter had arranged with Sidney that he would spend Christmas in Seattle. He would fly there from D.C. on Saturday, and Liz was trying to keep busy rather than actually thinking about that.

Now she read Nicole's message.

Dear Editor,

I'm sorry I was so grouchy last time. You are right to remind me how few writers actually make it into My Turn. And I'm grateful for all the time you have spent on me— maybe it gave me false hope, but that's not your fault.

I'm attaching another submission, and thanks for considering it.
All the best,
Nicole

The essay was about how Nicole got teased for being a bleeding heart and a Mother Teresa when really, she insisted, she was only doing what came naturally to her. Being kind to creatures in need was what gave her the most happiness. "The fact is," she wrote, "I just enjoy helping people, and animals too. I always have. When I was very small, I put out a dish of water on hot days for any passing dogs or cats. I refused to have a birthday party unless I could invite my whole class, because I couldn't bear to think of the unhappiness of those who weren't invited. I don't deserve any praise for this, because that's what makes me happy." In a broader context, the essay was about the cynicism of our time, where an unselfish love of others was more suspicious than admirable.

The piece was intolerable. Liz moved it out of the submissions queue to the queue where she stored miscellaneous files, so that she could vent her scorn on the essay itself, in italics. After the first, general paragraph, she wrote, *My grandmother always said, 'Self-praise is no praise.' Here's looking at you, Nicole Szabo.*

When Nicole wrote that the people who thought she worked hard, or even strained, at being a good person were wrong, "because helping other creatures—four-legged and two-legged—is what gives me the most joy," Liz responded, *May I kiss the hem of your garment? Seriously, enough with the humblebragging. Studies have shown that people prefer out-and-out boasting to your phony version.* She had no idea whether any studies had been done on humblebragging, but she liked the way it sounded.

After a paragraph about the stray dogs and cats Nicole had spoon-fed and otherwise sheltered, Liz wrote, *Wow. How's the beatification process coming along? Or are you already on the canonization track? You're a modern-day St. Francis when it comes to animals. But woe betide any children or wives who come between you and a man you want to love—because you're so loving, of course. I think you mentioned that once or twice. A vagrant dog is a lot easier to care about than children who want to keep on living with their father. You're so proud of the empathy that allows you to identify with a motherless kitten, but how about really imagining the life of a child whose father has moved across town so he can be with his girlfriend? Or about the wife who's left behind because her husband prefers a supremely loving person like you? Just a few questions you might want to ponder.*

At the end, when Nicole lamented the cynicism of our times, where goodness was dubious and altruism supposedly concealed more crass motives, Liz wrote, *Good ploy, Nicole. You're making it a societal thing. But don't you see you're undermining your own thesis? The only appropriate response to your tissue of self-praise is more cynicism.*

She wrote more, but those were the high points. By the time she'd finished, she felt calmer. She read over her interleaved remarks, smiling at her occasionally over-the-top contempt. There were some nice bits, like the beatification/canonization mockery and "your tissue of self-praise." She would keep it for a while, for the fun of rereading.

At home that evening, feeling blue about Peter and looking for distraction, Liz went online and found a new revenge story. The wronged wife hung a plastic bag of raw chicken thighs at the back of the closet she had shared with her husband, hidden among the closely packed, dressy clothes she never wanted to see again. Then she moved out. As the smell became overwhelming, the husband tried to sell the house, but no agent would take it on. Liz frowned. A successful revenge scenario has a lovely completeness. It persuades its delighted readers that a vengeful goddess is smiting the wicked, and all is right with the world. But this story left Liz with clumsy, dangling questions. Had the husband, who sounded clue-less, taken his own clothes out of the closet? Did he never think of inspecting his wife's clothes? Were all the real estate agents he consulted equally hapless? For a few minutes Liz thought of fixing the piece herself, but no, she was not going to start editing revenge stories. Which was a shame in a way, because that bag of festering thighs was such a promising start.

———

Paolo sometimes took a walk before he went to work, so on Friday Liz suggested that they could meet in Farragut Square, which was only three blocks from the paper. In spite of its glorious trees, Franklin Square was unloved, while Farragut, which was smaller, busier and more intimate, was a local favorite. After some brisk turns around the park, they sat on a bench while they were still warm from their walk.

He had been telling her a family story from Calabria. An aunt had had a longtime affair with a married man, and the villagers shunned her.

"When the man died, the procession of mourners filled up the village's only street. Everyone was in deep black and they shuf-fled silently along from the church to the cemetery. Suddenly, a figure in a bright red dress with a V-neckline appeared at the edge of the street. It was my aunt, without a coat, with her head held high. The villagers moved out of her way as she cut a long swathe through the crowd. Not from deference, but as if they were half-afraid of her."

Liz pictured the woman, on a dark, frosty day, half-smiling with fury as she moved slowly and defiantly through the mourners. "I wonder if acts like that, of vengeful craziness, are as satisfying as they look," Liz said. "When she went to bed that night, did she feel better?"

Paolo shrugged and said, "Most of us aren't cut out for that kind of drama."

Liz turned to him, admiring his profile, the long, elegant nose and the faint crow's feet in his fine skin.

"You and I don't seem to be," she said.

He turned to face her.

"You know, nothing's going to come of this. I'm a one-woman man." He smiled thinly. "And I don't see you as cut out for a threesome." He considered that number and laughed. "Or whatever you would call a relationship that included Natalie and her lovers."

Well, of course. It had been a goofy idea, that was obvious. And Paolo was so matter-of-fact that Liz wasn't even embarrassed. She was disappointed, but she had to admit that a relationship with him would have entailed a lot of adjustments. He didn't offer the usual, "And we'll always be friends," but she thought, privately, that they might become friends.

As the warmth of their walk wore off, they went up to the food trucks to get hot chocolate.

He asked her about Peter's visit home.

"Well, he wasn't home very much. And I happened to read a philosophy paper he wrote about forgiveness where a woman named Betsy, a.k.a. Peter's mother, seems to be making every mistake in the book. She even expects to feel better after she has forgiven her ex-husband and his wife, which apparently is the dumbest, most self-centered idea of all. It's pretty discouraging, trying to understand forgiveness. There're too many rules. It's too complicated."

"No," Paolo said. "It's simple. Someone hurt you. Someone chose their wants over your wants and needs. You can demand an apology, or not. You can forgive the person for his own sake, or for yours, or both. If forgiving the offender for his sake incidentally brings you some peace of mind, that's okay. The philosophers probably have a good idea or two, and so do the therapists. There's not just one royal road to forgiveness. There'll always be a gap between the experts' pronouncements and the messiness of human feelings, and that's okay too. Maybe the only rule is that you have to want to forgive."

Liz said, "And maybe that's the hardest thing of all."

Paolo took her empty cup and nestled it in his.

"Yes. I can see that."

He stood up, looking for a garbage can, and she followed him.

"Somebody told me once," he said, moving to the edge of the square, "that you never really get over anything. You just figure out a way of carrying it around as gently as possible."

They said goodbye at the corner of K Street and Seventeenth Street.

After a few steps, Paolo turned and said, "Liz."

She faced him and he said, "I wouldn't worry about forgiving or not forgiving if I were you. I think you've done what needed to be done."

She smiled and gave him a little half-wave, her elbow bent and her hand open at shoulder level. If only she felt that was true.

═══

Peter had arranged a ride home from Boston in a friend's car on Saturday, and within an hour Liz was driving him to Dulles Airport. He would return to D.C. for New Year's, so this was cheaper than flying from Boston. Mother and son were treating each other gingerly but civilly. Liz tried chatting about people Peter might see in Seattle. He would never look any of them up, but it seemed like a safe topic. Neutrally, Peter asked about her plans for Christmas.

"I'm not sure. There's an embarrassment of riches. Obviously, I'll see Greg and Gabe and Robert and their kids and of course we'll have Agnes for Christmas dinner. Honey will be celebrating in her usual loose Jewish-Buddhist way, and she's invited me for Christmas

Eve, and Freya and Paul want me to come over sometime during the holidays. Maybe I'll find time for all of them."

"Yeah. Sounds like fun." He sounded as if he could not be less interested.

When they reached the airport, she looked at the building's swooping profile with new eyes. "Would you call that Brutalist?" she asked her distracted son, who was checking his phone for his boarding pass.

He paid no attention to her. Well, at least she had learned something from William. Peter insisted that dropping him off at Departures was fine—he had no luggage to check—but she said no. She would find him inside once she had parked the car.

"Mom, that's stupid. I'll be waiting fifteen minutes for you just to say goodbye, which we can do right here. I'm not a child. Merry Christmas. We'll talk on the phone. We'll text. Love you."

He hugged her as much as was possible with a gearshift between them and a backpack on his lap, and then he was out the door.

Liz drove home carefully, watching for merging lanes and drivers maddened with gift-shopping rage. This was not a big deal, she told herself. She had been very lucky to have had Peter for Christmas all those years. Most divorced parents had a more equitable arrangement. And she had family and friends who wanted her to spend Christmas with them. She was a very lucky woman.

It was ten o'clock when she got home, and completely dark. Not a star in the sky. She parked in front of her apartment, put her head on the steering wheel and surrendered to loud, spasmodic sobs. In *The Odyssey*, when Penelope learns that Telemachus has left in search of his father, she collapses in grief and tears. Homer writes, "The house was full of chairs but she could not / bear to sit upright." It was such a resonant line, evoking archaic Greek chairs with slanted backs and legs, and a mother prostrate with sorrow. Now Liz could not lift her head from the steering wheel. It felt like the end of something bittersweet, and the beginning of something that was only bitter, but she could not have said precisely what was ending and what was beginning. She remembered another line from The Odyssey, a cry from Penelope: "I have lost my noble, lionhearted husband . . . and now the winds / have taken my dear son."

Among the saccharine Christmas scenes of Peter that scrolled through her mind, holding the famous knitted stocking, or choosing the one present he was permitted to open on Christmas Eve, were other, less sugary memories. On the first Christmas morning after she and Sidney had separated, she was making pick-up and drop-off arrangements with him on the phone, while Peter was enthusiastically singing "We Wish You A Merry Christmas" in the next room. He loved the line, "Oh, bring us a figgy pudding," although he had never encountered a figgy pudding, and he ramped up the threat in the next line, "We WON'T go until we get one, we WON'T go until we get one." As he blustered on, enjoying his own treble pugnaciousness, Liz heard Sidney crying on the other end of the phone. She could not remember her reaction, and probably she was still stony-hearted enough toward him that she registered it without much feeling. But now this memory took its place in the catalogue of what all three of them had lost. She did not know how long she stayed there, bent over the steering wheel, wailing in time to thoughts of abandonment, love, failure, loneliness.

There was a timid tapping on the window. Oh God.

A woman's voice said, "Liz, are you okay? What is it?"

It was pretty obvious that she was not okay, but who was this Good Samaritan? She rolled down the steamed-up window, and her neighbor Kara lowered her anxious face closer. Liz almost never saw Kara on the block. Where was her little boy, while she was out on the street at night, without even a carton of milk to justify her presence in front of Liz's apartment? Perhaps he was at home with Henry.

Smearing her hand across her streaming nose and wet cheeks, Liz asked, "Where is Ned?"

Kara stared at her non sequitur and said, "He's spending the weekend with my parents. But . . . what's wrong? Can I help you?"

"It's nothing, thank you. Well, not totally, but my son has gone to spend Christmas with his father in Seattle, and I'm not used to being without him for the holidays. That's all. I was just having a weak . . . minute."

"Well, that's not nothing," Kara said, the mother of a son. "Why don't you come in for a drink? I have a fire at home."

Liz pictured a snug scene in Kara's living room, with Henry watching the flames, anticipating a tender evening.

"That's so kind of you, but I'll be fine. Thank you. Maybe we can have a drink together over the holidays."

"Are you sure?"

"Very."

Kara looked as if she wanted to accompany Liz to her door, but Liz said, "You go on home. I'm almost done here. And merry Christmas."

———

Next morning, things seemed less dire, but without Peter, it didn't seem possible—or desirable—that Christmas was five days away. Liz had a few invitations to parties, none of which thrilled her, and she had presents to buy for her family, and for Freya and Honey. She thought she should do at least some minimal decorating, if only for her own morale, but she couldn't bend her dispirited will in that direction. She wondered if she should take a few of the boxes of ornaments out of the blanket chest in the hall and thank them for their years of service before storing them again. Marie Kondo recommended doing that when disposing of possessions. It sounded so fey that Liz repaired instead to a revenge site.

She had already read most of the schemes, but a new one appeared that was impressive. A woman had organized a formal dinner to celebrate her twentieth wedding anniversary. Most of the guests found a white plate at their assigned seat, but eight women had pink plates. The wife's speech was short and to the point. Asking "the special friends" who had pink plates to stand, she introduced them one by one. This one had been a college friend, this one worked with her husband, this one's first child went to nursery school with their daughter, and so on down the line. When they had all been identified, she added one more thing: they had all had an affair with her husband during the course of her marriage. Then, after picking up the new fur jacket and Vuitton suitcase she had stored under the tablecloth, she left for Paris. Needless to say, her husband did not give the toast he had prepared. Reading about that was more satisfying than thanking a box of Christmas balls, but even so it wasn't giving Liz her usual lift.

Just before lunch, the poet called.

"When do you want to see the Forrestal Building? It's maybe the finest of them all."

Oh dear. Now Liz did regret taking William home to bed. Their arrangement, or lack of it, had always been loose but, true to her feeling about afternoon sex, there had been something different that day. Paolo's words, "There is a promise made in any bed," came back to her. Arthur Miller's words, more correctly. She wasn't sure if that was always true, but she winced a little, remembering William's response to those inscrutable concrete buildings and her response to William.

"Not right away, William. I'm really busy for the next couple of weeks, until after Christmas at least."

William existed in a parallel universe without national holidays.

"Surely you've got a few hours to see a landmark building."

It was unlike him to press her. Another guilty twinge.

"You know what it is? I'm having a hard time with my son right now. With Peter. And I don't want to make any commitments that would interfere with spending time with him."

"Oh."

William knew almost nothing about Peter, nor did he ever show interest in learning more. Even now, when Liz told him things were difficult. Recognizing that, and William's general self-centredness, made her feel better about letting him down. But what exactly was she doing, pursuing one man who was helplessly in love with his wife and reigniting the spark with another, who was narcissistic, improvident and a serial freeloader? Peter's harsh summary of her romantic life came to mind, but she pushed it away.

The one social event she was looking forward to, because it was determinedly un-Christmassy, was scheduled for that evening. On the face of it, it seemed foolhardy for the Ladies' Dinner Club to meet on December 20, but Madeleine and Jane had argued that it would be a welcome night without family, shopping, holiday cooking and certainly no present-giving. Only Leona couldn't come. It was her busiest season and she texted them her regrets: *After New Year's, it will be my devout wish not to see another sausage ball or red velvet cupcake for at least six months.*

The group settled on a Persian restaurant, ignoring its blinking tree. Over her pomegranate chicken, Sally told a sad story about a friend who had tried online dating after she and her husband divorced. The only plausible candidate had been sabotaged by her children, who were actively hostile to the gentleman caller. All the women, even those who had no experience in the matter, agreed that dating when you had children was fraught. It was even worse when the new person also had children, which meant mingling them.

"We're taking that really slowly. We've hardly ever done things so far with both kids," Red Ann said, as if everyone understood what she was talking about. A few heads around the table did nod.

Liz had not heard the news and she turned to Red Ann, who on closer inspection did not look as completely comfortable as she had sounded.

"So, you're seeing someone?"

Ann spread her hands and lifted her shoulders slightly, as if to suggest that the situation was beyond her control. She had a red-head's sensitive skin, and her freckles were merging into her blush.

"Well, you know. Kara."

Kara? It felt to Liz as if Ann had dropped that name into a completely white and room-size box. It lay there for a minute in the emptiness, waiting to be recognized. Who in the world was this Kara? Finally Liz had a thought, although it seemed outlandish.

"Do you mean Kara, my neighbor?"

"Yes, of course."

Ann looked both faintly abashed and faintly affronted that Liz had to be told what was going on at the corner of her street. For one mad moment, Liz imagined that Kara, Ann and Henry were having a threesome. But they weren't. How was Liz supposed to know that Kara liked women? And what about that happy, first-flush-of-love scene between Henry and Kara at Costco?

"Ann, wow. What a nice surprise. And I do mean surprise. How recent is this?"

"Well, obviously, it started at Thanksgiving, thanks to you. . . ." Now everyone was paying attention to Ann, whose blush accelerated. "And things moved along pretty quickly."

Liz remembered that Kara had gone to the high school where Ann was a guidance counsellor. Their children were roughly the same age.

She said to Ann, hesitating only slightly, "You know, it's funny, but I thought Kara and Henry were dating."

"Henry?" Ann looked as blank as Liz had just looked at the mention of Kara. "Your friend Henry, the one who teaches . . . ?" She struggled to remember. "Why ever would you think that?"

"It's nothing, I guess. I just ran into them one night in the smoked salmon section of Costco."

Red Ann smiled. "That doesn't mean they came together."

Of course, Ann was right. They could have bumped into each other just as Liz had bumped into them. Liz suddenly felt very fond of Ann. And Kara was obviously a sweetheart, as seen in her solicitude last night. It seemed clear to Liz that Kara and Ann were going to be an ideal couple.

WEEK ELEVEN

December 21–27, 2015

*O*n Monday, Peter sent a half-apology from Seattle for his peevishness, based on one of their old routines. When he was naughty or miserable as a child, Liz would explain her upset by saying to him, "They say you can only be as happy as your least happy child."

He would answer, "That doesn't give you much choice."

"No."

Now he texted, *You know what they say: you can only be as happy as your least happy parent.*

The poet, meanwhile, had left a telephone message—he avoided writing anything except his poetry—saying that he had just finished a particularly lyrical passage about the Forrestal Building. It was one of the most despised Brutalist buildings, inexplicably, and he fumed against its stubbornly blind critics. Oblivious to the holidays as well as Liz's disinclination to see him, he suggested making a pilgrimage there on Thursday, which was Christmas Eve.

Liz did not want to think about either the poet or Peter in Seattle. She had finished her Tuesday page early and had come home to read submissions in peace and quiet. But first she would do a little Christmas wrapping. Arranging presents, wrapping paper, tape, scissors and gift cards on the dining room table, she started with the doctor bag and book she had bought for Poppy. The book was *Make Way for Ducklings*, and she took a nostalgic look at Robert McCloskey's drawings of Boston's Public Garden before she measured the paper. It was already a classic when her parents had read it to her, but she never tired of Mr. and Mrs. Mallard's search for a good home for their family, or of the policeman who stopped traffic on Beacon Street so that the ducklings could cross. When Sidney read it to him, Peter asked his father why Mr. Mallard went off for a week by himself to explore the rest of the river while Mrs. Mallard stayed home educating the ducklings. Sidney said, "It's different with ducks than it is with people." Liz had loved Peter for noticing that, and admired Sidney's careful answer.

She put the book in the middle of the paper and folded the sides so that the pattern lined up perfectly. There was nothing satisfying about swathing a present in tissue paper so it could slide around in a glossy, too-bright gift bag, and everything satisfying about enclosing it firmly in Ikea paper decorated with tasteful Scandinavian pine sprigs. Maybe one reason books had caught on in Western civilization was because gift-wrapping them was so pleasant. She was printing a gift card for Poppy, who couldn't read but made good guesses, when a text arrived from Peter. *The jig is up: Nicole knows. What were you thinking? Have you suddenly lost your mind or is this the slow creep of early onset dementia?*

Deliberately, she put down the gift card. Her hand was shaking too much to add LIZ to AUNT.

She took a deep breath and texted back, *How did she find out?*

How do you think? Dad asked me at breakfast how things were going at the paper and with your job, and I said you were always struggling to keep up with the submissions. What submissions? he asked. They thought you were still on the education beat.

That was what she had been counting on—that, and Sidney's and Peter's apparent lack of interest in her life. Or perhaps, Sidney's wish not to pry. Or not to remind his second wife of his first wife. Anyway, it didn't matter now. She sat holding the phone. Discovery had probably been inevitable, but even so she was shocked and covered in shame.

After five minutes without an answer from her, Peter texted, *I repeat: What were you thinking? And why didn't you tell me?*

She only answered the second question. *I hoped you'd never find out, because you'd think I was an idiot.*

Well, you got that one right.

A moment later, the phone rang and an angry Sidney told her how insensitive, callous and downright mean she had been to a hurt and confused Nicole.

Liz said she was sorry over and over, a pathetic, running undercurrent to Sidney's wrath until he added, "There you are, with your big job in Washington, making fun of a woman who hasn't done any writing. How could you take advantage of Nicole's innocence?"

That did it. Sidney had flipped a switch.

"Innocence!" she yelled, not caring how she sounded. "Excuse me, but *innocence* is not the first quality about your precious Nicole that leaps to mind."

She pronounced "innocence" as scathingly as possible. Then she hung up.

Okay, she told herself, her hands still shaking, calm down. There's no way that Nicole is not going to be the virtuous heroine in Sidney's version of things, and her part in the end of Liz and Sidney's marriage was an old story that everybody but Liz considered

past reheating. Whereas what Liz had done this fall was undeniably shabby.

She phoned Sidney.

"Hello." He sounded baleful.

"Sidney, could I please speak to Nicole?"

He put her on mute for a minute, and then said, "Here she is."

Nicole managed to convey with her "Hello" that her eyes were
red and burning and she had a large tear in her best skirt.

"Nicole, I am so sorry. I wish I understood myself why I did
that, but all I can do is say I'm sorry."

"You were playing me."

"I guess I was. You're right, I was."

"And you were enjoying it."

"It didn't feel that way."

"What did it feel like?"

A wilier opponent would not have asked that question, because
Liz's feelings were beside the point. The point was her guilt. But
Nicole was not a wily opponent.

"It felt wrong, of course," Liz began. "That was the main thing,
both as an editor and a person. It stirred up some anger, which I
thought I was done with. And some sadness. And mixed in was
something I have to admit was a guilty thrill, like peeking in the
window at a private scene between two people. Morally, it was
nauseating, like drinking too much or eating too much chocolate.
But I couldn't stop."

Silence on Nicole's end and then she said, "You gave me advice
about Sidney."

"Yes." Liz thought about that briefly. "Maybe that comes from
being a know-it-all as a schoolgirl. When I think I know the answer
or even a possible solution, I can't not tell it."

This was starting to sound almost friendly, perhaps too friendly.

Nicole said, "Well, you know Sidney better than most people."

And for a second they actually laughed together, ruefully.

"Tell me something," Nicole said hesitantly.

"Yes?"

"Did you ever use the trick you suggested, about connecting with him in his pessimism, just to start the conversation?"

"No, but maybe I should have. Maybe you only see a person clearly from a distance of time or space, I don't know."

It had never occurred to her to join Sidney in his glass-half-empty sensibility, even fictitiously, probably because she found it tiresome. But, even if she couldn't have play-acted, maybe she should have moved beyond her boredom and irritation and been more curious, if not sympathetic. Talked with him about the miasma of disappointment that shadowed him. Strangely, she had misquoted a line from *The Crucible* to Paolo recently and now another one from that play came into her head. She had never forgotten something said by the Puritan wife whose husband has been unfaithful. Taking responsibility for her part in their stale marriage, she admits to her husband, "It were a cold house I kept." In some ways she had kept a cold house for Sidney. It occurred to her that Peter had probably known that for years.

"Tell me something else," Nicole said, more tentatively. "Did you really plan on using my essay, ever?"

"No," Liz said, reluctantly. "You're a competent, clear writer. But only one or two percent of the submissions to My Turn ever get in the paper."

"Right." Their moment of quasi-friendliness was over. "Well, you should be ashamed of yourself."

"I am," Liz said. "And I think we should just leave it at that."

They said goodbye and hung up.

Liz settled the phone gently in its cradle, like a fractious baby, and stood up. What now? A Victorian heroine would have bathed her temples, but red wine sounded like a better idea. Before she could get to her wine-holder, the phone rang.

"Just one more thing," Sidney said coldly. "It's a bit rich, you disparaging Nicole's character. What about that woman who came up to us in the restaurant in Foggy Bottom, the one whose husband you had been seeing? Talk about hypocrisy."

Actually, no one had been talking about hypocrisy, but she decided he deserved an answer. "That was very wrong, my involvement with that man. Having sinned doesn't mean you don't know the difference between right and wrong. The fact that I erred doesn't absolve Nicole, or vice versa. We both did wrong—actually all three of us did, and I am critical of all of us."

Sidney was having his usual effect on her, and she was sounding like one of Peter's philosophy books.

Ignoring her answer, before he hung up, Sidney said, with an air of conclusion, "You should be ashamed of yourself."

So Nicole had said. Liz remembered that Martha had said that, too. Okay, it was official: she was ashamed of herself. It was early afternoon, but she would drink to that with a glass of red wine.

Luckily, she limited it to one glass, because Greg called shortly afterward. "Haven just called me. Mom is missing."

Agnes was not in a locked unit because she had shown no signs of wandering. Everything had seemed normal when her breakfast had been delivered to her room that morning. The person at the front desk, who kept a sharp eye on the main door, had not seen Agnes all morning. But her room was empty and a coat, too skimpy for December, was missing. So were her old leather purse and wallet.

Liz and Greg drove immediately to Haven and were shown into the director's office. Agnes must have left the building from the rear door in the basement, the director said. To get to the basement door, you had to enter a service elevator that was marked "Employees Only," but that would not have stopped Agnes. The director looked braced for accusations or anger, but Liz and Greg were not inclined to waste time on recriminations. As usual, Haven's holiday decor was a mashup of Christmas bells, Hanukkah candelabras and Kwanzaa flags. There was no Christmas tree, but there were boughs in abundance, hung with dreidels, Santas and Kwanzaa ears of corn. At the table in the director's office, Liz and Greg ignored one of these attempts at multicultural cheer to consult the map on their phones. Since Agnes had never taken any interest in the neighborhood, there were no likely cafés or shops, but Liz and Greg divided up the area and set off separately. A few Haven staff were already out searching, and the police had been notified.

After failing to find Agnes at the local library, grocery and several coffee shops, Liz looked at her phone in case she had missed a text or message from Greg. He hadn't sent one, but there was a message from Nicole. Odd. It was on her personal email, which Peter or Sidney must have supplied.

> *Hi Liz. It was good to clear the air a bit this morning.* (Was it? And had they?) *As you must know, I feel very clumsy and intimidated around you. Maybe we could manage to talk a little more, even have coffee or something when you're in Seattle. I don't know. Sidney isn't always the easiest person to read, and as I said this morning, you know him better than most people. ;-) I don't know, this is just a thought.*

Oh my. Liz stared at that for half a minute. But meanwhile her mother, in a thin coat and without hat or gloves, was wandering somewhere in temperatures that hovered around the freezing mark. Later, she said mentally to Nicole. Maybe.

By seven o'clock, she and Greg had been to all the cafés and food stores in the neighborhood as well as, farther afield, the streets around Agnes's former apartment. There were a few small strip malls in the vicinity, but no elderly, lost-looking woman had been spotted trolling the aisles of the stores. Greg had been put on hold when he called the local hospitals and he decided it would be faster for them to drive separately to the nearest ones and make sure Agnes was not sitting in the ER or on a gurney in a hallway.

On her way to the first hospital, Liz found herself in a neighborhood that looked familiar. The streets all had tree names and there was a Polish church on a corner with a life-size gold-colored statue of Pope John Paul II surrounded by little children. That landmark oriented her: Greg and Robert had lived around here with their boys, when Agnes had first moved to Baltimore. She drove to Sycamore Street, feeling her way slowly, and parked in front of a tidy brick box, its walk lined with the remnants of marigolds and geraniums, crunchy now and outlined with frost. Robert had kept the front yard weeded and raked in his day. He would have approved of the neatness but, a snob about annuals, he would have sighed over the flowers.

The petite, gray-haired woman who answered the door wore what used to be called a housedress. Without any preamble, she asked, "Have you come for Agnes?"

Still in her coat and holding her purse tightly, Agnes was seated in a pink velvet shellback chair in the living room. She looked at Liz calmly, but whether or not she recognized the woman in front of her as her daughter was unclear. There was a small, artificial Christmas tree in the corner, hung with silver paper icicles. Liz had only seen icicles on trees in movies from the 1940s or 50s. She wondered where you bought them. Mrs. Wroblewski, the owner of the house, was loquacious in her relief that someone was claiming Agnes.

"She knocked on the window, and that gave me a start. I was just finishing cleaning up the kitchen after dinner. When I opened the door, she marched right in and sat there. Wouldn't budge. Kept asking, 'Where is everyone?' 'Who is everyone?' I said. 'My husband is in the basement, watching the game, and I'm here. That's everyone.'"

As if he had been summoned, Mr. Wroblewski appeared from the basement and looked around.

"It's her daughter, come to get her," Mrs. Wroblewski explained, and that satisfied him.

He said, "How do you do" to Liz and returned downstairs.

"She wouldn't tell me anything except her name," Mrs. Wroblewski went on. "And not her last name, because she said that wasn't important. I wanted to look in her purse, in case she had some identification there, but she wouldn't let go of it. I'm telling you, I was at my wit's end. We called the police, but there's a big accident on the highway, so they said it could be some time before they got here."

"I'm so grateful to you," Liz said. "And I'm sorry you were disturbed. If you could call the police and say that all is well here, I'll call my brother and tell him."

Once she got off the phone, she took Agnes's hand.

"Mom, why did you leave Haven?"

"I didn't like their decorations. No point in spending Christmas there."

"Well, we were all very worried. And you came here, I guess, to see the boys?"

Agnes gave her the look that meant, Do you really need to ask that?

"I like to give them a little money at Christmas. That's why I wouldn't let her take my wallet."

She inclined her head toward Mrs. Wroblewski, obviously someone who couldn't be trusted with other people's money. With more apologies and thanks to Mrs. Wroblewski, Liz got Agnes out the door and into her car. She belted her in, and went over to the driver's side.

Before she started the car, she asked, "How did you get here?"

"I walked for a while, and took the bus part of the way," Agnes said, as if it were completely normal for her to travel miles from Haven to a long-ago destination.

"How did you know what bus to take?"

"Bus drivers get paid to know that."

The mysteries of the mind. All Agnes had needed to remember was Sycamore Street. Now that she had her mother back safe, still clutching her purse, and Greg had notified Haven that Agnes had been found, it seemed mean to deliver her back there immediately. The place of bad decorations.

"Do you feel like stopping for some coffee?" Agnes had never seen the point of tea.

"No, I don't. I'd like to go to a bar."

What a good idea. Haven served mediocre wine in the dining room at dinner, for those who wanted to pay extra, but the bright lights, pastel walls and walkers parked by the tables were not conducive to bonhomie. The bottles some of the residents kept in their rooms were not much better. It was cold and dark, a perfect night for one of Baltimore's welcoming bars. They found a likely one not far away, and Liz handed Agnes her own gloves before moving to unstrap her.

"Put these on, Mom. It's bitter out there."

"Don't be silly. We're a few steps from the door."

Agnes undid the belt herself, and got out of the car without too much trouble. Once inside, she headed straight for a banquette. Unlike many elderly women, she had not lost much height although she was thinner. She slid into the banquette and pushed her purse across the table to Liz.

"I'm paying for this, and you take the rest for the boys for Christmas."

"Mom, no. You're my guest. And you'll be seeing the boys on Christmas at Greg and Gabe's. I'll bring along a few cards for you to sign for them, and you can put the money in the envelopes. And probably you'd like to give something to Poppy too."

Although she'd had a good time with Poppy just a few weeks before, Agnes said, "I don't know any Poppy. What kind of name is that?"

"Yes, you do know her. She's Greg and Gabe's little girl."

"Does she like money?"

"She likes things you can buy with money. Toys and books. Why don't I get something for her, and you can sign a card?"

Casually, while they were talking, Liz had opened the purse and taken out Agnes's deflated pigskin wallet. Without smelling it, Liz knew that it would have a faint memory of a perfume or hand cream Agnes had once worn. Inside there were two dollar bills and some change. It was lucky she'd had enough to pay the bus fare—or had she? Perhaps the driver had let her ride with no charge.

Given a choice between wine and Scotch, Agnes chose Scotch. So, after some deliberation, did Liz. Its flames scorched her throat, first shocked and then grateful. The shock and gratitude spread further down, to her belly. Now that it was over, she could admit how worried she had been. Across the booth, her mother sat straight-backed and imperturbable. No, Liz told herself, "imperturbable" is a euphemism. She is oblivious.

"What about Robert?" her mother asked.

Perhaps visiting his house had sparked a memory.

"What about him?"

"Will he be there at Christmas?"

"Yes. I think Greg said Robert will have the boys for Christmas Eve, so he'll bring them and we'll all have dinner."

Agnes never pretended to understand when she didn't, and she looked evenly at Liz without nodding. Instead, she took a sip of her Scotch and said, "That's hard."

Liz thought, Is she saying that the ins and outs of Greg's two marriages and three children are beyond her right now? Or is she saying that she understands, however vaguely, the snags and hiccups involved in such a Christmas dinner?

Before Peter had decided to go to Seattle for Christmas, Liz had made arrangements for a floating editor to package My Turn over the holidays so that she could spend some time with her son. When the Seattle trip became a reality, she left the arrangement as it was. She hadn't had time off for months, and she might take up a friend's invitation to her country place in Maryland, or even make a flying trip to see her cousins in Boston. As usual, she left the temporary editor with a schedule of the essays she had chosen and their dates, identified by a word in the queue, called a "slug." The corresponding illustrations were carefully labelled. Occasionally, if she had the time or inspiration, she would leave a half-written hed and deck, or some ideas for them.

The essay scheduled for December 22 was a Christmas memoir. As a young man, the writer had volunteered in the kitchen at a homeless men's shelter and insisted on helping out at the shelter's Christmas dinner. His friends and some of his family called him a saint, but he knew that his motives were impure. It was easier to stand in a hot kitchen, ladling out soup or cutting mincemeat pies into eighths for nameless vagrants, than to be at home enduring his relatives' obnoxious political opinions or passive-aggressive comments on the food. The shift in the essay came when he couldn't bear his own pretense of charity anymore. Changing his ways, he stayed home for Christmas dinner and upped the ante by inviting a cousin and an aunt who were even more disagreeable than the usual guests. Now that they were all safely dead or past reading, he had written the piece. It had an agreeable, dry bite, and was slugged "saint." The illustration, which was not brilliant, showed a forearm and hand extending a bowl of soup.

Early on the morning of the twenty-second, Liz looked at her phone while she was still in bed, to see if Peter had written to her. He hadn't, so, although she was on holiday, she scanned idly through her work email and Twitter. She knew it was a bad habit, but she was cutting herself some slack this Christmas. There were more tweets than usual about the day's My Turn, but not so many as to raise alarm. A few readers admired the "sardonic" and "sarcastic" essay. Liz thought, Was it really that sardonic, and was it at all sarcastic? Another one admired the "double-sided" mind of the writer, which perplexed Liz for a minute. The reader must be referring to the writer's attitude during and after his retreat from his family. One reader said the illustration didn't do the essay justice, but surely a hand proffering a soup bowl, while a bit predictable, echoed the writer's experience in soup kitchens.

There was no predicting readers' reactions, she reflected, not for the first time, and turned back the covers. She had to do some last-minute gift shopping and grocery shopping for the ingredients for the Dutch Christmas cookies Greg and his sons requested every Christmas. The dough, including crushed shortbread and toasted almonds, was fiendishly hard to roll out, but once a year she inflicted sore arm muscles on herself for the sake of hearing her nephews' glad cries. Leaving the building, she picked up the paper from the porch and put it on the chair in the hall. She would read it later, if she felt like it. One of the most decadent parts of taking a day off was the possibility of not reading the paper.

An hour or so later, Liz was in a shop on M Street in Georgetown, trying to interest herself in a scarf for Honey. A sales clerk had set her poring over a tray of tightly rolled scarves, like patterned silk cigars, so she ignored the first vibrations and pings from her phone. Thanking the clerk, she returned the tray and turned to her phone.

The text was from Peter. *WHAT THE HELL? Can we get you a double room with Agnes? Did you think about the consequences of this for one single second? Is this your insane idea of atonement?*

What on earth was he talking about? There was also a message from Trina. *Wow. Quite the bombshell. I wouldn't have thought she had it in her. And well written, too, especially the comments from her dark side.*

Liz felt a creeping dread. It was 10:30 a.m. in D.C., which meant it was 7:30 in Seattle. She went to the paper's website and today's My Turn. The illustration, the hand and the soup bowl, was right, but the hed was confusing. "My Two Sides—Dark and Light— Finally Talk." What was that supposed to mean? People said that the floating editor was Gilman's latest conquest, but that was no reason for her to write such an inaccurate hed.

Then Liz's eyes landed on the signature: Nicole Szabo. She began dying a little. She read the first paragraph, and the dying speeded up. The idiotic editor had published Nicole's self-congratulatory piece with all of Liz's insulting italic responses. But how? Why?

Along with her frantically hammering heart came a strange clarity. She had removed Nicole's piece from the submissions queue before adding her own comments. The queue where she had stored it also held the pieces to be published over the holiday. The slug for the right piece for today, the soup kitchen essay, was "saint." Never imagining any connection between the two essays, Liz had sarcastically slugged Nicole's piece "saint francis." The damned subbing editor must have come to that one first in the queue, and read Liz's scornful remarks in italics as the writer's conversation with herself. The piece worked more or less with the illustration, so she must have thought that was what Liz intended for the paper. For the whole blinking national paper, which was now being read, in the print edition or online, across the country.

Oh. My. God. Obviously, she would be fired. After Sidney and Nicole sued her personally and then sued the paper. She had two more years of her share of Peter's college tuition to pay, and how was she going to do that? Who was going to hire a middle-aged newspaper editor when failing papers all across the country were operating with skeleton staffs? She knew all that, instantaneously, but it did not concern her as much as what she had done to Nicole. She had affixed a padded, embroidered, brazen scarlet A for Adulterer on Nicole's chest for the whole country to see. It was trimmed with sequins and battery-powered to blink on and off.

Like an automaton, she hailed a cab on M Street and went home. She could only write or telephone her useless apologies from her apartment, not on the street or from a café. By the time she got home, there was an email from Sidney.

> *Don't call or write. I don't want to hear your voice, and I'm not interested in your explanations or justifications. Even to dignify what you've done with those words infuriates me more than I am already. Whatever I may have thought of you when our relationship was at its worst, I never saw you as a bully, much less on this scale. Until now. I look forward to hearing your employer's reaction to this astonishingly irresponsible act. Naturally, I will be speaking with my lawyer about the appropriate response. If Peter were not as mature as he is, I would be questioning the amount of time he spends in D.C. during the school year. As it is, I will do whatever I can to see that he spends all of his summers in Seattle.*

There was no signature.

Later, Liz could only remember parts of the rest of that day. She did recall tearing a strip off the horrified subbing editor.

On the phone, she said, "One thing about editors, one *distinguishing* thing about editors"—here she had wished she could remember the woman's name because using it would have added to the caustic contempt of her tone—"is that they are careful readers. *Careful readers*, do you even understand what that means? And careful readers know that 'saint' is not the same thing as 'saint francis.' Why didn't you email me and ask if that was the right piece? Why didn't you at least *try* for the barest minimum of competence?"

She carried on until she heard sobbing on the other end of the line, and then she hung up. She did some crying herself, after drinking two glasses of wine.

The next morning, cleaning up the mess, she was impressed to realize that, rather than drink the half-empty bottle on the kitchen counter, she had opened a rather good Pommard in tribute to the day's awfulness. The Sancerre she'd been saving for a special occasion remained untouched: sick contrition, fear and horror clearly called for red. She must have called Honey at some point, because Honey arrived after work. She'd read the piece at the paper, but now, over the remains of the Pommard, Liz told her the backstory. This interested Honey as much as the current catastrophe.

"But why didn't you tell me about all this?"

"Because I didn't know why I was doing it and it was so wrong on several levels . . ."

That didn't feel like a complete sentence, but Liz couldn't think of any way to add more.

"And would you ever have told me about the whole Nicole charade, if it hadn't blown up?"

Liz thought. "Probably not. Why are you looking at me like that?"

"Because you need to talk to me more. Or to somebody. You're going around with these dramas in your head, keeping all these secrets, and you're losing perspective."

"Yeah, okay. Maybe you're right." She couldn't possibly tell Honey about Seamus. "But what about the piece?"

Honey read it again.

"It's actually pretty cool, the way it works as the woman's dialogue with herself."

"How can you say that? This isn't about a 'cool' piece of writing, this is about a nightmare for Nicole and for me! I wonder if publishing this"—Liz hit the paper, as if it were to blame—"is actually illegal."

She saw herself in Douglas's office, as someone, probably Norris, put her in handcuffs. Seamus and Douglas would stand by, the faces of all three men indicating that there was a natural progression from the inflammatory pieces she had published in My Turn to a jail sentence.

"Don't worry about that. It was an accident. But if I'm wrong, I'll visit you in prison."

"Very funny."

"But back to the nightmare for you two," Honey said, looking over the piece once more. "Okay, subtracting the annoyed responses from her cynical self, it's embarrassing for Nicole because she comes across as sanctimonious. But the comebacks from her other self save her, because the reader sees that she understands how obnoxious she can be."

"But I wrote those," Liz said, stating the obvious. Why was Honey being so obtuse?

"The reader doesn't know that. You might have some apologizing to do to Nicole, but the woman who appears in this essay is more than capable of criticizing her goody-two-shoes side. And that's a saving grace."

"And you think Nicole can make that distinction. I doubt it. But the worst thing is that I've exposed her as a home-wrecking adulterer."

"My God, Liz. The twenty-first century is fifteen years old, and you're still living in some Victorian melodrama where the impure woman is going to have to throw herself onto the train tracks. If this century is too much for you, at least try getting into the twentieth. This is *not* the huge deal you imagine it."

But it was. At least, that was how she saw it, and how she imagined Nicole saw it. On the other hand, Liz had several friends and acquaintances, nice women, married and not, who seemed perfectly blithe about the affairs they'd had with married men in the past or were having in the present. Liz remembered a furious

Martha asking her if she also cheated at cards or shoplifted. The women she knew would not dream of such petty dishonesty, but they were okay with adultery. And as for herself, she would not have described herself as blithe about her affair with Seamus, but she had been more than capable of sweeping any ethical worries under the carpet for a few years. So, maybe she should think about Honey's reaction. Maybe later, when she did not feel so wretched. If that ever happened.

Honey left after eleven, and Liz resigned herself to a night of no sleep. She did drift off, occasionally, but her dreams were so dreadful that she preferred being awake. They involved losing custody of Peter (could anyone be said to have custody of a twenty-year-old?), having a scarlet A affixed to her own clothes by Martha and serving time in a jail where she still had to read all the My Turn submissions.

—

After a few hours of early morning sleep, Liz staggered into the kitchen shortly after eight to make coffee. Even her feet hurt. This is what old age is going to feel like, she thought, remembering her father's gingerly steps first thing in the morning, as his joints protested. She wished she could skip this purgatory and be thirty years older right now. Things like this didn't happen to old people. She had several ignorable messages and texts congratulating her on how yesterday's My Turn was trending on Twitter. One person did remark that it wasn't very Christmassy.

There were also two texts she would not ignore.

The first was from the floating editor, whose name turned out to be Deborah. She wrote, *I assume you're going to tell Norris?*

Liz answered, *I'm not telling Norris. He may find out, but it won't be from me.*

The second one was from Nicole, who had sent hers a few minutes before: *Can we talk?*

Liz had never understood the expression about screwing your courage to the sticking place. If there was ever a time when she needed to know where the sticking place was, it was now.

Of course. Should I call you?

No, I'll call you.

Muddled, Liz thought, She doesn't want Sidney to hang up on me if he answers the phone. Then she realized that it was 5:00 a.m. in Seattle.

Liz sat next to the phone, feeling as if she were going to be sick. She should have made coffee before she read her messages, but now she was afraid to stop staring at the phone. When it rang, she started as if nothing could have been more unexpected. She began talking before Nicole could say a word.

"Nicole, I know it won't do any good to apologize. It was a horrible, horrible accident and it was never meant to be published. I've already chewed out the editor who misunderstood my instructions."

Silence.

"Of course, I can't deny that I wrote those irritated comments. But they were only intended for me. To let off some steam. There was no way in the world I would ever have made them public."

Silence.

"I'm so sorry. You didn't deserve this."

Wait a minute. Did she really mean that? She had time to think about it, since Nicole was still not talking. She decided that yes, she did mean that.

Finally, Nicole spoke, in her smallest, poor-me voice. "Sidney is so upset."

"Oh, stop it!" Tactically, it was not the best time to lose her temper with Nicole, but it felt remarkably satisfying. "Now you sound like the plaster saint who wrote the essay."

"You mean, before you corrected it."

Meow. So she could give as good as she got.

"Yes, before I corrected it. I'm not interested in Sidney's reaction. I imagine you have one of your own. And can you please talk a little louder."

"Everyone is sleeping. I'll close the door."

A door closed, and then more silence.

Then Nicole said, "So you really despise me."

"I just find your holier-than-thou stance preposterous."

"And you decided to announce that to the country."

Why was she making Liz go over this? Peter had explained to her what had happened yesterday and Liz had just explained again. Probably it was part of her punishment.

"I just told you that the editor made a terrible mistake," she said, trying to sound patient. "The name on your piece was similar to the name of the piece that should have been published."

"You mean, the name on *our* piece."

"If you want to put it that way, yes."

Another pause.

"And don't think I haven't thought of the things you wrote in your half," Nicole said. Semi-belligerently, to make it clear there were no revelations there for her.

This time the silence was on Liz's side. She wasn't sure what was going on. Nicole had said "our piece" and "your half." Were she and Nicole collaborators now?

"Okay . . . so why didn't you write them?" Liz thought of adding, "It certainly would have made the piece more readable," but she decided not to push her luck by playing editor.

"I don't know. Maybe because people do seem to see me as kind. And I did want to make the point that it comes naturally."

"Except when it doesn't." Liz was risking another eruption, but things could hardly be worse than they had been.

"Except when it doesn't. I wasn't ready to show the other side of myself, I guess. And I probably don't have the writing chops, yet, to express what it would be like to look at myself that way."

Liz thought, Was it all about writing? But that made sense in a way. Trying to get the right words in the right order to describe a situation or motive or cast of mind was almost always clarifying. Maybe there was a book or a course there: Writing as a Way to Understand Yourself. She would no doubt be looking for employment in the near future.

"It wasn't fun for me to read," Nicole was saying, "but together we wrote a more full self-portrait."

Before Liz could even begin to absorb that astonishing statement, Nicole whispered, "Sidney's up. I have to go."

The line went dead. Liz sat staring at the phone, as if it would explain to her what had just happened. Was it even remotely possible that Nicole didn't resent her for the things she had written, or hadn't she had time to get to that? And there had been no mention of the A-word. Maybe Honey was right and Liz—Liz alone, without Nicole—was the last standing Victorian.

There were no more messages or calls from Nicole. The day dragged on. In her sleep-deprived, confused fog, Liz made the Dutch Christmas cookies. The dough was its usual defiant, punitive self, not so much a dough as clumps of flour, butter, shortbread crumbs and those damned almond flakes that refused to coalesce until Liz had beaten it into submission with Agnes's old wooden rolling pin. Tomorrow her arms would ache as if she had been lifting bags of cement, and it felt properly penitential.

By late afternoon, she couldn't bear the silence from Seattle. She texted Peter, *Call me, please.*

At first he was truculent. "So, have you plotted your next little crisis? I have to admit you're full of surprises."

"I think I'm done for a while. I'm still too covered in shame to grasp why Nicole seems to be taking it better than your father. How are things going?"

"Dad's in a bad mood, no surprise. Nicole goes back and forth between being embarrassed, mad and proud."

"Proud?"

"She's getting a lot of calls and messages about what a good writer she is. And that makes her happy."

"That makes her happy. Wow. Even though she only wrote half of it."

"Yeah, and some of the people mention how they especially like 'the dark side.' But it all has her name on it. Don't ask me to figure it out."

This was a new twist. Was it better to be a good writer, or even a reputedly good writer, who commits adultery than a not-good one who doesn't?

"And she's not upset that I've outed her affair with your father?"

"Dad told her he thought that was left kind of vague in the piece, that it could come across as a fantasy and not a reality."

He listened to Liz pondering that one.

"Yeah, I know. Wishful thinking. But Nicole liked the idea. At one point, she did say that most of their friends knew how she and Dad got together, so . . ."

"So enlarging that circle to include the country is okay?" That sounded more aggressive than she had intended.

"Mom, I'm just the reporter, okay? Stop asking questions if you don't want to hear the answers."

"You're right, I'm sorry. Other than that, how is Christmas? Or is there nothing much other than that?"

"Well, Nicole and her kids have this sacred Christmas cookie-making tradition that we carried on with yesterday when we were still in full crisis mode. Apparently Tamsin and Andrew have been doing this almost from the womb. The cookies are pretty random. And we spent more time cleaning up than we spent making the cookies."

Like father, like son, Liz thought.

"On the bright side, or at least Nicole thinks so, Andrew is learning how to knit. Part of a home economics course boys take in Seattle now. He's trying to knit himself a Christmas stocking, which he'll never finish in time. But Nicole is acting as if he's making the Bayeux Tapestry. And for Christmas dinner, they always have some strays. Not on the menu, I mean on the guest list. Some broken-hearted or homeless or otherwise desolate people Nicole picks up somewhere. Should be jolly."

Liz thought, Well done, Nicole. Another Mother Teresa knock-off.

As if he had just remembered that his mother would be home alone for Christmas, Peter asked again what her plans were. But, unlike their conversation on the way to the airport, this time he sounded as if he really wanted to know.

"Well, Honey is having a potluck Christmas Eve supper tomorrow. It's past the solstice but it's partly a solstice thing, partly Buddhist and partly what she calls Judeo-Christmas. I don't know what the Buddhist part entails or the Judeo-Christmas, except that Honey says Jesus wasn't the only Jewish boy with messianic tendencies. Then I'll go to Greg and Gabe's for Christmas Day. We'll spring Agnes from Haven for the day and bring her to Greg's. Robert will be there, and we'll have your typical blended-family, gay Christmas."

"With you and Agnes and the kids as the outlier heteros," Peter said.

"So far, yes."

"So, is that your next surprise for us?"

"I was thinking of the kids."

"You're right, it's probably too late for you and Agnes."

They laughed. It sounded more friendly than it had for some time.

———

Nicole called again on Christmas Eve, before six in the morning in Seattle. That seemed to be her time.

"Sidney is still kind of miserable," she began, as if that were a problem Liz would want to help solve. Maybe Sidney's resentment was easier to taunt Liz with, rather than admit any lingering bad feelings of her own.

"He'll come around. He just needs to stew in his own rancor for a while. You know that."

"Yes, I do know that."

Liz could imagine Nicole's semi-smile.

"I just wish I could lighten his heart," Nicole continued. "In general, I mean."

"I'd forget that if I were you. I don't think that's going to shift. You've already made him happier than I could in lots of ways. At least, Peter says you have. And you know what? Sidney's a good man. Everybody, including him, seems to be doing the best they can. Nothing is perfect."

And with that basketful of clichés, she hoped to bow out of marriage counselling. Gravely, she and Nicole wished each other a good Christmas. "Merry" sounded like too much of a stretch, but even the tempered alternative would have seemed impossible the day before yesterday.

After lunch, Sidney called.

"Nicole is strangely okay," he began, accusingly.

"Yes, I'm very grateful for that. I didn't expect such magnanimity."

"I still think your behavior to her, starting with the deception about editing, was despicable. And you have no reason to feel morally superior to her, or to me, after your affair with that married man."

Hadn't they already had this conversation? Why was he still harping on that? Liz guessed that her affair was a nice dry piece of turf Sidney could stand on, when water threatened to swamp him on all sides. She decided to make him a peace offering. Or maybe, a Christmas present.

"Actually, that affair was worse than the run-of-the-mill kind, in a way. I think that unconsciously I hoped that if I had an affair with a married man that it would cancel out the need to forgive you and Nicole. If we were all rowing in the same morally leaky boat, I was just as guilty as you were, so I could skip the forgiveness part. Which doesn't make sense, but it was easier to have an affair than to do the hard, sad work of forgiving. The man was a convenient way to put things I needed to address on hold."

"You were really using that guy."

Liz understood Sidney—how he shied away from the obvious, difficult question, retreating to a safe, impersonal place until he was ready.

"Yes, I was," she said. "And I must apologize to him for that."

It felt as if she had to beg pardon from everyone—at least from Seamus and Martha and Nicole and Sidney. And from Peter, because she had not loved his father well enough. Perhaps Nicole and Sidney might think about apologizing to her, although she did not particularly care about that. (But Peter did not need to apologize. She accepted his anger as part of the dues of parenthood, and also because it was deserved.) Since people were no doubt going to go on putting their own wants over those of other people, the need to pardon each other was also going to endure. Everybody had better get used to it. In her mind, she adjusted the nursery rhyme Poppy liked to sing about the mulberry bush to "Here we go round the forgiveness bush, the forgiveness bush, the forgiveness bush."

Now Sidney was ready to ask the hard question, in his own way. "And how's that going, the forgiveness work?"

"Who knows. Such a hydra-headed beast, forgiveness. But somebody whose opinion I respect thinks I've forgiven enough."

Abruptly, Sidney asked, "How is Agnes?" He must be buying time to process her answer.

"Not great, but holding her own."

"You know, I should really thank you for one thing," he said, relenting only a little grudgingly and returning to feelings. "You boosted Nicole's confidence about her writing. And she needs that boost. She doubts herself, doesn't think much of her talents. And that can make her kind of needy at times. With you, I think sometimes I wished for more neediness. You had a kind of flinty independence that could make me feel left out. Now I can see some advantages in that."

After they said their goodbyes and hung up, Liz thought about what Sidney had said. Maybe modern marriage was too demanding for only two people. It needed others—therapists, friends, ex-spouses (ideal in some ways)—to share the burden of perfect love, erotic exclusivity and best-friendness we now call marriage. But Liz wasn't going to be part of that. She had retired from couples therapy. Sidney and Nicole would be fine without her.

Honey put her usual organized self on hold for her Christmas Eve party, which was relaxed to the point of unplanned. People slid their potluck contributions out of boxes and plastic bags onto the kitchen table, and as usual with potlucks, it all somehow worked out.

Liz was now treading cautiously in the world. She felt as though she should not make any sudden moves, in case the fragile new bridges and scaffoldings that surrounded her should collapse. Cooking was beyond her, so she managed to buy one of Leona's sweet potato pies. Leona had made eight of them for a big party, but she said, "People are too full by dessert to have more than a micro-slice. Take this one, the crimping on the crust is less perfect than the others."

Honey's ex-husband, Sol, and her boyfriend, Dave, were there, along with Sol's current wife and a dozen other friends. Sol's canine namesake, Shlomo, craved his customary attention and Sol indulged him.

"Watch the onanism," Honey whispered to Liz, as Sol kissed the bulldog's big sloppy lips.

If there was an acknowledgement or celebration of the solstice or Buddhism, Liz missed it, but Judeo-Christmas was richly observed. Sol's wife played the piano, and they gathered around the battered upright to sing Christmas songs written by Jews. Once they had belted out "Chestnuts Roasting on an Open Fire," "Have Yourself a Merry Little Christmas," "Let It Snow" and, of course, "White Christmas," Liz wondered if there were any Christmas songs not written by Jews. A majority refused to sing "The Little Drummer Boy"—too mawkish—and there was resistance to "Rudolph the Red-Nosed Reindeer," but the traditionalists won, so they sang that too. The singing had made Liz feel more normal and less wrapped in gauze. Finally they reached her favorite, "Winter Wonderland."

As a romantic teenager, she had loved the part in the song where the couple build a snowman and pretend he is the local minister who will marry them. She sang happily,

> Later on
> We'll conspire
> As we dream by the fire
> To face unafraid
> The plans that we've made
> Walking in a winter wonderland.

Dave, who was standing next to her, said, "You have a nice voice. You should sing more."

"Yes," she said. "Maybe I should."

———

Unlike Honey's party, Christmas at Greg and Gabe's house was meticulously choreographed. They had even managed to organize four-year-old Poppy, who was not allowed to open her stocking until 7:00 a.m. and then had to wait until the guests arrived mid-morning to open her other presents. She greeted her grandmother and Aunt Liz with more than her usual warmth and then paced the front hall until her half-brothers and their father showed up a little late. Robert gave Greg a quick half-hug and shook hands with Gabe.

Poppy ushered them all into the living room. Looking over the Christmas tree, Agnes asked, "What happened to the icicles?"

Icicles would have been an almost funky addition to Gabe and Greg's stylish tree, decorated only with tiny LED lights and Poppy's choice of gold and pink balls. Liz understood that Agnes was thinking of the tree in Mrs. Wroblewski's living room.

She put her arm around her mother, briefly. "It's so hard to find places that sell icicles now, isn't it?"

Poppy seemed to realize that Christmas depended on her. Casting off her natural skepticism, she rose to the occasion, rifling through the gift wrappings and greeting each present with enthusiasm. She ran off to her room with the doctor kit to treat her stuffed animals and when she returned, satisfied with their progress, she wore her stethoscope around her neck. Liz, sitting next to Agnes on the couch, reached for her mother's hand.

"I wish Dad could see her."

"Yes," Agnes said. "He was always sorry he hadn't become a doctor."

Liz hadn't known that about her father. He had always seemed so thoroughly absorbed in his pharmacy she had never imagined he'd had other dreams. When Agnes became incapable of remembering anything, the undisclosed family lore would die with her memory. I need to spend more time with her, Liz thought, capturing some of those stories.

After all the presents were opened, Greg went into the kitchen to attend to dinner.

Robert asked Gabe how long they had soaked the turkey in brine, and Gabe said, "Not for a minute. Brining is over."

Liz tensed. Robert had been in charge of brining in his days with Greg, and had taken it seriously.

But Robert said equably, "Yeah. That's probably overdue. Some years it affected the texture, I thought."

Gabe said, "And the drippings were so salty, they were hopeless for gravy."

Robert nodded in agreement.

Since the men were bonding over brining, and her teenaged nephews were absorbed in their new phones, Liz suggested to an overstimulated Poppy that she would read *Make Way for Ducklings* to her. Poppy, who had not seen many books with black-and-white illustrations, was at first reluctant but then yielded. No, she was too big to sit on Aunt Liz's lap, but she sat welded to her side, her slightly sweaty body still warm from all the excitement. Agnes sat on Liz's other side, looking closely at the pictures. The boxy 1940s cars and the swan boats in Boston's Public Garden puzzled Poppy, but not as much as the phone booth where Michael the policeman called for reinforcements to help the ducklings cross the road. She asked, "But why doesn't he just use his own phone?"

Unsurprisingly, the dinner was superb. The unbrined turkey was moist and flavourful, and a new addition, a garlicky beet and prune salad, from an Eastern European cookbook Gabe said was all the rage, brought a burst of zest to the usual bland vegetable offerings. Most miraculous of all, everything was hot. Liz had offered, as always, to bring a dish in addition to the Dutch Christmas cookies and, as always, her offer was declined. She suspected her cooking was not up to their standard.

In between the main course and dessert, when it was late morning in Seattle, they called Peter. Everyone wished him Merry Christmas, with the grownups asking about Seattle's weather (very similar to D.C.'s) and Greg's children asking about his presents.

Poppy gave a detailed account of her gifts, and Agnes asked a few times where he was. Liz missed him, of course, and she thought Greg's boys did too. She had never had a Christmas without Peter. But her mother, brother, nephews and niece were good people, and so were Robert and Gabe. She found she wasn't feeling horrible, thinking of Peter at Sidney and Nicole's. She could even imagine his presence there as her gift to them, which she knew was a stretch. And there was one compensation for Peter's absence: the stuffing could cook inside the bird.

On December 26, Liz called Paolo to hear about his Christmas and to wish him a happy New Year. She had bought him a copy of Ian McEwan's novel *Saturday*, thinking it might suit him, but she decided not to give it to him just yet. She didn't want to rush things with their friendship. Paolo and Natalie had had their usual convivial, densely populated holiday, he told her. Natalie came from a big family and they went to her brother's house in Chevy Chase, where all the kids retreated to the basement and the grownups visited in the living room.

In turn, Liz gave him a censored but still full version of her own Christmas. Perhaps, just perhaps, she might someday tell him more of the story. But meanwhile she had plenty to report about Peter being in Seattle, Honey's Judeo-Christmas party and dinner at Greg and Gabe's. They promised each other they would fit in a walk early in January.

He said, "It's getting easier with the kids, because now they have their own clubs and activities one or two days each week."

Later the same day, there was an email from Nicole.

Hi Liz, I hope you had a good Christmas. We're enjoying having Peter with us, and I hope it's not too lonely for you without him.

*This afternoon everyone went skiing except me, so I
had a little time to myself. I started trying to write
something about the ins and outs of forgiveness. It seems
like a good subject for My Turn. You'll hear from me again
if I can make anything of it. There's something addictive
about writing, don't you think?*

*I don't want to be presumptuous, but I can't help saying
that I'm so relieved and happy that we're becoming friends.*

Happy New Year,

Nicole

Liz sighed. At the very least, she needed to declare a conflict of
interest and have some other editor deal with Nicole. But she had
been thinking about Norris's suggestion that it was time for a change.
She'd had a two-year run with My Turn, and a new assignment was
appealing. Although her colleagues looked on the religion beat as
the journalistic equivalent of Siberia, there was a gold mine of under-
reported stories there. The newish pope whose liberalism might or
might not be window dressing, the rise of evangelical Christianity
and its connection to politics, the resurgence of the abortion
question, the debate over medically assisted death, the cover-up of
priestly abuse, gays and their relationship to organized religion,
Jews and Israel, Muslim immigrants and Western values. That was
just the tip of the iceberg. She would give it some thought.

As for being friends with Nicole, she would write a kind, solid
answer. She began drafting it mentally: "Nicole, I'm hoping that I'll
feel less clumsy with you and Sidney. I think I will. But there's probably always going to be some messiness, no matter what the experts
say. So, no, I don't think we are going to be friends. We're going to
be friendly, or anyway more friendly, and that will be a big improvement, or at least some improvement, at least on my side."

She would have to work on that. There were enough qualifiers
and second thoughts in there to sink a ship.

YEAR'S END

December 30, 2015

Peter's Christmas present to Liz was a single ticket for *The Seagull* at the Arena Stage, for December 30. Liz thought it was rather odd that he hadn't bought two tickets, so that she could invite a friend, but no matter. He wrote on the card, "This is short notice, but I know you like *The Seagull* and the run is almost over. This was meant to be one seat over. Sorry! Hope you enjoy the evening."

At the theatre, she slid in past the knees of a couple on the aisle, the kind of gray-haired people dressed in good wool who frequented the Arena. Academics, maybe, or senior government bureaucrats. Her seat was the third from the aisle, next to the wife, who looked to be wearing Eileen Fisher, a tweedy pumpkin-colored top that didn't quite have the courage to be a poncho but was edging in that direction. On Liz's other side, a smallish balding man with a faint aura of mothballs was checking his watch and turning off his phone. A fussbudget. Wondering why Peter had wanted her to be one seat over, she settled her coat behind her and began reading the program. She was deep in the story of the play's disastrous premiere when she heard someone taking the seat on the other side of the fussbudget. Feeling that the newcomer was looking at her, she raised her head and saw that it was Henry, his coat still folded over his arm. They laughed in surprise, a little shyly. Liz thought, what a coincidence. Henry seemed to be alone too.

Once he had dealt with his coat and sat down, indicating the man between them with the merest flick of his eyes, Henry asked her, "Do you think this is Peter's idea of symbolism?"

The man, who was folding his program precisely and filing it in his pocket, paid no attention to the two people talking across him.

"What do you mean?" Liz asked, feeling slightly disoriented.

"Peter wanted to thank me for some help I had given him with his history paper. He did mention that by the time he bought my ticket, there were very few seats left."

So that was why Peter had wanted her to be one seat over. He just hadn't been able to get two seats together. It was typical of him, a clever idea that came close to materializing but didn't, quite.

At that point, the house lights dimmed and the fussbudget looked sternly at each of them, to make sure they would stop talking. The play began, with Masha in mourning for her life, and Liz tried to pay attention. She knew the play well, all the stifled lives, the doomed hopes and the middling artists, whether determinedly unintrospective like Arkadina or miserably aware of his shortcomings like Trigorin. And yet she never stopped being aware of Henry. She remembered their meeting in Costco, when Henry seemed to know that Peter was coming to D.C., and that made sense now.

At the intermission, without needing to talk about it, they walked out to the lobby together.

In the line for drinks, Henry asked, "Are you getting a whiff of mothballs?"

"Yes. He's a planner. He probably took that jacket out specially for tonight."

Liz wasn't sure what to talk about next. She had an impulse to say, "Isn't Peter kind of darling?" but that would be speeding ahead too fast. Instead, she said, "It looks like a sold-out house."

Henry had already mentioned that, but she was at a loss.

"Yes. It's not exactly Christmas fare, but they extended the run because it was such a success."

"I didn't know you and Peter were in touch. Or that you were helping him with a history paper."

"He didn't need much help. He was writing about education in colonial America and I suggested he narrow it down to a few signers of the Declaration of Independence, to show the range of possibilities. He focused on Madison and Hancock, who had gone to Princeton and Harvard, and two lesser-known signers who had hardly any formal education. Those were his choices, and I thought it was a good paper. But I don't know much about colonial America."

That was the kind of thing historians said: "I don't know much about colonial America." Whereas a journalist would consider himself or herself an expert on the subject after an hour or two spent googling.

"Would you like some Prosecco?" Henry asked. Prosecco was possibly too celebratory, and she looked uncertain. "It's a good antidote to mothballs," he said, and ordered two.

Once they had their flutes, he steered her, just confidently enough, to an empty space in the lobby. It reminded her of the adroit way he had managed the umbrella on the way to their first date.

He asked, "Are you enjoying the play?"

"Yes. But as I get older, I'm more impatient with all the artists in the story. I realize theatre people love to write plays about the theatre, and writers love writing about writers, but I think I'd like to see more plays about teachers or farmers or shopkeepers."

"Look," he said, "there are your sort-of friends. The ones who didn't want to talk to you at the Phillips concert."

It was the Dubroffs, and they were smiling and nodding at them through the crowd. Liz smiled and nodded back, but made no move to join them.

"I know what you mean about all the artists," Henry said. "But don't forget, the stage is littered with unhappy lovers. And the non-artists and the artists are about equal when it comes to making bad choices in love. You probably know that Chekhov said the play had 'little action, tons of love.' I'm concentrating on that."

She liked the idea of Henry intent on all the disappointments in love. She excused herself, and just inside the ladies' room she found Jana Dubroff in line ahead of her. They asked each other about their holidays and both reported that they were quiet, which was what they wanted. Not really the case with Liz, but she wasn't going to go into it.

Jana said, "He looks like a nice man."

"Henry, do you mean? The man I'm standing with?"

She didn't want her to think they were a couple.

"Yes, that one," Jana said, looking slightly puzzled but still friendly. Liz relented. "Yes, I think he is a nice man."

It appeared that Liz had been forgiven. Maybe Jana was just plain tired of resenting Liz for publishing the cat piece. When it came to forgiveness, Liz also felt spent, as if she had run a long race and did not need or want to do that again. The experts didn't talk about fatigue, but it too had a place in the forgiveness hopper.

During the second half of the play, Liz came to resent the fuss-budget. It almost seemed as if he had inserted himself deliberately between Henry and herself. While Trigorin waffled back and forth between Nina and Arkadina and Treplev edged closer to disaster, she thought how pleasant it would be to feel Henry's arm brushing hers or even to bump briefly into his leg when she shifted in her seat. He wore what looked like a new sweater, in a beautiful soft shade of heathery green. She wondered if it was a Christmas present, and who had given it to him.

Henry was right to point out the unrequited love: Liz counted

six instances, and the only character who had even a remotely satisfying personal life was the bachelor doctor. Was love, and self-
knowledge, really that hard? Torn between irritation and sympathy,
she watched the young writer, Treplev, berating his mother. As
always, she was riveted by Arkadina, too narcissistic to give her
son what he needed, and dreading the shot that ends the play. She
and Henry filed out into the lobby in silence.

Putting on his coat, Henry asked, "Why do we want to keep
seeing a story that we know is so unutterably sad?"

She said, "I guess because it is so perfectly told."

He nodded. They traded accounts of their Christmases. He had
had his children and his parents for Christmas Eve, and he went to
his sister's on Christmas Day.

"It's never perfect, but it was pretty good," he said. "And my sister
gave me the Ottolenghi cookbook, so I'm set for honey-roasted
carrots."

They smiled. Their tiny past.

"Just don't roast them for forty minutes, as the recipe says.
They'll be limp noodles by then. Twenty minutes is plenty."

Now they were at the front door. They both had driven to the
theatre, so they walked together to the parking lot. Liz thought,
Will he never make a move? But why would he, when she had only
responded to his farewell message with the usual boilerplate of "It's
not you, it's me and I don't know why that is, et cetera." Her standard exit lines. They ascertained that they were in roughly the same
part of the lot, but she was farther away. Henry said he would walk
her to her car.

Without thinking, she said, "No, don't do that, I'm fine."

Disappointment crossed his face rapidly, and she could not bear
it. His nut-brown eyes and that nose that occasionally twitched.

"But wait," she said. "We need cheering up after that beautifully
told heartbreaking story. I'm on your way home, so why don't you
come to my apartment for a glass of wine?"

Henry's face opened up.

"Corcoran between Sixteenth and Seventeenth Streets," she said. "Number 1622."

"I remember."

And they smiled.

Acknowledgments

My thanks to the following for their inspiration, expertise and technical know-how: Chuck Jones, Damiano Pietropaolo, Gregor Robinson, Harriet Sachs, Bruce Townson, Kate Townson-Carolan.

Thank you to Elizabeth Renzetti, who read the manuscript for accuracy about the newspaper world, and saved me from several errors. I am also grateful to Jane Dammen McAuliffe, who read the book with a lifelong Washingtonian's eagle eye for D.C. bus routes, opening days, neighborhoods and other local arcana. She and her husband, Dennis McAuliffe, were my generous, knowledgeable hosts during a stay in Washington.

My first reader was Marni Jackson, and I was the lucky recipient once again of her uncanny ability to welcome a book on its own terms and, with probing questions and subtle suggestions, to make it even more itself.

At Knopf Canada, my thanks to Anne Collins, Sharon Klein, Rick Meier and Deirdre Molina for their keen professionalism. To Angelika Glover, whose copy editing provided a valued safety net. And to Kelly Hill, for another elegant book design and splendid cover.

At HarperCollins, Sara Nelson, who asks excellent questions, became *Her Turn*'s eloquent champion. Thanks also to Joanne O'Neill for the sleek U.S. cover, and to Mary Gaule and Amy Baker.

My agent, Samantha Haywood, embraced this book with her usual blend of brains, enthusiasm and determination. Thank you, Samantha.

Lynn Henry continues to be the model editor—discerning but flexible, attentive to the details as well as the big picture, alive to writerly sensitivities but never shirking a point that needs to be argued. And no matter how many drafts she read, she always convinced me that she was enjoying the read. Thank you, Lynn.

Thanks to W. W. Norton & Company for their permission to quote from Emily Wilson's translation of *The Odyssey*. Wilson's wonderful version appeared in 2018, but I advanced its publication by a few years so that Liz could read it.

The philosopher Peter quotes in his paper ("Forgiveness is a moral issue with psychological implications; it is not a psychological issue with moral undertones") is Anthony Bash, in *Forgiveness and Christian Ethics*.

Paolo's idea that we learn to carry painful memories with us comes from Bronwen Wallace in her story "Heart of My Heart" (in *People You'd Trust Your Life To*). She writes, "Now, I think maybe you never get over anything, you just find a way of carrying it as gently as possible."

KATHERINE ASHENBURG is an author and journalist who has written for *The New York Times*, *The Globe and Mail* and *Toronto Life*, among other publications. Her nonfiction books include *The Mourner's Dance: What We Do When People Die*, and *The Dirt on Clean: An Unsanitized History*, which was published in twelve countries and six languages. In former incarnations, she was a producer at CBC Radio and was *The Globe and Mail*'s Arts and Books editor. In 2012, she won a Gold Medal at the National Magazine Awards for her article on old age. In 2018, she published her acclaimed fiction debut, *Sofie & Cecilia*, which launched her career as a novelist. *Her Turn* is her second novel.